THE DANCE SETTEE AND OTHER STORIES

The Dance Settee
and other Stories

Ruth Thomas

Polygon

Polygon
An imprint of Edinburgh University Press Ltd
22 George Square, Edinburgh

Typeset in 10.5 on 13.5 pt Galliard by
Hewer Text Ltd, Edinburgh, and
Printed and bound in Great Britain by
Bell & Bain Ltd, Glasgow

A CIP record for this book is
available from the British Library

ISBN 0 7486 6247 2 (paperback)

The Publisher acknowledges subsidy from

towards the publication of this volume.

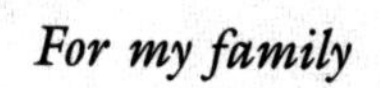

For my family

Contents

Acknowledgements

Some of these stories have appeared in the following:
Groundswell: 'Sensible Footwear'
Shorts (Macallan anthology): 'Cave Paintings'
Scottish Crime Stories: 'Whistling, Singing, Eating Fruit'
The Late Book (BBC Radio 4 broadcast): 'Mabbo'

For their encouragement while writing these stories I would like to thank the Digger's Pub Writers Group; Margaret Burnett, Anne Hay and Sue Wilson; my editor, Marion Sinclair; Larry and Toots; and as always, Mike – for his understanding, support, and ability to rescue word-processors in distress.

Cave Paintings

CARLOS GONZALEZ WAS two years older than Linda. He drove a moped but he still wore childish shorts. In his first letter to her he had written *'Hallo Linda! I am pleased to be your pen-pal! I am fifteen and my eyes are blue, brown, green.'*

'He sounds as if he's got three eyes,' said Linda's father, when she read the letter out at home. Now she was in Spain, staying with him, and she realised that he was not pleased to be her pen-pal. The whole thing was embarrassing.

The Gonzalez' house, *Casita Bonita*, was the furthest out of town. It had a wishing well, a kidney-shaped swimming pool and palm trees. Mr Gonzalez worked for an insurance company, but he spent a lot of the day sitting at the side of the swimming pool wearing thick rubber flip-flops. He never swam. He had a dark tan and chest hair. He would play a tape recording of chirping crickets if the weather wasn't warm enough for the real thing. 'You swim,' he said to Linda, and she would have liked to leap into the pale, shining water, holding her breath, but the sight of his chest and his striped swimming trunks deterred her.

Mrs Gonzalez had a gold handbag. Everything about her was gold and sparkling. Her hair was dyed blonde and her perfume was the colour of amber. She was out working all day and when she came home in the evenings and saw Linda she sometimes made a strange noise with her mouth that sounded like disapproval. 'You're really lucky,' Linda said to her friend Trish after the first weekend. 'Your family's really nice.' Trish had got a traditional Spanish mother with black hair. She made ratatouille and had *jamon serrano* hanging from hooks.

On her first Monday there, Mrs Gonzalez had knocked on her bedroom door, given her money and asked her to walk to the bakery to buy bread. 'Good for your Spanish', she said, 'You know how to say *I would like bread please*?' and Linda had got dressed and walked down the lane, feeling jettisoned but almost exhilarated to get out of Casita Bonita. There was a wide view from the town, of navy-blue sky and beige mountains. Casita Bonita, from a distance, made her think of sugar cubes; she could imagine picking it up with tongs and dropping it into a cup of tea.

The bakery did not have any bread on the shelves, just a small framed picture of the Virgin Mary. The bread was kept in a large sack under the counter. 'Queria pan, por favor,' Linda said. The bread woman looked at her with small brown eyes. She went to the bread sack, took out a curiously-shaped loaf and thumped it on to the counter. 'Cien pesetas,' she said. There was a plate of biscuits at the back of the shop, under another Virgin Mary picture. Linda pointed at them. 'Cien,' said the woman. Linda gave her the money in small change. Then she walked out of the shop with the bread and biscuits. The biscuits were good – crumbly and tasting of cinnamon. People appeared from doorways and watched her as she ate. People stared a lot, she had noticed – the men playing dominoes in the bars; the women washing the pavements, the women dressed in black. 'Hola,' she said, but the women just stood there with their arms folded across their big stomachs. She took another biscuit out of the bag and turned up the lane that led back to the Gonzalez' house. She walked slowly, sliding her sandals in the dust.

Casita Bonita was white and cool. It was like an igloo. When she got back she let herself in through the kitchen door, walked through the house and out again into the garden, where Mr and Mrs Gonzalez were sitting, silent, on plastic chairs. The garden was the beautiful thing about the house. She had never seen anything so colourful. There were roses and lilies and olive trees and a peach tree. She approached the table and Mrs Gonzalez poured her some coffee. She pulled pieces of bread off the loaf Linda had bought, and put them on a plate.

'Linda, why not pick olives?' Mr Gonzalez said almost as soon as Linda had sat down. Mrs Gonzalez put her sunglasses on and smiled a thin smile.

'OK,' said Linda. She wasn't learning much Spanish. She got up from her chair, walked up to the top of the garden and sat on a tree-stump. There were little lizards sitting on the tiled roof, blinking, sunning themselves, and when she looked up she could see the Gonzalez' neighbours sitting like bigger lizards on their terraces, reading and sunbathing. Carlos had gone out somewhere on his moped; she could hear the noise it made, the echo of it in the lanes, ricocheting against the white walls of the houses.

When she walked back down the steps Mr Gonzalez had gone, but Mrs Gonzalez was still sitting there, reading a book. Linda had picked a handful of olives from the tree, and she put them on the table. Mrs Gonzalez looked at them. 'Very green,' she said, and she made the disapproving noise with her mouth. She put her book down.

'Linda,' she said, 'In Spanish, Linda means *nice*. Do you know that?'

'Yes,' said Linda. 'My teacher told me.'

'And you are a nice girl, Linda,' said Mrs Gonzalez. 'You are very English,' she said.

'I'm Scottish,' said Linda.

Mrs Gonzalez put her head on one side, like a big bird. Then she leaned across the table and patted Linda's arm. The sun had created prickly heat bumps already, on the backs of Linda's hands. 'Oh look,' said Mrs Gonzalez. Her voice caught. 'Oh no,' she said, dramatically, and she picked up her tube of sun-tan cream and squirted inches of it on to Linda's hands. 'Pay attention of the sun, Linda,' she said.

'Yes,' said Linda.

'Now I must go,' said Mrs Gonzalez. She stood up and adjusted her bikini. There was a zig-zag pattern impressed into her thighs.

Linda was meant to walk to school with Carlos but he seemed

to spend all day skiving with his friends. Some of them had thin moustaches. They went up into the mountains with their mopeds, and threw sticks at tourists as they walked past.

After Mrs Gonzalez had left, Linda walked back into the house and lay on the leather couch, behind the Venetian blinds. Mrs Gonzalez kept a little caged bird in the sitting room. She called it Chico. It looked like a sparrow. Linda felt like opening the cage door and letting it escape. She got up from the couch, walked towards the cage and put her fingers against the bars. The sparrow came and pecked at her fingernail for a while, then it flew away again. Linda went into the kitchen and opened the fridge door. It was full of things that she had never seen before; strange cheeses and vegetables and milk that wobbled about in plastic bags. She took a four-pack of crème caramel from the top shelf and snapped off a carton. She peeled back the lid, upended the carton on to a saucer and watched the dessert slide slowly down the plastic. It was a perfect castle-shape. She found a teaspoon and ate the crème caramel slowly, cutting little curves into its sides so that it resembled the mountains around the town. She left the caramel sauce until last. Mr Gonzalez came into the kitchen as she was putting the final spoonful of it into her mouth. 'What are you doing?' he asked in Spanish. She couldn't think of the Spanish for 'I am eating,' so she just smiled. 'Hola,' she said. That was all she could think of. Mr Gonzalez looked at her. He didn't smile. He walked out of the kitchen and into the living room. He started to move things around loudly in there, as if he had mislaid something.

When she got to Carlos's school she couldn't see anyone she knew so she walked back up the lane, past the bakery and the women standing in doorways, and into the town. There was a little café in the square. During the daytime it was full of old men in hats playing dominos. The old men turned in their seats and stared as she walked in. Then they turned back to the dominoes. There were tupperware boxes standing on the counter. They were full of dried-up tapas – olives and chorizo and a kind of potato mayonnaise. Linda asked the barman for a coffee and he looked at her as if she amused him, and gave her a tiny cup of espresso. After a while, he walked away and started throwing pastry into a pan of oil.

Linda sat at a table next to the domino players. She took some postcards out of her bag and looked at them. They were views of the town: one of the church, one of two old men with walking sticks, and one of the mountains. They looked like the kind of postcards she received at home that said nothing about anything. She turned one of them over. *View of the stunning 16th-century Church of the Virgin Mary.*

Dear Mum and Dad,
It's hot here. The Gonzalez have a swimming pool and an olive tree. I am sitting in a cafe next to some old men playing dominoes.

The door opened. There was a tiny breeze, and in walked Trish with her penfriend, whose name Linda had forgotten. They were both wearing suede trousers.

'Linda,' said Trish, 'what are you doing?'

'I'm writing postcards,' said Linda.

'But shouldn't you be with Carlos?'

'Yes I should,' she said. She felt angry suddenly, and sad. 'I should,' she said, 'but Carlos is on his moped in the mountains'.

'Oh,' said Trish.

Trish's penfriend put her hands in her pockets and looked at her.

'We thought we'd get a coffee before school,' Trish said.

'I thought you didn't like coffee,' Linda said. Trish ignored her.

They went to the bar and Trish's penfriend asked the barman for two coffees with milk. She said something else to the barman and he winked and gave her a little bowl of sweets, wrapped in coloured paper. Then she and Trish walked back to Linda's table.

'Do you want some of mine?' Trish asked Linda when the barman brought the coffee over. 'I could pour it into your cup.'

'No thanks,' said Linda. 'I've had plenty.'

Trish looked at Linda's tiny espresso cup and didn't reply.

'So, Linda,' said Trish's penfriend, 'what have you been doing at the weekend?'

Linda gripped the tablecloth and tried to think of something interesting to tell them.

'I went swimming,' she said, 'and I looked at the church of the Virgin Mary'. She couldn't think of anything else. 'How about you?' she said.

'We went to Ronda and got these trousers. You should go, Linda,' said Trish. 'They're really cheap. You should get a pair. And we went to Alcatraz. And we looked at a cave yesterday. It's got stone-age paintings in it.'

'It is not far,' said Trish's penfriend.

'It's just in the mountains up there,' said Trish, pointing through the window, 'but you have to make an appointment with a man.'

'Right,' said Linda. Mr Gonzalez had asked Carlos to take her to the cave on Saturday, but Carlos had just shrugged and said something Linda didn't understand.

Trish's penfriend drank some coffee. 'Linda,' she said, 'do you know that in Spanish, Linda means nice?'

'Yes,' said Linda, 'people have told me.' She unwrapped a sweet and sucked it for a while, until it was a sharp diamond in her mouth.

Her bedroom was at the far end of Casita Bonita. When she had arrived from the airport, Mrs Gonzalez had taken her to see it straight away. She told her she had papered the walls herself. The paper was the colour of apricots, and there were pictures of flowers on the walls. There was also a picture of Mr Gonzalez, taken several years earlier, when he was thinner and better looking. He was sitting at a table drinking beer.

Mrs Gonzalez told her she should have a siesta at lunchtime, and Linda had tried to sleep, lying on top of the duvet, but she had kept sneezing. She wondered if she was allergic to the Gonzalez' pillows. When she came back from school, she would sit by the swimming pool if Mr Gonzalez wasn't there, but if he was she went to her room. There was a fan in the corner, and she would switch it on to try and dispel whatever it was that was making her sneeze. At around eight o'clock, Mrs Gonzalez came back from work. Linda would hear her throw her bag and keys on the kitchen table, sigh, walk into her dressing room and shut the door. She would spend about twenty minutes in there, then she would emerge in different clothes: crisply casual things with motifs and bits of fake jewellery sewn on to them. She would begin to cook dinner while Carlos and Mr Gonzalez sat by the swimming pool. Every so often, Carlos would throw something into the water – an olive stone or a leaf – and Mr Gonzalez would shout at him.

Linda walked into the kitchen when Mrs Gonzalez got home. She stood at the sink, flexing her toes inside her trainers.

'Can I help you?' she asked.

'No,' said Mrs Gonzalez.

She walked lightly over the kitchen tiles in a pair of gold mules. She gathered things together – vegetables, ham from plastic packets, a bottle of Coca-cola.

'I am making tortilla,' she said. She cracked four eggs into a bowl and started to whisk them together. She looked through the window.

'Carlos is not a nice boy,' she said.

Linda leaned against the cool marble worktop. Mrs Gonzalez stopped whisking the eggs and looked at her. 'Too much sun today,' she said. 'You are very pink. Very English.'

'I'm Scottish,' said Linda.

When the tortillas were ready they put plates on the table and Mrs Gonzalez called to Carlos and her husband. 'My husband is angry,' she said, closing the window.

Carlos and Mr Gonzalez came in, sat at the table, folded their arms and said nothing. Carlos had wet hair, and Mrs Gonzalez tapped him on the head with a wooden spoon and said something to him in a sharp voice. Carlos shrugged. He didn't eat any of the tortilla. He sat with his elbows on the table and made small comments. Occasionally he picked up the mayonnaise jar and dipped breadsticks into it. Mr and Mrs Gonzalez ignored him.

They cut up slices of tortilla and broke off pieces of bread from the loaf Linda had bought. From time to time, Mrs Gonzalez would get up from the table and feed pieces of ham to Chico the bird.

On Saturday, when everyone else was at the beach or visiting the Alhambra, Mrs Gonzalez decided that they would stay at home and have four o'clock tea. 'You do this in Britain?' she said to Linda. 'Tea at four o'clock?'

'Not really,' said Linda. 'Not any more.'

Mrs Gonzalez said it again: 'Tea at four o'clock,' as if she wanted to confirm something, some belief. 'You must tell your parents we have cakes and sandwiches,' she said, 'like in England.'

'We don't have four o'clock tea,' said Linda. 'We aren't often at home then.'

Carlos sat in the armchair behind them and sniggered – from where she was standing she could just see the edges of his big, beige knees. Mrs Gonzalez sighed. Before the shops shut she went out and bought cakes at the bakery – chocolate eclairs and strawberry tarts and more of the cinnamon biscuits. She opened the packet of Earl Grey tea that Linda had given her, and made ham sandwiches with very white, crustless bread. This time Linda didn't offer to help. She just sat and watched her buttering bread. It was a still day; the air in the kitchen hung.

Mrs Gonzalez placed the cake stand on the table. She put some orange blossom in a vase and placed it on a crocheted doily. At four o'clock they sat down. Mr Gonzalez cleared his throat and rubbed his hands together. He was still wearing his T-shirt and swimming trunks, but Mrs Gonzalez had changed into a red dress and high-heeled shoes.

Just as she was pouring the tea, Carlos suddenly got up from his chair and went into his room. He came back with a video camera. He sat down again and began to film them all. 'Carlos!, said Mrs Gonzalez, but he didn't reply. He sat opposite Linda and pointed the camera at her. She didn't look up. She pretended not to notice him. She talked to Mrs Gonzalez with all her concentration, twirling a strand of hair around her finger, holding her head in an unnatural position to make it as annoying as possible for Carlos. She thought of his first letter to her: *Hallo! I am pleased to be your pen-pal! My eyes are blue, brown, green.* When she had received the letter, she had imagined somebody nice.

'Now, Linda,' said Mrs Gonzalez. She smiled and offered Linda a strawberry tart. 'They are little,' she said, 'have two.' She filled her cup from a very ornate teapot, and glanced across the table at her husband. Mr Gonzalez was just sitting there, with a linen napkin tucked into the top of his T-shirt. He was glaring at his son, who had finished filming the tea-party and was now playing the picture back. From where she was sitting, Linda could see them all, tiny and upside-down on a little screen. Even from that distance she knew that she didn't want to look any closer. The sound-track had Mrs Gonzalez' loud voice, and Linda's inane, ungrammatical mumblings, and shrieks from Chico in the background.

'That is enough, Carlos,' Mr Gonzalez said, but Carlos didn't look up. He continued to play the film.

'That is enough,' said Mr Gonzalez, and he suddenly burst up from his chair like some big, dark wave, projected himself across to Carlos's side of the table and grabbed the video camera. He opened the back of the camera, pulled the film out and strode, swearing, through the back door with it. Carlos sat with his mouth open and his hands still in a camera-holding position. Then he started to shout in a hoarse, cracked voice. Tears came into his eyes. They all watched from the table as Mr Gonzalez reached the edge of the swimming pool and hurled Carlos's film into the water.

After that, Carlos changed. He became quiet. On Sunday, while Mr Gonzalez was out, he opened the door to Chico's cage and let the bird fly away. He stopped going out on his moped; he just went into the garage and stood, looking at it. He didn't speak to his parents, but suddenly he started to talk to Linda, about three days before she was due to leave. He took her for walks. On her last day in Andalucía, he took her to see the cave paintings. Not because his father asked; he just took her there. He knew a way in. The cave was massive inside, like a cathedral, and as cool as a well. After they had been in there a while, the lack of oxygen made it difficult to breathe. Carlos said that people would never have been able to live in the cave; nobody really knew what they had used the cave for. There were just these paintings. They walked further in and it took a few moments for their eyes to become accustomed to the dark but when they were, they saw pictures on the walls: drawings of horses, fish, people. There was one of a deer and one of a seal with a fish, upside-down, inside its belly. 'These are twenty thousand years old,' Carlos whispered. They were older than anything Linda could imagine. Looking at them, it was hard to believe in things like swimming pools and four o'clock tea. It was hard to believe that these things mattered.

Silver Coin

WHEN JANE ARRIVES for her interview, there is a woman sitting at a typewriter in Reception. She is wearing a tweed skirt and a lilac jumper. She smiles and stares, and Jane smiles back and clutches her new, leatherette handbag. She is carrying this bag to project a no-nonsense image. Her image is usually more nonsense. These are clothes she wears only for job interviews: smart, womanly clothes. Her blouse wraps itself statically around her; she can feel the silk clinging to her like little hands. The woman stares for a while longer. Then she resumes typing.

There is a wooden chair by the fireplace. The woman does not invite Jane to sit, but she does, anyway.

'This is a nice fire,' Jane says. It is; it is like a fire that you might toast crumpets by, cosy, in your living room.

The receptionist looks up. 'It's cold today, isn't it?' she says.

'Yes,' says Jane, 'not warm.'

She wonders if this conversation might be a secret part of the selection process.

'I think snow may be on the way,' says the woman, and she pulls a digestive biscuit out of its packet and puts it in her mouth.

'Are you working at the moment?' she asks.

'No. I was made redundant.'

'Oh. That's a shame,' says the woman. Then she stands up, smoothing her skirt into place, and goes to the window. It is hard to tell how old she is: she could be Jane's age. She peers between two bands of Venetian blind and gazes at a seagull that is standing in the middle of the road. She sighs and looks at her watch.

Inside the interview room there are two people sitting on one side of a very shiny table: a man in a blue blazer and a woman in a maroon jacket.

'A cup of coffee would be nice, Sandra,' the woman says to the receptionist.

'Surely,' says the receptionist and she walks through a doorway marked *Kitchen*.

It is four in the afternoon. The interviewers look drained.

'My name is Carol Dickson,' says the woman in the maroon jacket. 'This should take twenty minutes.' She looks at her little gold watch.

Jane sits down, holding her handbag.

'Now,' says Carol Dickson, 'perhaps you could talk us through your last job.'

'I worked for a music company,' says Jane. 'I edited a magazine,' and she shows them the copy of *The Music Stand* that she has brought with her. It is the one she likes best, with the picture of a piano on the cover. It has a subtitle: *Striking The Right Note.*

'I devised it,' she says, 'and did all the editing. It was good fun.'

'So why did you leave?' asks the man.

'I was made redundant.'

'I see.' The man strokes the ends of his moustache. 'And you have been out of work for a number of months, I see.'

'Yes. It's a low time of year for jobs. I mean, I wanted to wait until the right one came along.'

'I see,' says the man again. He frowns. 'And I see, also, that you devised crosswords.' He has turned the magazine over and is looking at the competition page. His eyes widen a little. 'Nine across,' he says, 'seventies band; it's elemental!'

Jane smiles. '*Earth, Wind and Fire*,' she says.

'I don't understand,' says the man. He looks at her and flicks the ends of his moustache, and Jane has a feeling that the interview has lurched perilously, swung in a sudden, unexpected direction, like a jack-knifing lorry.

The kitchen door opens and Sandra clanks in with a tray of coffee and shortbread biscuits. Jane smiles. 'Thanks,' she says. She takes a biscuit, because she feels woolly-headed suddenly; in need of sustenance. Her ears are buzzing. Biscuit crumbs fall on to her blouse.

At the end of the interview, Carol Dickson asks Jane to do a typing test. She leads her into a small room containing a table, a chair, an instruction sheet and a typewriter. The view through the window is of two very tall galvinised bins.

'I'd like you to imagine that you have double-booked an appointment, and are writing to arrange another date,' says Carol Dickson.

'OK,' says Jane.

'There's no rush,' says Carol Dickson, and she leaves the room. She shuts the door very gently, and Jane hears her creeping away.

Jane sits at the table and looks at her instruction sheet. She has to write to someone called Mr Brown.

Dear Mr Brown, she writes, and then she stops. The typewriter hums. She looks through the window. There is a starling sitting on one of the galvinised bins, with twigs in its mouth. It appears to be staring at her. It has its winter plumage: white dots, as if it has been splattered with paint.

I am writing to apologise for the fact that I have double-booked your appointment with – Jane looks at her instruction sheet – *'Crystal Clear Window Systems'*.

She writes 'Crystal Clare' by mistake. She presses the delete button. A small metal arm appears from the innards of the typewriter and attacks the word with little teeth. It is vicious, like a Velociraptor. When Jane peers closely, she can see that the top surface of the paper has been removed. She types 'Clear' over the abrasion and continues.

I wonder if Friday 11th February would be a suitable alternative date? she writes. It seems odd to be asking a non-existent man a question. *I shall telephone you in a couple of days' time to discuss this. Yours,* – she stops again; *faithfully or sincerely? faithfully or sincerely?* Her mind tries to retrieve what it learned at school.

Yours sincerely, she writes, and then she presses a little button marked UPPER CASE. Nothing happens. The paper is stuck. She pulls at it but it is stuck fast. The typewriter begins to make a buzzing noise. Jane leans across to shake the roller, and her sleeve catches a chrome lever, and something falls off the back of the typewriter. Something smashes against the floor.

She doesn't move. She sits absolutely still and wonders what she is going to do. After a few seconds she gets up, walks around the back of the table and picks the pieces of broken plastic off the floor. There are eight pieces. She swears quietly and stands up again. Then she walks to the window and looks out. The starling is still on the galvinised bin, still staring at her. It hops around for a while longer and then flies away. It is replaced almost instantly by a large, brown and white pigeon, which seems to have a broken foot. The pigeon limps and holds its pink foot up under its chest, as if it is a little, gnarled hand. Jane breathes in very deeply and returns to the interview room, holding the bits of plastic.

'I'm really sorry,' she says, 'but I think I may have broken your typewriter.'

Carol Dickson's smile wavers slightly but does not disappear altogether. She is very composed. Perhaps she has achieved her director's status by being composed.

'These things happen,' she says. 'It could have happened to anyone.'

'I'm really sorry,' Jane says again.

'Never mind,' says Carol Dickson, leading her to the door.

The man with the moustache doesn't say goodbye. He sits and helps himself to another piece of shortbread.

It is only 4.25, but there is already a very pale moon in the sky. A full moon. Jane has always been a little supersitious about a full moon. Her horoscope that day had said:

> *A full moon on Wednesday is sure to make you emotional. Keep some cash back for emergencies; you will need it.*

Her limbs feel tired but she does not wait for the bus. It is cheaper to walk home. When she gets there, John is already back from work. He is in the kitchen making coffee with the espresso-maker, the one she gave him. The blue gas flame underneath it looks pretty; like a flower.

'How did it go?' John asks.

'I destroyed their typewriter.'

'Oh dear.'

When the coffee is ready John pours it into two mugs. There is hardly any milk left in the carton, so he pours it all into her mug and hands it to her.

'You didn't want to work for Smart Glass Windows anyway,' he says.

'It's called Classy Glass,' she says.

'That sounds even worse'

'I want a job,' she says, 'that's all I want.'

She has another interview the next day, with the National Brownies' Association. Her appointment is at ten o'clock, and she has to get a taxi to make it on time. She sits and stares through the taxi window, aware of the dark rings beneath her eyes.

'I used to be a boy scout,' the taxi driver tells her. 'I know all my knots.'

'I'm glad someone does,' says Jane.

When they get there, the driver says 'Remember, pet: Be Prepared.' Then he winks, counts out her change and drives away.

Jane knocks on the Brownies' door and waits. A woman in a floral dress appears after a while, holding a plastic jar filled with silver milkbottle tops. She leads Jane into a narrow green corridor and tells her to sit down.

'You may find this interesting,' she says, handing Jane a magazine, and then she goes into another room.

The magazine is brown. It is called *The National Brownies' Association: Brownies Helping Older People.*

When people get older, is it time for them to start winding down or time to get more active?

In the contents page there are headings:

Brownies help with:
Tea Dances
Singalongs
Jumble Sales

The chapter headed 'Singalongs' talks about camp-fire songs. It talks about community centres. It talks about Brownies working towards Brownie badges.

The woman's head appears around the door. 'Mrs Parker is ready now,' she says, and she leads Jane along the corridor and into an office. Mrs Parker is sitting at a desk by the window, signing pieces of paper. Pinned to her bosom is a little badge of an owl.

They talk briefly about the weather, and Jane is halfway through a sentence about snow when Mrs Parker interrupts her.

'It doesn't say here whether you are a Miss or a Mrs,' she says, looking at her notes.

She shuts her eyes then looks up, smiling, her canines showing very slightly. She waits for Jane to answer. It is very quiet in the room and Jane can hear a man whistling on the street outside. It sounds like Flash Gordon; complicated to whistle.

Mrs Parker says 'Just difficult to pronounce Ms, isn't it?'

She writes something on the paper. She fingers her pearl necklace, then looks through the window at the pale, waving trees.

Jane is about to speak when the receptionist comes into the room with more pieces of paper. 'Angela' says Mrs Parker, 'what do Brownies do with old people? Any thoughts?'

'Cooking,' says Angela.

'Anything else?'

'Erm,' says Angela.

Mrs Parker frowns because Angela is so stupid. Then she takes the papers that Angela has given her. She snaps them into shape and places them on her desk.

'Ten-pin bowling?' Angela suggests, but Mrs Parker does not reply, and Angela walks out again, sighing, slightly stooped.

Mrs Parker is in the middle of a speech about liaison when Jane begins to feel unwell. A strange singing has set up in her ears, becoming louder and louder, blanking things out. Her head feels heavy. She is still answering questions but her voice has cut its links with her head. Any minute now she will have to interrupt her. She will have to say something strange and inappropriate.

'I –,' she says.

Mrs Parker stops talking.

'Are you alright?' she asks. 'You have gone terribly pale.'

The room lengthens and twists. Mrs Parker seems to be speaking from the end of a mile-long desk.

'I'm feeling faint,' Jane says. She tries to remain polite, to stay upright, but everything is disconnected. The room starts to wobble like a mirage. Her mouth opens and shuts and the voice that floats out of it doesn't seem to belong to her. She is aware of Mrs Parker standing up; of the pink and blue flowers on her dress looming towards her. There is the sound of chair legs scraping against the floor.

'I'm sorry about this,' Jane says. Everything is slowing down; receding. She feels frightened. She puts her hand out and grabs on to the drawer handle of Mrs Parker's desk. The drawer handle has suddenly become very significant, as if it is the only thing that will keep her attached to the world. Her hands are sweating. She watches herself pulling the drawer out of the desk and scattering its contents. Then she hits the floor.

She is only unconscious for a couple of seconds. When she comes round, Mrs Parker is standing above her like a giant. She is holding a green First Aid box.

'You were out for a moment there, dear,' she says. She sounds excited. Jane sits up slowly. Then she stands up, and sits down again on a chair. She can feel the sweat on her face, drying and cold. There are sheets of A4 paper all over the floor.

'Not the best thing to do in an interview,' she says.

'Ha,' says Mrs Parker. She does not disagree. Angela comes in and hands Jane a cup of sweet, orange tea, and Jane wonders how many Brownie badges Angela acquired when she was young. She only ever got the pet lover's badge. Angela and Mrs Parker stand over Jane and watch her while she drinks.

'Shall I call you a taxi?' Angela asks in a sweet, undulating voice, the kind that she perhaps reserves for children. 'You look really pale,' she says.

'I'll be alright,' Jane says, and she smiles at her. 'Thanks,' she says.

'Go home and have a lie down,' says Mrs Parker.

'Yes, I will.'

Jane steps out of the Brownies' Association slowly and carefully. She walks home.

She tells John about the fainting fit while they are eating supper.

'Maybe there is something wrong with me,' she says.

'Nothing more than usual,' says John. He is amused. He goes to the cooker and returns with the saucepan of soup, the nice soup he made.

'Maybe I'm anaemic,' she says, 'maybe I've got low blood pressure.'

'It's more likely to be your subconscious,' he says, 'telling you not to work for the Brownies.'

'But I've got to get a job,' she says.

'You will get a job.'

Her third interview, the only one she has left, is for a sales assistant in a department store. She has never worked in a shop before. She has an appointment with a man called Mr Dougal.

She decides, this time, to get a bus there. While she is standing at the bus stop she looks in her purse for her fare and finds a foreign coin, almost hidden in the lining. A half franc. She doesn't know how she got it. The bus fare is 65p, and she has

55p and a half franc. When the bus arrives, she gives it to the driver with the rest of her change and hopes he won't notice. But he does.

'Someone's been abroad,' he says.

'Sorry?' says Jane. She sounds so innocent. 'Oh,' she says, 'I thought that was a ten pence piece.'

'Did you now?' says the bus driver.

He drives very fast for the rest of the journey. He keeps hooting at taxi drivers and braking very hard at all the junctions, and Jane wonders if he is angry, or late, or if he always drives like that.

Mr Dougal's office is up four flights of stairs. Each flight has a different surface, getting more primitive as Jane ascends; carpet, linoleum, wood, stone. The steps are difficult to negotiate in her pencil skirt and court shoes.

'You get fit working here,' says Mr Dougal when she reaches the top.

Mr Dougal has an office door that looks like something out of a gangster movie. It has greenish glass set into it and gold lettering saying 'Mr Dougal: MD'. He opens the door and lets Jane walk in first. There is a view through his window of the grey backs of other department stores; she can see steam coming through a grille in John Menzies' wall.

'Sit down,' says Mr Dougal.

'Right,' says Jane.

Her chair is slightly broken. It lurches to one side and makes a tiny groaning noise.

'I shall tell you a little about the store,' Mr Dougal begins, and he leans forward. His eyes flick very quickly to Jane's bust and then away again, as if they were accidentally looking in the wrong direction.

'The sportswear department is either very busy or very quiet,' he says, 'depending on the time of year.'

'Yes.'

'At the moment it is very quiet so we can break you in gently.'

'I see.'

Jane clears her throat and crosses her legs. Her chair makes a sound like a plaintive cello string.

'Could you cope with that, do you think?' Mr Dougal asks. 'The fact that it is either very busy or very quiet?' He furrows his brow.

'I like variety.'

'Well,' says Mr Dougal, 'they say it is the spice of life.'

'Yes.'

They both laugh in a tiny way and stare at the walls. Mr Dougal looks at her CV.

'I see here that you used to edit a magazine,' he says.

'Yes,' says Jane, 'it was fun.'

Mr Dougal smiles and looks up. 'Well, I'm sure we could find something fun here for you,' he says. 'Window display, perhaps.'

'Yes,' Jane says. She shuffles uncomfortably in her seat.

Before she leaves, Mr Dougal shows her around the store. He takes her down to the stock-room, which is like a series of little white caves with low ceilings. She bangs her head against an unexpectedly low door arch and it makes a hollow sound.

'Oh,' says Mr Dougal, 'I felt that.'

'My head sounds worryingly hollow,' says Jane. She laughs loudly and rubs her forehead. She wonders if she is going to get a bruise. Mr Dougal looks at her. 'Alright, dear?' he says. Then he opens a cupboard door. There is a member of staff in the cupboard, eating a sandwich.

'Sorry to disturb you, Rita,' he says, and he shuts the door again. 'That is an alternative rest area for staff working on the lower floors,' he explains.

The main tearoom is almost at the top of the building. It is full of empty cardboard boxes. The side of each box is covered with thick, marker-pen script: *Gym Slip, Navy, Size 30 – 32; Football Strip, Red, Size 28 – 30.* An old man is sitting beside a huge stack of boxes, alternately smoking, eating a pie and reading the *Daily Record.* He does not speak to Jane and Mr Dougal when they walk in.

'Gordon's been here forty-three years,' says Mr Dougal. 'Isn't that right, Gordon?'

'Too right,' says Gordon.

One floor further up is the repairs room. It is inhabited by an elderly woman called Pearl, who is sewing name-tapes into shirt collars.

'You'll get plenty of exercise running up and down these stairs,' she says to Jane.

'Yes,' says Jane, and she smiles. Her head is still throbbing, keeping time with her heart.

'We might ask you to sew name-tapes on during the summer,' says Mr Dougal.

'It's a relief to work up here, dear, it really is,' Pearl says, slowly, threading a needle. 'Far from the madding crowd.'

When John gets home in the evening, Jane tells him straight away about the job. 'I didn't faint,' she says, 'and I didn't break anything. So I got the job.'

'What's the salary?'

'£3.60 an hour.'

'It's a start,' says John.

'But I'd already made a start. I'd made a much better start.'

John takes his coat off and throws it on to one of the kitchen chairs. It lands on top of her new leatherette handbag.

'I can't even afford a real handbag any more,' she says. 'I'm going backwards.'

'You're not going backwards,' says John.

'What has happened to my career?' she says.

'It'll be alright,' says John, 'you'll find something better.'

In the middle of the night she has to get up because she is so thirsty. She goes into the kitchen and runs water from the tap into a glass. She drinks very quickly, in big gulps, and stands looking through the window. The moon is waning very slightly now; she can see a tiny sliver pared off one side of it, like a worn-down silver coin.

When she gets back into bed, John is muttering in his sleep as if something is scaring him, and she touches his hand.

'It's alright,' she whispers, 'it's alright,' and he stops muttering at once. Asleep, people are so easy to calm. She lies completely still for a while, with her hand on top of his.

The Dance Settee

NAOMI HAD ALWAYS been choosy with boys, not liking the little details of them. She was suspicious of their flattery, and of the fact that they all liked her hair. Long hair on a girl seemed full of strange significance.

'Your hair,' said one of the poetic ones she had met early on – they had been sitting in a gloomy churchyard – 'In the sunlight it's like . . .' and he couldn't think what it was like.

'Tumbleweed?' she asked.

'No,' he said. She had noticed that boys liked to have the last word, particularly the romantic ones. The poet had had pale hair, thinning already, even at the age of seventeen. His eyes were pale, too, and slightly protruding. None of the boys she knew had been very attractive up to that point.

When she left school she found a job in a recording studio. This was an oddly static place to work, held together by habits: digestive biscuits at 11.30; small word-processing calamities; early home-time on Fridays. It seemed that only Naomi was changing. Since she had started working there, her hair had been getting shorter and shorter until it had eventually grown into a compulsion, curling awkwardly at the front, sticking out at the sides. She sat typing letters – *Dear Mr Hounslow. Ref: 'Pet Owners' Broadcast* - knowing that her hair looked a mess. She thought of the long plait she had once had, hanging simple and beautiful down her back. When she saw long-haired girls walk past she would stare and feel a tiny stab of grief. At home she would hover at her dressing table, opening wooden boxes and metal tins and looking at the hair slides inside. They were like lost toys.

She'd had six haircuts within a year. She'd become fickle, visiting different hairdressers across town, but they all failed to understand what she wanted.

'What would you like today?' they asked, and they picked up a limp piece of her hair and let it flop back again, like a spaniel's ear.

'Well . . .,' said Naomi. She didn't know which words to use. 'I'd like a trim, please,' she said, 'a kind of bob,' but maybe a 'bob' was not what she thought it was. Maybe a bob was a curious creature that sat on your head and made you despair.

'It's gamine now,' the hairdresser had said on her last visit. Naomi looked at the reflection of her hair on the floor.

'You've cut a lot off there, I see,' she said.

She touched the back of her head, and her hair sprang back against her fingers, short, like a boy's hair.

'It's gamine,' said the hairdresser again, and she stomped away, jowelly-jawed, to get a bottle of Hair Fix.

'I don't want any spray, thanks,' Naomi shouted across the room. She stood up and pulled off her grey plastic cloak. She didn't look gamine; she looked nothing like Audrey Hepburn. She paid and fled, fumbling in her bag for her hairbrush.

'You used to have such lovely hair,' said her parents when she got home, and she felt hollow, as if she'd done something irreversible.

There was a sound engineer called William McCann who worked at the recording studio. Naomi would cover her bobbed head with her hands when he walked into the room.

'I'm going to call myself Bob,' she whispered to Lindsay Pringle, the administrative assistant.

'Sorry?' said Lindsay. Lindsay looked at her anxiously sometimes, as if she might be on the edge of something worrying.

'Didn't you have long hair when you came here, Naomi?' William asked, walking past with a set of headphones.

The first time she had met him she had been handing out coffee around the office. 'Cheers,' William had said, lifting a cup from the tray. He was so deadpan and sure of himself, and 'Cheers' was the sort of word that sound engineers used – casual, slightly odd. She'd noticed that. Underneath the sound-desk he wore very old black trainers, unlike the studio manager, who wore shiny brogues. She was intrigued by someone who could work quietly with electric cables and headsets, diverting whole shows from disaster. William was in control of Studio 2, which was tiny, egg-box like; he would sit there for hours with his cups of coffee, flicking switches.

Naomi began to collide with William, surreptitiously. She would turn up in Studio 2 at the tail-end of the afternoon when he was in there, sitting in the corner, soldering something.

'Still here?' she'd say, knowing that, of course, he was still there. Or she would suddenly need to collect things from Studio 2 during his shift. 'Hi,' she would say, abruptly. She would pick up his empty plastic cup and couldn't think what else to do. 'Cheers,' said William. The smell of soldered flux filled her heart with a kind of pained happiness. At home, watching television with her parents as they balanced plates of macaroni cheese on their laps, her thoughts would be strangely unfocused and full of him.

A week after her shortest haircut, leaves began to emerge on the trees. They grew almost as she watched, turning from a green haze to real leaf shapes within a few days.

'The growing season,' she said to Lindsay Pringle. 'How ironic.'

During lunchbreaks, she started to take her sandwiches out to the park. The weather was beautiful suddenly, unexpectedly bright and still. People were out throwing frisbies and lying on the grass.

One Friday, as she was biting into her fourth sandwich, she saw William McCann appearing over a low hill. She breathed in a tiny crumb of bread but managed to prevent herself from choking by swallowing very quickly. She just had time to brush the tears from her eyes before he arrived at her bench.

'I was going for a walk by the canal,' said William, 'would you like to come?'

'Have we got time?'

'Does it matter?'

And Naomi was gripped by an odd mix of elation and anxiety. 'Is he asking me out?' she thought. 'Is he asking me out?' She didn't have a clue. And she wasn't sure where the canal was – it slunk around the edges of town without her ever knowing how to get to it.

She squashed up her pieces of silver foil, put them back in her sandwich box and they left the park.

'Nice day,' said William.

'Yes,' she said, 'sunny.'

'Left,' said William, and he began to lead her along unfamiliar pavements, down unknown streets. They turned into strange, graffitied alleyways, whose walls bounced back the sound of their footsteps.

'Snickets are useful,' said William.

She didn't know what a snicket was but she supposed they were walking along one. The town she knew seemed to be disintegrating the nearer they got to the canal. All the shops were boarded up, and thin dogs limped past with smiles on their faces. After a while they came to a small iron bridge, which had steps down the side of it. They climbed down and stood on the towpath.

'Look at the towers,' William said, and he pointed at a couple of industrial chimneys in the distance. Smoke was waving whitely, sadly, from the tops of them.

'I love this place,' he said.

Naomi looked down at the edge of the water. There was a broken bicycle wheel and a squashed cigarette packet. She didn't know what to say, but the fact that he liked rubbish-laden canals seemed sweet and poignant. William breathed in and closed his eyes, and she stared at his long eyelashes and his pale face. His cheeks were slightly chipmunkish, if she really analysed them.

'Are you going to the fancy-dress party at the weekend?' William asked, opening his eyes.

'I don't know,' said Naomi. She was alarmed by abrupt questions.

'I just wondered,' William said, and she felt a little rush of hope and embarrassment running up her exposed neck. 'Which evening?' she asked. She tried to inject a note of boredom in her voice. She stroked the back of her head. This had become a habit; a test to see whether her hair had grown in the past half-hour. 'Is there a theme?' she asked loudly. 'Is it tarts and vicars or something?'

'No,' said William, and he looked startled. Naomi felt her face growing warm.

'I just wondered if it might have a theme,' she said.

'The Wild West,' he said.

Some urbane ducks swam past, quacking and rooting for weed amongst the litter.

'That sounds interesting.'

Her voice came out over-enthusiastic and jolly. A little breeze began to blow across the water, cooling her neck.

The party was in someone's flat, on the first floor, up a narrow street. Naomi walked there by herself, when it was already dark, dressed as a cow. Over the weekend, she and her mother had sewn white cotton circles on to a long black T-shirt and leggings. She had also spent a number of hours creating horns out of a coat hanger, felt and cotton wool. She had attached the horns to her hair with some of her redundant kirby grips.

'What are you supposed to be?' her father asked, sitting, astonished, in front of the television.

'A cow,' said Naomi.

'Oh. Very good,' said her father, and his eyes re-focused quickly on the television, as if they were searching the screen for something normal.

Outside the party flat, Naomi rang the doorbell and waited. There was the sound of thudding music and heavy footsteps on carpeted stairs.

'Oh,' said a girl, opening the door. She was dressed as a

cowgirl, in a suede skirt and cowboy boots. She had long, blonde hair. 'What are you?' she asked.

'A cow,' said Naomi.

'Oh,' said the girl, and she didn't seem to know what else to say. She led her upstairs, and it occurred to Naomi that they were falling into their cowherd and cow characters quite naturally.

'There's drinks and stuff over there,' the cowgirl said. She pointed at a table which held wine bottles and bowls containing crisps. Naomi's horns slipped slightly as she walked towards the table. She poured herself some wine and went to join a group of people she recognised from the recording studio. There were several sound engineers, but William was not there. Naomi sat down. Her cow horns were just visible, black objects, in the corner of her eye.

The recording-studio girls were discussing school. They were just far enough away from schooldays to reminisce about them, to feel almost fond of them.

'We used to sing "Kum By Ya" in assemblies,' said one of the girls, the one with long brown hair. 'I never used to know what it meant.'

'Me neither,' said someone else.

Naomi tipped a handful of crisps into her mouth. 'I used to wonder what the Dance Settee meant,' she said. 'You know, in that song, I am the Lord of the Dance Settee.'

Everyone was suddenly looking at her, their faces looming in the half-light.

'It was "*said he*",' said the long-haired girl.

'Yes,' said Naomi. Her anecdote had collapsed into an alarming shape. 'I just used to think it was "settee", she said. 'You know, I just used to wonder what it was.' She clonked more wine into her glass.

William McCann didn't turn up until she had already drunk too much wine and was feeling slightly unwell, and one of her horns had fallen off and disappeared behind a sofa. When he finally walked into the room Naomi was talking to a man with a thin moustache who reminded her of her first admirer. 'I like your hair,' the man was saying, 'it's very definite'. Weeks later, she remembered him asking her how old she was, and when she said 'eighteen,' he said, 'So young. So mysterious. So kissable.' She couldn't recollect any kiss through the fug of wine, although she did remember that he had been wearing a poncho with little wollen pom-poms, and sitting crossed-legged with a bowl of peanuts in front of him, and when she stood up to go and talk to William she managed to tread on the bowl of peanuts instead of the gaps on either side. 'Sorry,' she said, 'sorry.' When she had picked up the broken china and peanuts and rearranged the remaining peanut bowls, William was already in the kitchen talking to the cowgirl. She didn't remember any more about the evening.

She was letting her hair grow now. By June it had got to the messy stage, standing woven, frightening, above her head when she got up in the mornings. But with a comb and hair gel she was able to start curling it around her ears. She bought a new packet of kirby grips to remind herself not to return to the hairdresser's. It was easy to get your hair cut in a moment of weakness. It was like being in love: a simple thing, temporarily good, which you might weep about for months afterwards.

In the middle of the summer she moved out of her parents' house. She loaded all her possessions into her parents' car and they drove across town together, to a large flat which she had agreed to share with Lindsay Pringle. She and her parents spent an afternoon unloading her clothes, cheese plants, cushions, stereo, speakers, duvet, books, and plodding up four flights of stairs with it all. It looked incongruous in a different setting. Standing on her desk was the yogurt maker which her parents had bought for her eighteenth birthday. She had still not used it. She had thought at the time that it was an odd present to receive when you reached eighteen, but she kept it in her room now and made thin yogurt in it, and looked at it sometimes with a deep, shuddering sense of homesickness. Her new room was large and cold. The bathroom was draughty with an extra-small bath, which it was impossible to lie straight in. She sat upright, listening to the top forty, surrounded by cooling Rambling Rose bubbles. She stared at the tiling, which was falling away from behind the taps, and at the strange, mosaic plug which didn't fit the plughole properly.

After she had been in the flat for a couple of weeks, William began to visit her there. They would stand in her room and kiss for minutes on end. Sometimes, when they had stopped kissing, they wouldn't know what to say to each other.

William's bedroom faced west; it was much warmer than Naomi's room. At dawn, sunlight would come in and shine across the bed, and it felt womanly and slightly melancholy to be lying there, with William asleep next to her. She lay on her back, listening to the milk float and the birds, and watching the tops of the trees. Then she would look at William and wonder whether to touch him.

'I'm getting up,' she said. William pressed his face further into the pillow.

'I'm going to get some breakfast,' she said.

Being naked in front of someone else felt strange. She'd forgotten how to walk in the nude. The only confident part of her were the soles of her feet against the floorboards. She looked at herself in William's mirror. Then she put William's dressing gown on, and it was amazing, to be a woman, aged eighteen, wearing a lover's clothes, and to walk out into his kitchen and look around and find some bread and coffee, even though the kitchen was the most unhygienic, the most fetid place she'd ever been in. Lining the walls were ancient jars of pickled vegetables and tins of chicken soup.

She expected to be with William for years, and when he left and moved to another city she was broken-hearted for months, maybe a year, afterwards – through autumn, winter, another spring. She was still grieving when she had left the recording studio and her first flat; even when her hair had become long enough for kirby grips again.

'You can always come back if it doesn't work out,' her mother had said, standing outside the flat that Naomi was about to share with Lindsay Pringle. 'There's always room.' She looked at the peeling front door doubtfully.

'I'll phone you tomorrow,' Naomi had said, and she hugged her parents and waved to them as they drove away, and wasn't quite aware, even then, that she would not be going back.

Stopping Distances

EILEEN'S DRIVING TEACHER, Gary King, had a little white Rover. It was squat and bright, like a child's toy, and everything about it clunked. Sitting in it, Eileen felt cherished; protected from the world.

She had two lessons a week, after work, just when the sun was setting. Sometimes, in the low light, she and Gary drove around Salisbury Crags. She was not very good at corners, so driving around a small mountain was ideal.

'OK,' Gary said. He said that a lot. He was the calmest man Eileen had ever met. He had a blond beard and blond arm hair.

'OK,' he said on her fifth lesson, 'I am just going to sit here and not say anything. I want you to start the car without any help from me.'

Eileen's heart raced. She put the key in the ignition, checked the mirror, checked the road behind them and set off. She drove as fast as she could to the quietest road she could find.

'You forgot something,' Gary said, when they were safely in the backwaters, churning around Tantallon Place.

'Did I?'

Eileen often got a little flirty with Gary; a little coquettish. Sitting in the driving seat, she always felt very confident.

'You forgot to adjust your position,' said Gary.

'But it didn't need adjusting.'

'If I was the examiner I wouldn't have known that. You have to pretend to adjust things, even if everything's OK.'

'Right.'

Sometimes, she didn't really listen to what Gary was saying, because she had to concentrate on the road. She had to slow down so she didn't drive over kerbs.

'Examiners need humouring,' said Gary, sitting, calm and cosy and belted in. Maybe that was why she flirted with him – because he couldn't escape.

Her husband Jim had learned to drive at seventeen. He had done so many sensible things at a time when she was just loafing around.

But their car was difficult to drive. It was thirteen years old and made strange grinding sounds. It was filled with unnecessary things: half-empty screen-wash bottles, dog-eared maps, empty Irn-Bru cans, chocolate wrappers. There was an ugly little nodding dog on the back shelf, bought as a joke by a friend.

'You need some practice,' Jim said one weekend in September, so they drove to the beach. There were big, empty roads there, simultaneously safe and terrifying, like an empty ice-rink. 'These roads are nice and calm,' Jim said, as they crawled past the sand-dunes and the weedy verges.

But Jim was losing the ability to be calm. Eileen had only been driving for a few minutes when he started to shriek and grip on to the handle of the passenger door.

'You're practically in the ditch,' he shouted. He moved his arm across her, his big annoying arm, and turned the steering wheel. 'Aim nearer the white lines,' he said.

'I would if you weren't holding the steering wheel.'

The problem was he anticipated her mistakes before she made them.

'I was doing fine till you did that,' she said.

And the weekend had been fine; they had gone to the beach because it was a nice afternoon. Autumn; but still warm, still late-summery, and there was a man selling ice creams from a caravan, and they had bought two cones and walked along the damp, puddingy shoreline, watching people's dogs leaping in and out of the water. They had picked up seashells and slithered over the bubbly seaweed. They were a young couple eating King Cones.

The row had come halfway home, shortly after Jim had said 'Why don't you drive?,' and she had just taken over when a mauve Allegro suddenly came bowling out of thin air, over the brow of a hill, with an old man sitting behind the wheel. She could see him very clearly. He had a long thin neck and was wearing a cloth cap. He was sitting bolt upright and driving a little erratically. And just as she was about to turn the wheel, deftly, confidently, Jim had suddenly grabbed it and swerved the car towards the edge of the road.

'You're doing it again!' she shouted.

'You were far too close.'

'I was perfectly in control.'

'It didn't look like it.'

Eileen turned to frown at him. He had become pale. She turned back, moved the wheel, and noticed they had come to a bend in the road that was more curved than she had realised and had a branch sticking out into the middle of it. There was no time to do anything about it. So she drove straight through the branch. The windscreen was filled with squeaking twigs and leaves.

'What the hell are you doing?' Jim said.

'I didn't want to drive on the wrong side of the road. It was either the branch or the blind bend.'

'You could have smashed the windscreen.'

'I thought it was better than driving into an oncoming vehicle.'

'You don't have any road sense whatsoever.'

Eileen didn't reply. She pulled up, calmly, expertly, in a layby that had a sign in it saying '*Look – Potatoes!*' She switched the engine off, got out of the car, slammed the door and made her own way home. It grew dark, and she couldn't see what kind of surface she was walking on. The path was sometimes hard and sometimes squashy. It took her two hours to get back.

The weather in September was very windy.

One Friday morning, when she woke up and switched the

radio on, a woman was talking about high-sided vehicles not being allowed to drive over the Forth Road Bridge. She mentioned the words 'gale' and 'speed restrictions'. So Eileen phoned up the British School of Motoring and asked to speak to Gary.

'One moment,' said the receptionist. Then she pressed a button, and Eileen found herself listening to 'Für Elise'. The notes plunked like punctured squash balls. After a while the receptionist pressed a button again.

'He's on his way,' she said, and Eileen could hear Gary walking to the phone, saying something to someone about a cheese and coleslaw roll, and laughing. There was also the sound of women laughing. It all sounded very warm and flirtatious. Not dull, dull and cold, like the teabag company where Eileen worked. Or frenetic and ridiculous, like Jim's open-plan office. The motoring school sounded real.

'Eileen,' Gary said.

'Do you think we should go out this afternoon?'

'The wind will have died down by then,' Gary said. 'I'll come and pick you up as per normal.'

He said that a lot. As per normal.

'Yes, but . . .'

Eileen picked up a pen and began to doodle a picture of a small, boxy car on the side of the Weetaflakes packet. She could feel herself becoming nervous, just at the thought of driving. Driving in the wind.

'Don't worry,' Gary said, 'we won't go out if it's dangerous'. He made a small, chuckling sound; it was the kind of sound he made when she overrevved the engine.

In the evening, she and Jim sat in the living room. At 5.45 Jim found the remote control behind a cushion and switched on the news.

'Can you move your head?' he said.

Eileen moved her head a couple of centimetres, but she knew it would still be obscuring his view of the Houses of Parliament. She sighed. Jim folded his arms.

'I saw your driving instructor today,' he said.

'Really?'

She picked up a magazine and looked at an article on marriage. The article was called 'For better, for worse?' It was discussing the way marriages could slip, suddenly; the way they could go into freefall. You could realise, one weekend, that you had become entirely different people.

'He was trundling around the Grassmarket,' said Jim. 'He was teaching an old biddy.'

'Really?' said Eileen. And her heart went out to him: calm, kind Gary, sitting in his Rover, teaching an old lady how to drive.

Jim stared at the television screen.

'He needs to get his clutch looked at,' he said.

Gary arrived at six on the dot, just as the newscaster was shuffling her papers together and about to speak. He tooted the horn, and Jim looked up. Then he went to the window.

'Here he is,' he said.

'Yes.'

'He has a very neat beard.'

Jim walked out of the room, down the hall, through the front doorway and across to Gary, who was still sitting in his car. Gary wound down his window and they talked for a while. Eileen watched them from the living room. The whole scene reminded her of something. She couldn't think what it was. Then she realised it reminded her of her father quizzing her boyfriends before they drove off for the evening.

Even though it was nearly winter, Gary always wore T-shirts. He had a fresh, lemon-yellow one which went particularly well with his blond arm hair.

Eileen was practising the little, difficult manouevres now. The ones where you could easily damage the bumpers. Parallel parking; reversing around a corner; three-point turns. Maybe one day, she thought, I will be good at these things.

For the three-point turns Gary had chosen a road with a very steep camber, which they kept falling into. She was in the middle of turn number five – she had manoeuvred the car full-square across the middle of the road – when a large red Estate car appeared at their side. There was a middle-aged man sitting in the driving seat, frowning at her. She could almost hear him sighing.

'Damn,' she said. She took her foot off the clutch and stalled the car.

'Don't panic,' said Gary. 'He will just have to wait.'

He moved forward in his seat, smiled and waved at the car driver. The car driver stared.

'Some folk get so pompous,' said Gary. He moved back again.

'Right,' Eileen said. She turned the key in the ignition, put the car in first gear and stalled again. The car driver hooted his horn.

'Keep your hair on,' Gary said to him, through the closed window.

Eileen tried again and it worked. Like Robert the Bruce's spider.

'Like Robert the Bruce's spider,' she said.

'Yes,' said Gary, 'concentrate on the road.'

The car lurched forwards and rolled down the camber, and the Estate car edged around them with only a few inches to spare. The man glared and mouthed some words which Eileen was quite capable of lip-reading. He drove off very fast. There was a sticker on the back window that said '*Baby On Board*'.

'Excellent,' said Gary, and Eileen wanted to put her arms around him.

She was able to speak and drive at the same time now, so sometimes they had conversations. Or Gary might put one of his cassettes on. They bowled along at nearly thirty miles an hour, listening to a cassette he had called 'Jazz on a Summer's Afternoon'.

'So,' said Gary, 'what do you do?'

'I work in a herbal teabag company.'

'Really?' Gary glanced out of the window. 'Interesting,' he said.

'At the moment I'm working on Marvellous Mango.'

Gary looked at her. He was silent for a moment.

'Have you ever been to the States?' he asked, after Eileen had successfully negotiated quite a large mini roundabout. 'They have things called four-way stops there.'

Their conversations were often a little disappointing. Eileen changed into third gear. 'I haven't, no,' she said, glancing up at the rear-view mirror and realising that there was a lorry on their tail. It was driving very fast and getting nearer. It was nearly touching the bumper. The driver seemed oblivious. Eileen could see him slouching forward, leaning his elbows against the steering wheel, chewing something.

'I've been there,' said Gary, 'a long time ago. When I was young and carefree.'

Eileen could see nothing behind them except the lorry's front grille and headlights.

'It's my ambition to drive across the States,' Gary was saying, staring out of the window at the shopfronts, and she was about to say 'Gary, there is a huge lorry bearing down on us, what do I do here, Gary, what do I do?,' when the lorry turned up a side street and the road behind them cleared. After a minute or so her heart-rate slowed again.

'Freeway driving seems quite strange,' she said breezily. She gulped and felt sick. 'There don't seem to be any rules.'

Gary folded his hands together in his lap. 'I like your perfume,' he said. 'What is it?'

'Marvellous Mango.'

'Ha!' said Gary. He always laughed at her jokes.

They made their way past a garage and a long, grey row of tenement flats, and Eileen changed up into third gear.

'Excellent,' said Gary.

The way the sun was shining, low and oblique, Eileen could see their silhouettes printed against the stoney walls of the buildings. The shadows of their faces moved towards each other and kissed.

Sometimes, packing teabags at work, and thinking how much they resembled little pillows, she would think of Jim. She would think of hugging him, kissing him, sleeping with him. But often, when she got back home, he was not there. He was caught up with work, with a deadline, and had left a message on the answerphone. Or sometimes there was no message. Sometimes the lights would be on in the flat, and she would call out 'Jim?,' but there was no answer. Sometimes she would walk into each room, to see if he was in one of them because she wanted to see him so much; she wanted him, suddenly, to be there with her. But after a while, she would give up. She would make herself some toast and tea and sit in the kitchen. She waited.

Sometimes she couldn't settle to anything.

On Monday Jim walked in at half past seven. He was carrying some strips of Contiplas.

'Where were you?' Eileen asked, walking out into the hallway. He had been late for so long that her enthusiasm for him had turned into resentment.

'I went for a drive,' Jim said.

'Are you just saying that to annoy me?'

'No. I just went for a drive. I got some Contiplas to make the bathroom shelves.'

'I didn't think we were planning to have Contiplas shelves.'

'What's wrong with Contiplas?'

'Why are you shouting at me?'

Gary would never have Contiplas shelves in his bathroom, she thought. Jim glared. Then he went outside again. Eileen watched him through the window, removing another sheet of ugly white Contiplas from the boot of the car. Then he came in again, went into the bathroom with it and shut the door. After a while, Eileen could hear him sawing the Contiplas and drilling holes with the electric drill his father had bought him. She went into the bathroom.

'They'll be useful,' she said, doubtfully.

She walked up to him and touched his arm.

'Don't do that,' he said, 'it's dangerous.'

'Sorry.' She stood there for a while. 'Do you want some tea? Work gave me a hundred Marvellous Mango sachets to try.'

'I'd rather have a cup of coffee,' he said.

At the start of her next lesson, Gary suggested they drive up to Salisbury Crags again. He thought it should be nice and quiet. Also, it was picturesque.

Eileen drove for quarter of an hour or so, almost reaching forty miles an hour, and ascending at quite an angle.

'Speedy Gonzalez,' said Gary.

The sky was full of mackerel clouds. It felt so remote around Salisbury Crags that Eileen almost expected to see sheep. Or the Queen, out for a walk.

'Nice view,' said Gary, sighing.

'It's beautiful.'

'We should do this route more often,' said Gary.

When they got to the lake, Eileen pulled over, parked, switched off the engine, and they got out. They stood, leaning against the car bonnet and looked up at the sky. It was pink; a wintery pink, with birds flying in it. There were some geese, honking and flying in small, broken Vs. They made Eileen think of Jim and her – big, awkward birds going off in straggling directions.

'Gary. . .', she began, 'do you think. . .', but he interrupted her.

'Pink-footed geese,' he said.

'Yes,' she said, and she stopped talking.

She turned and pulled open the car door, climbed in, hitting her head against the rear-view mirror and knocking it out of line. Then she just sat there, behind the steering wheel. She watched Gary through the windscreen. He stood, smoking a cigarette and looking across the lake, and Eileen felt something dragging her down: a little undertow of sadness.

After a while, Gary got back into the car. He smelled of cigarettes.

'OK,' he said, and Eileen switched on the engine, put the car into gear and drove back on to the road. It was difficult to see clearly. It was the time of evening that confuses the eyes.

At the weekend she and Jim stayed at home and drank a lot of wine.

'How are the driving lessons going?' Jim asked.

'Fine.' She could feel herself blushing.

'What's what's-his-name like?'

'OK. Capable.'

She turned her face and poured herself another glass.

Jim looked at her. Then he got up, went out into the hallway, and stood, looking at the bookshelves. He returned with a battered copy of *The Highway Code.* He dropped it on to the carpet in front of Eileen.

'A present,' he said. Eileen opened it and looked at the front page. It was published in 1979, the year Jim learned to drive. There were diagrams of people doing hand signals out of the window.

'That's very nice of you,' she said, 'but I think I'll need something more up to date.'

'Thanks.'

'Jim. . .,' she said, crawling towards him across the carpet, 'I'm very touched. . . '

'Never mind,' he said, and he got up again and went to sit on a chair.

Her theory test was in the Central Library. She had circled the date in her diary: Wednesday, 8 October. She had learned all the roadsigns but there were some obscure ones she kept forgetting, like the blank circular one. It seemed appropriate that she kept forgetting the blank one. And she still couldn't remember the stopping distances.

Gary thought she would be fine. On the day of the test they arranged to meet, so he could test her. He suggested they went to a café he knew, across the road from the library. It was called Dumbo's. This also seemed appropriate.

When she arrived he was already there. He was sitting at a table for two, reading the plastic menu that stood three-faced in front of him. There was also a little vase of plastic flowers. He was wearing a long-sleeved shirt, and a BSM tie. There were little cars printed on it.

'Hi,' he said.

'Hi.'

Eileen edged around the table and sat down. She thought 'I am drinking coffee with my driving instructor.' The night before, she had been dreaming about him. Her heartbeat was audible in her head.

'What would you like?' Gary asked. 'A cappuccino?'

'I think I'll have an espresso.'

'A woman of refined tastes.'

'Espresso's the opposite of refined though, isn't it?' she said. 'Espresso's pretty strong and unrefined. Is it? Or maybe not.'

Gary stared at her, and she looked down at the plastic menu. She wondered if this curious little dalliance was making her hysterical.

Gary put one finger in the air and a hopeful, handsome expression on his face. Two waitresses rushed up to the table, and he asked them both for an espresso. The waitresses giggled. Eileen smiled. Then she just sat and knotted her fingers together for a while; she knotted them into a little architectural knot. *Here is a church, here is the steeple, lift up the roof, and see all the people.*

She wondered if she and Gary had anything at all in common, apart from his Rover.

After a few minutes the older waitress returned with her espresso and another cup of cappuccino for Gary. She smiled and spilled a little of both on to the table-top.

'Whoops,' said Gary, 'butterfingers,' and the waitress giggled again and went away.

'You're looking very smart,' Eileen said, a propos of nothing.

'I had a meeting,' Gary said.

Then they fell silent. Eileen put her elbows on the table, her fingers outstretched to cover her hot face. She wound her ankles around the rungs of her chair.

'Well,' she said, 'here we are in Dumbo's.'

Gary chuckled and shook his head. Eileen noticed that, as well as the tie and the long sleeves, he was also wearing aftershave. It smelled a little like Magic Tree.

'How's life in the teabag industry?' he asked.

'I'm packing Berry Bonanza at the moment.'

Gary looked slightly disconcerted.

'And how are you getting on with the Highway Code?' he asked.

'Not bad. Although there are some bits that are confusing.'

'Some bits that are confusing,' Gary repeated, as if he found this very sweet.

Eileen looked at some notes she had brought with her.

What if the car rolls back on a hill? Can I drive faster than 30mph? Will I be asked to drive up a cul-de-sac?

They all seemed to signify something.

'So you live on Albany Crescent,' Gary said. 'Nice street.'

'Yes. How about you?'

'I live near the bypass.'

'Oh. Any flatmates?'

'No. Just the wife.'

Eileen began to make a fuss with her espresso. 'So,' she said. She wanted, suddenly, very much, not to be there. Gary pulled at his sleeves as if he was not used to the length of them. He looked around the restaurant. Then he looked at her again.

'Is there anything that you want to ask before the test?' he said. 'Anything you're still not sure of?'

'One thing.' She cleared her throat. 'I wanted to ask about box junctions. Whether you can sit in them.'

Gary smiled. 'Women drivers,' he said, and something chilled the back of Eileen's neck suddenly, when he said that. Something made her shudder.

'The things you come out with!' Gary said.

'Oh,' said Eileen, and Gary smiled again. 'Sorry,' he said, 'did that sound sexist?'

Then he told her about box junctions. You can enter a box junction, he said, as long as you can get out of them.

She knew, anyway.

By the time she was out of the library, it was already dark. She sat on a concrete bollard at the main doors, waiting for Jim. It was raining, and she didn't have an umbrella, and Jim was late. He was an hour late. The rain was cold and plastered her hair against her head.

When he finally arrived, it was nearly eight o'clock. The ugly nodding dog nodded at her as the car turned the corner and stopped.

'Hi,' she said. She got up from the bollard and walked over to the car, ashamed.

'How was it?' said Jim.

'OK, I think,' she said. She held on to the silver handle of the door.

'Did you get the stopping distances right?'

'I think so.'

Jim stopped the engine and looked at her face. Then he moved across from the driving seat to the passenger seat.

'You drive,' he said.

'OK,' said Eileen, and she got in. She adjusted the seat position, the rear-view mirror and the wing mirror. She breathed in, her heart thumping, and put the key in the ignition. She was still thinking about the questions in the exam; the signs that indicate diversions; cul-de-sacs; detours. She was thinking about the ones you see on motorways sometimes, that say '*End Of Roadworks. Thank You For Your Patience*'.

Round the World

SOMETIMES, I GO into changing rooms to get away from my friend. I stand behind the curtain, or I sit, on the little chair. Sometimes I don't even try anything on. I just hang the clothes up on the hook, close my eyes and picture Saturday, when my friend will be on a plane, flying away.

On Monday we went to the park; we sat on a bench and ate the expensive Marks & Spencers sandwiches Amanda bought. Chicken tikka, tasting slightly of plastic. On Tuesday we stayed at home and she forced me to show her all my holiday photographs. 'Who's that?' she asked, pointing at the picture I have of John, my new man. She has always been nosey. Today we are shopping. Amanda has bought two candlesticks, a silk dressing gown, a red coffee pot and six teaspoons. I have bought a pair of ankle socks.

'You should buy tights,' she says. 'Ankle socks are not flattering.'

In the changing room, I imagine I am in a bathing hut, being wheeled out to sea. I am walking down the steps; free, alone, and running into the waves. But in the distance I hear her – she is shouting 'Are you going to be in there until the next millennium or what?,' and the sea evaporates. I pick up my coat and bag, come out of the cubicle and walk towards her. Amanda is leaning against a chrome clothes rack that has purple smocks hanging on it.

'How did it look?' she asks.

'It made me look shouldery.'

'But you have nice shoulders,' she snaps. She moves away from the clothes rack, and all the smocks swing back and forth, like people swaying too enthusiastically at a disco.

'I'm going to try on this top,' she says, and she turns and walks towards the changing rooms. There is a small queue now. Two old women and two young ones, all moving up the line, very slowly. An assistant stands at the head, facing forward, like a figurehead. She takes circular tags off pegs and hands them to people. She says 'How were they? Any good?' After a few minutes Amanda reaches the top of the queue. The assistant holds up a tag and she grabs it and disappears. The blouse she has found is flaming scarlet with a ruffled front. I don't understand Amanda's dress sense.

While I wait, I touch one of the smocks, just out of curiosity, and it falls off the hanger into a little heap on the floor.

I have known Amanda since we were twelve. We are now thirty. When she was sixteen she moved away with her family and we didn't see each other until we were twenty-one. When we met again we had evidently grown apart. We had nothing in common except our ages. Amanda was very pretty and went clubbing. I was plainish and liked staying in. My boyfriends had names like Dave and Steve and worked in electronics shops. Amanda's were called Sebastien and Lucas and worked in advertising.

Amanda always had things that I didn't have. She had pixie boots and a ra-ra skirt and once she went to a Bay City Roller concert. The year we first met, she had a horse. His name was Stardust. He was brown with a white star on the centre of his forehead and he used to froth at the mouth. He was a birthday present, bought for Amanda by her father, and for about two months she would go and visit Stardust in his bleak little field on the outskirts of Croydon, and clear up his dung with a shovel. The weather always seemed to be cold, with grey rain-clouds. Stardust sulked and ground his teeth, and Amanda got bored with him after a while and started going out with a boy called Christian. So her father ended up shovelling dung for the next ten years.

Amanda once showed me something she called 'in-saddle exercises'. There was one called 'Scissors' and another called 'Round the World,' where you were meant to turn 360 degrees in the saddle. Halfway through, you'd be perched the wrong way round, eighteen hands up, staring at the horse's shiny bum. You would start to perspire; to imagine falling and knocking yourself out. Amanda would be standing somewhere with a little, fading torch, miles away, saying 'Come on, slowcoach, it's getting dark,' and after twenty minutes or so, you'd pluck up the courage to hold on to the tail, praying that Stardust didn't move, and swing one leg around very carefully and slowly until you were sitting sideways, facing nothing but blank space. A gap, with hard, flat mud ten feet below you and a barbed-wire fence twenty yards away. You'd be wobbling in a void, your saliva tasting of fear. After another pause you'd heave yourself the right way round again, so that your head pointed the same way as the horse's, and you'd climb off; you'd climb off as quickly as you could.

Earlier that morning, when Amanda had tried to do it, she had fallen off. Smack, onto the hard, wet ground. Her mother told me that, in secret, when we went indoors for tea.

Amanda lives in Berlin now and is very successful. She is a contract manager for a big music company called Koolkat. She lives in her own apartment and has tropical fish and boyfriends with names like Marcus and Antoine. But she still visits me. For the past eight years she has been visiting me every year, en route from somewhere to somewhere else. She has sat in my kitchen and lamented my lifestyle. My flat, she thinks, is weird and plain, and so are my men. And I wear funny clothes now – clompy shoes which are very strange. And my job, working in a garden centre, is very non-aspirational and badly paid. I say 'I like working in the garden centre. I like wearing these clothes and being with this man,' and Amanda smiles.

In Debenhams we spend a long time looking at the bath-towels. They have been arranged in beautiful layers of orange and blue. On the top towel there is a sea urchin, and it makes me think of holidays at the beach; but not the kind Amanda would approve of, involving black cleavagey bikinis and tanned, lip-curling men. I am thinking of the kind that involve skinny-dipping at night, and cassette players, and drinking beer. Also of one particular man, John, whom I haven't introduced to Amanda. I am meeting him tomorrow night, after waving goodbye to Amanda.

'Don't these colours look lovely together, Mandy?' I say, picking up one of the orange towels.

'A bit garish, aren't they?' says Amanda. She is looking at the silver-plated toothbrush holders.

'I'm going to get one of these,' I say, holding up a plastic soap-dish. It has a hole in the middle, for the water to run through. It costs £7.50, almost as much as Amanda might spend on a soap dish, and buying it makes me feel a little devilish, because she will hate it; she hates unadorned, peculiar, plastic things, and that makes me feel good. I take it to the till, along with a metal lemon squeezer and two recycled wine glasses, which are slightly warped. I am in the mood for buying domestic objects; plain practical things for my home. When Amanda is with me, I am as defensive as a snail about my home.

The woman at the till has her hair up in a bun, but it needs re-doing. It looks as if it has had a hard day.

'What's this?' she asks, picking up the soap dish.

Then she smiles, but not at me, the customer; she smiles at the smart, affluent young woman who has come to join us, clutching a hand-towel with embroidery on one corner. The embroidery says 'Guest Towel'. Why? Why would you want to own a towel that says 'Guest Towel', as if you can't say 'Here's a towel' when someone comes to stay?

'Those towels are lovely, aren't they?' says the woman at the till. 'They're stylish. They're very popular.'

And Amanda smiles at the woman; a quick, beautiful smile. There seems to be some sort of telepathic communication going on between them. Something like 'Why the hell is this woman spending £7.50 on a piece of plastic?' Maybe they are thinking that.

The assistant rings the prices up on the till.

'That's £21.95 altogether then, please,' she says, smirking, and tearing off a strip of tissue paper to wrap the glasses in.

Sometimes we talk about Stardust. I say 'Do you remember when you used to show me those in-saddle exercises?' and Amanda says 'Oh, yeah, Stardust'. But Stardust is in the past. Amanda has spent several years in America, where horses are part of the scenery.

'Let's eat,' Amanda says as we're leaving Debenhams. 'I'm starving.'

There is a department store across the road which I have never been into. It is called Nieves and Brown. It has very expensive and horrible suits in the window.

'Let's go there,' says Amanda.

'Why?'

'Because I want to look at the clothes.'

The entrance is full of Accessories. Hosiery, hats and bags. The light is dim; you would never know it was sunny outside. It's as dismal as a swamp. Shop assistants sweep around the floor in quiet, thick-soled shoes. A piped arrangement of 'I am a Woman in Love' is playing over the circular skirt racks, and in the middle of the window display, an assistant is creeping about, arranging fake lemon trees in groups.

'Those little suits are dead sexy,' says Amanda, and I feel I am intruding on something; something mysterious to do with being Amanda – a woman who has her hair *colour-rinsed* once a fortnight; who wears designer jackets; who earns $45,000 a year.

I walk fast towards the stairs. On my way there, I reach out and touch a shirt on a hanger, just to grab on to something different, something unrelated to Amanda, and it falls off.

Up in the restaurant we queue for lasagne and coffee. Amanda also asks for a jug of extra hot milk. The assistant behind the counter looks annoyed.

'We don't do hot milk,' she says.

'Is it really that much bother?'

Amanda stares at the assistant with her dark, pretty eyes. The assistant stares back. 'We don't have a separate price for hot milk,' she says. She looks about twelve. She sets her mouth at a belligerent angle and stares for about three seconds. Then she loses her nerve, apologises, looks close to tears suddenly, picks up a small metal jug and pours hot milk into it.

'Thank you,' says Amanda, gathering together cups, saucers, napkins, lasagne, cutlery, milk pot, putting it all on a tray, squaring it up neatly, getting out her soft, leather wallet and paying. I don't offer to pay. I have stopped trying to be mature about things like that.

We plot our way balefully around the restaurant furniture like a U-boat. Amanda chooses a table by the window which is not too near the Ladies and not too near the noisy till. It is behind the plastic plant display and has a view of the bus depot. We sit in silence, watching people queuing at the bus stances.

'I wonder if those people are off to the beach,' I say, trying to force jollity into my voice.

'If they try swimming in that sea,' says Amanda, 'they'll go down with something nasty'.

She looks through the window and sighs, as if the people at the bus stances, the people who live in my city, are as strange and unsuccessful as me. She shakes her head and pokes at the lasagne with one fork-prong.

'There aren't any real beaches here,' she says, 'not like California.'

'There are plenty of beaches. California is not the only bloody place with a beach.'

Amanda looks at me. She does not reply. She is the same as she always was – the bossy twelve-year-old with the horse called Stardust. She sits there, with her expensive handbag on her lap, and frowns out of the window. She looks as if she is staring through the window of an aeroplane. Sitting, plotting her next move, in executive club class.

There is a delicate hush of voices and side-plates. I saw away at a hard piece of lasagne. Amanda blinks, breathes in and looks down.

'I've bought you something, actually,' she says, in the high voice she has when she is upset, and I feel myself flinch. I have hurt Amanda. My oldest friend. And she has bought me a present. I put my cutlery down, grip the wicker of my chair, and watch as she unclips her handbag and pulls out a paper bag. She hands it to me.

'It's probably not your kind of thing,' she says.

'I'm sure it's very . . .', I say, opening the bag, '. . . very . . .'. Inside there is a very shiny silk scarf. I pull it out of the bag and shake it open. It is printed all over with pictures of horses. And they all look like Stardust – brown, with crazed expressions, and white stars on their foreheads.

'I got it when you were in the changing room,' says Amanda. 'I couldn't resist it'. She smiles at me. And I smile back. And I don't think she will ever quite forgive me for that day: when I went round the world, and she fell off.

Sensible Footwear

MRS CLIMBER IS the careers officer. People make jokes, to do with climbing the careers ladder. It is an old joke, because Mrs Climber has been there for decades. She has a long face and a long nose and dyed chestnut hair that swoops, in an eighties, *Cosmopolitan* kind of way. Her face is too old for her hair. She breathes through her mouth and looks very sadly at Heather as she walks into the Careers Office in her customised school uniform. Mrs Climber always looks very sad. Her voice is lisping and melancholy.

'You must have definite plans, Heather,' she says, 'You're sixteen now. It's no good vaguely thinking what you want to do. In just over a year,' she says, pulling a blue folder from a pile on her desk, 'you're going to be out there, in the World of Work.'

She looks at Heather.

'What do you want to do?' she says. 'Any ideas?'

'I want to be a singer-songwriter,' says Heather.

'That is most laudable,' says Mrs Climber, 'but not very realistic.'

'It's what I'm good at,' says Heather, 'singing and writing songs.'

'Yes,' says Mrs Climber. She tosses her chestnut hair to one side, and glances at Heather's purple-varnished nails. Heather has drawn a little smiling face on one of them. 'Unfortunately,' she says, 'you can't spend your life singing and writing songs.'

'Some people do,' says Heather.

'But not most people.'

'I'm not most people.'

Mrs Climber looks at Heather. Then she looks at some writing she has on the subject of Heather.

'What else do you like doing?' she asks.

'Mainly I like going for walks,' says Heather.

Mrs Climber looks relieved. 'Well, why don't you sort out some outdoorsy-work over the summer holidays? That'll give you some idea whether you want to pursue that Particular Avenue. You could do conservation work.' She pauses. 'Planting trees,' she says, a little wildly. 'Mending walls.'

'I mainly like walking around town,' says Heather, but Mrs Climber is not listening.

'. . . then you can think what A levels you might want to do,' she is saying, 'because unfortunately there are currently no singer-songwriting A levels.'

'There's music,' says Heather.

Mrs Climber does not seem to hear.

The stone-walling course that her mother has read about is suitable for fit people of all ages. All you need is a willingness to learn, the ability to lift stones and some sensible footwear.

'That sounds as if it might be fun,' says Heather's mother. 'You might meet some nice boys.'

'Mother,' says Heather. She can't imagine that there will be any nice boys. And she doesn't have any wellingtons. So she looks in her wardrobe and gets out her worst shoes: the squashy, childish ones she bought in a department store sale. She also packs her black jeans, her black jumper and her father's yellow kagool.

All the other volunteers are wearing shades of green. She noticed that from quite a distance. They are standing at the bus station, hovering in a small, laughing group around Stance B.

'Are you the conservationists?' Heather asks a tall man.

'Yes,' says the man. 'How did you guess?'

'I saw the wellingtons,' she says, and the man looks at her with pale, unblinking eyes.

'Indeed,' he says. He looks away and continues talking to his friend.

Heather finds a little gap towards the back of the group and squeezes herself into it. She puts her rucksack and her bag of sandwiches on the ground. She wonders whether to take her kagool off. Now she is there, surrounded by people in green, she feels inappropriate. Like a canary in a swamp.

'Have you been a volunteer for long?' she asks a woman standing beside her.

'This is my first trip,' says the woman. She shivers, turns away slightly and coughs.

'I have been stone-walling for twenty years,' says a man. He moves and treads, very slightly, on the edge of Heather's foot. He is the only other person not wearing wellingtons. He has on a pair of shoes with leather flaps across the toes.

'And you?' he asks.

'This is my first time.'

'Always the worst,' says the man. 'On hols?'

'Sorry?'

'School holidays?'

'Yes.'

'Gainfully unemployed, then?' says the man.

'Yes.'

'Welcome to my world,' says the man.

The minibus arrives. It has a painting of an acorn on the side, and a sign over the door that says *Seating Capacity: Ten Persons.* It feels as if there are more than ten of them. But after they have got in, milled about, trod on feet and coils of rope and shovels, they all find seats. They settle down suddenly.

'All aboard?' asks the driver, like Noah in the ark. No one replies. It is airless in the minibus, and there is a smell of paraffin.

The driver is wearing green and sitting beside a green-T-shirted woman. As soon as he has started the engine up, the woman leans over, whispers something and starts to rub the back of his neck. The driver laughs, changes gear and pats her arm. Heather wonders if touching comes naturally to people who spend their time digging ditches together.

When she looks out of the window, she can see her mother's office. She can see her mother's colleague, Hilary Jamieson, wearing her silk-effect green blouse, and she can see the Easter Cactus and the telephone. Next door is Il Gardino, the café where she and her friend Sandra go for coffee sometimes, after school. She can see Tony the waiter handing someone a cappuccino. She can see his white shirt and his dark, solid haircut and his smile. She puts her hand up and waves but he doesn't see her. And suddenly she wants to get out, she doesn't want to be on her way to Lancashire, on her way to a stone-walling course. She wants to be walking into Il Gardino with Sandra, going up to the counter and saying 'Hi Tony, how are you?, but here she is, sitting in a minibus with nine strangers, trying to prove that she likes being outdoors; and the driver has accelerated to 40 miles an hour, and the city is disappearing behind them. Everything is disappearing. Within quarter of an hour they are on the motorway, and there isn't any city left; only warehouses, shopping malls, computer centres and the occasional, small field of sheep.

There is no room to move. Her kagool sits around her like a hot, plastic tent. She is wedged between the man with the shoes and the short woman who doesn't speak.

After a while the driver begins to sing. 'Ten green bottles, sitting on a wall, ten green bottles . . .'

'Please,' she thinks, 'please stop,' and as if he has heard her, he stops.

The short woman sniffs.

'So,' the man with the flappy shoes asks, 'why are you volunteering?'

'I need to do something definite,' Heather says.

'You need to like nature,' says the man. He raises his eyebrows, smiles and gets out his sandwich box. It is metallic with a little plastic clip.

'I'm Frank,' he says after a moment.

'I'm Heather,' she says, and she bites her lip. She wants to laugh, suddenly. She wants to remember this, so she and Sandra can write a song about it. They could call it 'Frank'. Or 'Frankly Frank'.

Frank frowns. Then he prises one of his sandwiches apart, looks at the filling, presses the bread back together again and puts it in his mouth.

'I always finish my lunch before we get there,' he says.

Sitting there, being driven, reminds her of holidays when she was small. Of sitting behind her parents, beside her sister, and staring through the car window at the side of the road; hedges, cattle, farm-gates, strange posts with consecutive numbers on them. On the verges there are dandelion clocks and purple lucestrife.

After a mile or so she sees a short, bearded man standing in a field, surrounded by a pile of stones. The man lifts one arm and waves at the minibus. And then they move on. They drive, fast, across a small, hump-backed bridge, and for a second she is thrown into the air. Her head knocks against the roof of the minibus.

'Sorry,' the driver shouts. He looks at Heather in his mirror. 'You don't have as much ballast as some of us.'

'Enjoy the trip?' says Frank. 'Send us a postcard next time.'

Then the minibus turns suddenly, sharp left, through a gateway, down a stoney track and up on to a grass verge. Heather can feel her brain rattling inside her skull.

'Right,' the driver shouts. He stops the engine abruptly. 'Everyone out,' and they all bend their heads, step across the ropes and shovels, and jump.

The barn is made up of one long kitchen, two dormitories and four showers.

'This is the Ritz,' says the bearded man, the one who had been waving at the minibus. His name is Adrian. 'This is five-star luxury,' he says, 'compared to most of our barns.'

Nobody speaks. They walk into the kitchen and look around. There is a long, formica-topped table, a sink, a cooker and a fridge.

'It looks quite nice,' says someone quietly.

'It *is* quite nice,' says Adrian. 'Most of our people sleep on the floor. Here we give you beds. Isn't that right, Dave?'

'That's right,' says the minibus driver.

Heather is sharing her dormitory with two middle-aged women: Prue and Tina. There is nobody Heather's age. It's embarrassing. They toss a coin to see who has to have one of the lower bunks. 'Tails,' Heather says. She always says tails. She gets the lower bunk.

'Perhaps we could swop halfway through the week,' she says.

'It hardly seems worth it,' says Tina. She is already making up her bed, plumping up the pillows.

The view through the window is of a rusted tractor chassis and some tall, quite pretty weeds. In the sunlight, feathery seeds blow about, and Heather stands by the window for a while and watches it. It isn't too bad a view. It is something you can look at when you don't know what else to do.

There is a wardrobe in the corner of the dormitory that smells of pinewood, and they unpack and put their empty rucksacks in it. Heather has packed too many summery clothes and only one jumper. Her jeans and kagool and squashy shoes are the only other practical things she has. And a pair of her father's socks. She has packed her new black dress and a swimming costume, even though they are in the middle of fields. The nearest place to swim is the sea, twenty miles away.

'That's a nice dress,' Prue says, as Heather is trying to smooth the creases out against her hip, 'very sophisticated.'

'Are all your clothes black?' Tina says. She is hanging her own clothes down the side of the bunkbed. They are all shades of green.

'I brought it because I thought we might be going out in the evenings,' Heather says, and Tina makes a strange little laughing noise. 'I didn't think people who wear purple nail varnish went out much,' she says. Heather is beginning to dislike Tina already, and she has only known her for an afternoon. She looks out of the window again. At the far corner of the yard, she can see a ginger cat crawling around beneath a pile of pallets. After a while it pounces on something. She wonders if it is a rat.

They spend the evening playing whist with a very dirty pack of playing cards that somebody found down the side of the fridge.

‘So are you going off to uni next year?’ Frank asks Heather, halfway through a game of rummey.

‘I don’t know,’ she says. ‘I haven’t decided.’

‘What do you want to do?’ he says.

‘I want to be a singer-songwriter.’

‘Ooh,’ says Frank, ‘get you.’

At about nine o’clock one of the men goes out to a small shop at the far end of the nearby village. He comes back an hour and a half later with two bottles of Thunderbird.

‘It’s the only alcohol they had,’ he says.

Frank gets drunk very quickly on the Thunderbird. As they’re beginning their seventh round of whist, he suddenly puts his arm around Heather and draws her towards him.

‘I write the songs that make the whole world cry,’ he slurs into her ear. His breath smells of sour pears.

‘Yes,’ says Heather. She struggles from beneath his arm. She resists the temptation to run out into the night.

In the morning they all meet up in the kitchen and make breakfast. The women slice up mushrooms and tomatoes and the men take them away and fry them in a lot of oil.

At nine o’clock they assemble at the barn door, get back into the minibus and drive to the stone wall. It stands on top of a windy hill. There are gaps all the way along it, like the edges of a postage stamp. Before they begin work, Adrian shows them what to do.

‘The beauty of stone-walling,’ he says, ‘is that you just need stones and your hands.’

He holds his hands up in the air, and then a couple of stones.

‘It’s like a big jigsaw puzzle,’ he says. ‘You just need to find stones the right size, and make sure they fit neatly.’

He crouches at the side of the wall and places the two stones on top of a larger one. They make a clumping sound.

‘You just have to watch your fingers,’ he says.

They are put into teams of three, along the length of the wall. They are so far apart that they can’t hear each other; they are all just small, silent figures, wielding rocks on the brow of a hill.

Heather's group contains the very quiet woman and a boy whose name is Gordon. He is very tall and has a pair of green army trousers. He tells Heather that he is doing geography at Glasgow University.

'So I suppose stone-walling is quite relevant if you're studying geography,' Heather says, sensibly; in a sensible voice.

'That would be geology,' says Gordon. He looks at Heather. 'I'm just doing this,' he says, 'because I get free rent and food for a week.'

He picks up a huge rock and crashes it into a gap in the wall. Heather watches him for a moment. *That is the thing about boys*, she thinks, *they can pick up heavy weights.*

At lunchtime, they all stop working and huddle around a small fire that Frank has made. Adrian arrives with some bags of things to eat: white bread and orange cheese. For pudding there are Mars Bars.

'Enjoy,' Adrian says, dropping the bags on the ground and walking away again. He is going to eat lunch in a pub.

Everyone looks at the bags.

'This is like being a cave-person,' says Prue.

'Why?' says Tina.

'Because of the fire and everything,' says Prue, dismally. Frank makes a strange humming noise through his nose, and begins to dispense plastic plates.

'So,' Heather says, sitting beside Gordon on a little hummock of grass, 'how long have you been at university?'

'Three years,' says Gordon, spreading a thick layer of margarine on a slice of bread.

'Are you studying any particular region?'

Gordon puts the slice of bread between his teeth and pulls. 'It doesn't really work like that,' he says.

Heather can't think how to pursue the conversation. She feels it has been exhausted already. Nobody seems to want to say anything to anyone. They just want to move rocks around. She reaches forward and searches in the food bag for something with vitamins in it. The only thing she can find is a small, hard tomato.

She is biting into it when something colourful suddenly whizzes past her left ear. It is a plate. Frank and Prue have started to play frisbies with the plates.

She wonders how far away the nearest phone box is. Maybe there is one in the village. But perhaps it is best not to phone Sandra. They might have hysterics.

She gets up, still eating the tomato, and walks away from the group. She goes and stands on the wall. She just stands and looks around. The view from the top of the hill is very beautiful; the colours are green, brown and mauve, and there is a smell of woodsmoke. She can see in the distance a line of dark-green fir trees, and beyond that, the sea, shining like a slug's trail.

When she gets back, Frank is sitting on the ground, with his hand over his left eye. He has been hit by a plastic plate.

They start work again just as it begins to rain. Heather puts up the hood of her kagool, and the edges of her view are framed with yellow. She can just hear the swishing noise that the plastic makes as she moves her arms, and the rain spitting against her head. She picks up a rock and drops it into a gap. Once, when she was sitting in the car behind her parents, beside her sister, she looked out of the window and saw prisoners in uniforms doing community service. They were just plodding about in a field, moving rocks around. The conservation group makes her think of that: everyone working silently on their own little sections of wall, looking for suitable-sized stones. Heather fills in the gaps in the middle. She looks for stones that will fit into the palm of her hand, that she can curl her fingers around.

After a while she looks up and sees a landrover driving fast across the field towards them. It is Adrian, back from his pub-lunch.

'Here comes the slavedriver,' says Frank. He has a faint bruise at the side of his eye.

Adrian draws up, switches off the engine and jumps plumply out.

'How's it going, folks?' he shouts. Everyone swings their heads up like livestock, and looks at him.

'That section's coming along nicely,' says Adrian, pointing at Heather's bit of wall. He looks at her. 'Nice kagool,' he says.

Halfway through the afternoon, she does what you are not supposed to do. She drops a rock on her foot. It is such a sharp, awful pain; it makes such a terrible squashing noise, that it brings tears to her eyes. She swears and sits down, clutching the end of her shoe.

Frank looks up.

'Nee-naw, nee-naw,' he says, imitating an ambulance.

'What's up?' Adrian shouts, lifting his head up over-dramatically, like someone in an action film. He squints into the rain, and then he frowns, bounds in a strange kind of slowmotion across to Heather, and squats athletically beside her.

'Alright, love?' he says.

'No,' says Heather. A phrase her mother uses has suddenly come into her head: *Between a rock and a hard place*. She often says that when she talks about her work colleagues. Her colleagues are rocks and hard places. Heather's foot throbs. She can feel something strange happening to her big toenail.

'Alright?' Adrian says again.

'No,' she says, 'I'm not alright.'

'What did you do?' Adrian says. 'Drop a rock on your foot?'

'Yes,' says Heather.

'Shame,' says Adrian, 'because you were doing a nice job there, very neat.'

'I can't walk,' says Heather.

'You'll be fine,' says Adrian.

He sighs, puts his hand on her shoulder and peers into her eyes. 'You're too airy-fairy for this kind of work, aren't you?' he says, after a moment. 'I thought that as soon as I saw you. Do you want to go back to the barn? You could make a start on the tea.'

'Yes,' says Heather, 'I think I would like to go back to the barn.'

'Come on then,' Adrian says, and he opens his arms, picks her up and carries her across to the landrover. 'Ooh,' says Frank behind them, 'cradle-snatcher,' and he starts to wolf-whistle.

Tina hums the theme tune from *Love Story*. Heather ignores them. She enjoys being carried away, over the mud and the stones; she can't remember the last time someone lifted her up and carried her.

The barn, after Adrian has sat her on a chair and returned to the field, is very, very quiet. It is bigger and barer than anywhere she has ever been. She hobbles to her bunkbed, takes her shoe off and looks at her foot. She was not wearing sensible footwear. There is dark blood beneath the nail of her big toe, and a greenish swelling across the top of her instep. It is a real injury; the kind that is impressive to show people. When she gets back home, she will show Sandra. She will describe the whole event. She will set it to music. She will call it 'Sensible Footwear.'

Her bruised foot seems like evidence of something. She had to drop a rock on her foot to prove it. She stretches her leg out, leans back on her pillow and looks out of the window, but the yard is empty – even the ginger cat has gone. *Here I am,* she thinks, *a girl in a barn with a bruised foot. A singer-songwriter in a barn with a bruised foot.* She wants to phone Mrs Climber, she wants to rush out and find a phone box and dial her number and say *'Mrs Climber, I do not want to work with nature. I have definite plans.'*

It begins to rain. She gets up and hobbles into the kitchen. She looks in the food boxes that Adrian has brought. There are bags of pasta and packets of processed ham and orange cheese. She goes to the cupboard and finds a large, aluminium pan which she takes to the tap and fills with water. She tips in enough pasta for the ten of them, adds salt from the big plastic tub, lights the gas, puts the pan on to boil.

Oh Never Leave Me

AUNT NORA ARRIVED from the station in a small, muddy taxi.

'Hallo, sweetheart,' she said. She stooped low in the front doorway. She was holding a very strange tapestry bag. 'I won't say "Haven't you grown?",' she said. She stood up again. 'I remember how awful that was,' she said to Janet's mother. 'All these grown-ups saying "*Haven't you grown?*"'

'Yes,' said Janet's mother. She was hanging on to Nora's wet raincoat. 'I've put you in the guest room, Nora,' she said. 'It's a Z-bed, but it's quite comfortable.'

'I can't tell you what this means to me,' said Aunt Nora.

'I've put a towel at the end of the bed,' Janet's mother said. 'I thought you might like a freshen-up before tea. Why don't you have a nice bath?'

'Oh Anita,' said Aunt Nora, and she started to cry.

'Janet,' said Janet's mother, 'why don't you go and see how many jam tarts we have left in the tin?'

'There are seven,' said Janet. 'I counted them.'

'Well,' said her mother, 'why don't you go and put three teabags in the teapot? So tea's all ready?'

'OK,' said Janet. She looked up at Nora, who was still sobbing. Her nose was running slightly, and so was her eye makeup. She had found a packet of paper hankies in her handbag.

'Janet's growing up so fast,' she said. Then she put a hanky up to her nose. She just stood and held it there.

* * *

At teatime they sat at the table, eating boiled eggs. Janet had turned the empty shell of her egg upside-down so it looked as if she hadn't eaten it.

'Eat your egg, Janet,' her father said suddenly, interrupting something Nora was saying.

Janet didn't reply. She sat very quietly and looked at the upturned eggshell masquerading as an egg. She felt very proud of it.

'And I see that the poppies are coming up too, now,' Aunt Nora said.

'Yes,' said Janet's mother.

'How long are you planning to stay, Nora?' Janet's father asked.

Nora cleared her throat. 'Well,' she said. She frowned. She buttered a piece of bread and cut it in half. Then she said 'Excuse me,' got up and ran out of the room.

'What was all that about?' Janet's father asked. 'I only asked her a question.'

Janet's mother looked at him. Then she pushed her chair back. The legs scraped against the floor. She walked out of the kitchen, down the hall and into the sitting room. After a few minutes Janet could hear her voice. It sounded like the grey pigeon that sat sometimes on her window-sill and cooed. Nora's voice didn't sound so good. After a while, her father sighed, and Janet felt something sad gripping the room. She looked at the empty eggshell.

'Daddy,' she said, and she held the eggshell up.

Her father looked. He smiled. 'Very good,' he said.

Janet put the eggshell back in the cup. Then they just sat there. They sat for a long time and listened to her mother's pigeon-voice and Aunt Nora's honking one. Janet's father sighed and stared at the gas boiler behind Janet's head.

Aunt Nora went out to the newsagents the next day, and bought Janet a copy of *Twinkle.*

'I thought you might like this, sweetheart,' she said, 'because you are such a good reader.'

'Thank you,' said Janet.

On the cover there was a drawing of a girl with a yellow ponytail and enormous eyes. She was holding a doll which had a yellow ponytail and enormous eyes. Above the drawing, there was a sentence which said 'Springtime Fun For Little Girls'. But *Twinkle* was not fun.

'Thank you,' Janet said again, and Aunt Nora smiled.

'A pleasure, sweetheart,' she said.

Her parents always seemed to be talking about Aunt Nora when she wasn't there, but Janet didn't often listen. They would speak very high up and a long way away, and she would sit apart from them, at another end of the room and make things out of paper and cardboard. Her parents would talk about Nora's husband, a man called Clive – how terrible he was – and money, and sometimes they would shout and sometimes they would tell jokes and laugh very loudly and for a long time, and she didn't listen.

When her father came home from work, Janet would sit on his knee and he would recite nursery rhymes.

Fuzzy Wuzzy was a bear,
A bear was Fuzzy Wuzzy.
When Fuzzy Wuzzy lost his hair
He wasn't fuzzy, was he?

Sometimes she would press her ear against his blue-jumpered chest and listen to his voice that way. It was like the sound of a huge bee buzzing.

At school her class was making things for Easter. You were allowed to make anything you liked as long as it had something to do with rabbits or chickens. Janet was making a rabbit out of yellow wool, green satin, buttons and a toilet roll. The toilet roll was the body and the green satin was the dress. At the end of the lesson she walked up to Mrs Humes' desk and showed her.

'Very good, Janet,' said Mrs Humes. 'Is it a chicken?'

'It's a rabbit.'

'Oh,' said Mrs Humes. She looked at it. 'Are you going to give it a tail?' she asked. 'You could make a tail out of cotton wool.'

'There isn't any cotton wool left,' said Janet. 'There's none in the box.'

'Oh,' said Mrs Humes, and she paused. 'Is it a present for someone?'

'It's for Daddy,' said Janet.

'Well,' said Mrs Humes, 'I'm sure Daddy will think it's very nice.'

'Yes,' said Janet. She stared at Mrs Humes. There was something rather frightening about her. She smelled of smoke and had a mouthful of silver fillings. You could see them when she opened her mouth.

When school had finished, Aunt Nora was waiting for her outside the classroom. She was leaning against the creosoted wood of the fence, staring into space. Janet ran to her, clutching the rabbit.

'Look what I've made for Daddy,' she said.

'That's lovely, dear, what is it?'

'It's a rabbit,' said Janet. 'I'm going to give it to Daddy.'

'Yes,' said Nora, 'you told me.'

Then she put her hand out, spreading her fingers like a big star for Janet to hold. But Janet didn't want to hold Nora's hand. She hopped up on to a little wall that ran along the side of the pavement.

'Be careful, darling,' Nora said, when they came to the edge of a road.

'I am being careful,' said Janet.

'Why did the chicken cross the road?' Nora said, as they crossed.

'To get to the other side,' said Janet.

'Yes,' said Nora. 'You know that one, then,' and she became rather quiet.

'I know lots of jokes,' said Janet. 'I know the ones about the elephant in the fridge.'

Then she began to skip, and while she skipped, she pulled at the tall grasses that grew at the side of the pavement.

Nora walked behind her in silence, carrying Janet's coat and her tapestry bag.

'Don't pull the grass,' she called out after a while, 'you'll cut your hand.'

'No I won't,' said Janet, and she pulled at another grass. When she was with Nora she always answered back.

It took Nora a long time to open the front door. She had been given a set of keys but she kept trying the wrong ones. 'Oh dear,' she said. She shuffled through each key in turn and none of them seemed to work. As they stood on the doormat it began to rain.

'It's the gold key,' said Janet.

'I don't think it is, dear,' Nora said.

It was the gold key.

When they got indoors, Janet ran into her bedroom and hid the Easter rabbit in her plimsoll bag. 'Rabbit,' she said, out loud. She wondered if she should give it a name. She thought Clive might be a good name for it. Clive the Rabbit.

When she ran through to the kitchen, Nora was crouching on the floor, staring into the cupboard.

'Your mummy asked me to make the tea,' she said, 'but I don't know what to make.'

She turned and looked at Janet. Her eye makeup was running again.

'Why are you always crying?' Janet asked. She stared at her.

'Because I'm not very happy,' said Nora.

'Why?' Janet asked. 'Is it because of your husband?'

'Yes,' Nora said, 'it is'. Then her chin started to tremble and she turned to look at the cupboard again. She sat back on her heels and looked at the tins of food.

'Let's have that tin of ravioli,' she said.

'Yes,' Janet shrieked. They hardly ever had ravioli but she loved it – she loved unfolding the little serrated pillows and looking at how neat it all was.

While Nora was trying to puncture the tin with the tin-opener, Janet went into the bathroom. She pulled her knickers down, sat on the toilet and stared at the patterned tiles on the wall. Then she looked up at Nora's dressing gown and sponge bag that were hanging from the peg on the back of the door. The sponge bag was enormous with a pattern of ducks on it. The dressing gown was pink and lined, like corrugated cardboard. She tried to remember the peg being empty. But it was difficult to think that far back.

Janet sighed. Then she started to sing a song that she had learned at school.

'Early one morning,' she sang, 'just as the sun was shining, I heard a maiden singing in the valley below.'

She didn't know the rest of the words, so she sang the same lines again. She paused, then she sang them again. Then she got off the toilet, wiped herself, pulled up her knickers and pulled the flush. She went to the basin, put the plug in and turned on the taps. When the basin was full, she turned off the taps and looked at them. And something occurred to her. Hot and Cold. The Hot and Cold labels on them were loose. 'Yes,' she thought. And she leaned forward, prised them out with her fingertips and swopped them around. It was so clever. It was hardly even naughty, she thought, because it was so clever. It was more clever than naughty. She turned on the hot tap and the water was cold. She turned on the cold tap and it was hot.

She unlocked the bathroom door, pulled it open by the cord of Nora's dressing gown and went back into the kitchen. Nora had got the ravioli tin open. She was standing at the cooker, stirring the ravioli around with a wooden spoon.

'That was a nice song, sweetheart,' she said. 'Do you know the rest of it?'

And before Janet could say anything, she started to sing.

'Oh never leave me,' she sang,

'Oh don't deceive me, how could you use a poor maiden so?'

She had a very loud, warbling voice, and when she sang 'you use' the words sounded too long.

'Now,' she said, and she turned the gas off, got two dishes out of the cupboard, emptied the ravioli into them and placed them on the table with a couple of spoons.

'I'm just going to wash my hands,' she said.

Janet sat at the table and watched Nora walk into the bathroom and close the door.

She picked up her spoon and listened.

She heard the taps being turned on, and the sound of water running into the basin. Then there was the noise of Nora turning the soap around in her hands, splashing water, and clearing her throat. That was all. Janet waited for some shout of surprise. But there was nothing. There was just the sound of Nora pulling the plug out and turning to the towel-rail. Then, after a moment, she unlocked the door and walked back into the kitchen.

'Now,' she said, and she smiled, 'let's eat.' But the ravioli wasn't hot through; she had heated it too quickly. 'I'm sorry, dear,' she said. They had to empty it back into the saucepan and heat it again.

It was strange, Janet thought, how her parents didn't notice things. She would have noticed straight away about the Hot and Cold labels. But her father didn't. When he got home he went into the bathroom and a few moments later the door opened and he came out again. His face was bright pink. He had the look on his face that made her want to run, very fast, into another room.

'What a stupid thing to do,' he shouted. 'I could have scalded myself.'

'It was to make you laugh,' Janet said.

'It wasn't funny,' said her father.

Janet stood and looked down at the round tops of her new shoes. As she looked, the shoes seemed to divide and dissolve. Tears were rising into her eyes, from wherever tears rise.

'It was not funny,' her father said again. 'It was stupid.'

And he crashed back into the bathroom, took the Hot and Cold labels off the taps and put them back onto the right ones. He slammed the door behind him.

Aunt Nora was very tall and thin and when she sat down in chairs she looked cramped, like a daddy-long-legs. She folded up, like her Z-bed. Janet went to the doorway of her bedroom and stood, watching her. She was writing something. She was writing very fast with a black biro. After a moment she stopped and looked at Janet.

'Hallo, darling,' she said.

'Hallo,' said Janet.

'You shouldn't have done that to the taps.'

Janet didn't reply. She came into the room and stood beside Nora. She looked down at the strange tapestry bag.

'Aunty Nora . . .,' Janet said, and she sighed and looked at the letter Nora was writing. The paper was very, very white and sharp-edged. Paper for grown-ups. Janet spelt out the first word under her breath. C–L–I–V–E.

'When Mummy writes letters she puts Dear,' she said.

'Well,' said Nora. She looked down at her biro. She didn't say anything else.

'I've got you a present,' Janet said. 'Guess which hand.'

'The left one.'

Janet shook her head.

'The right one.'

'No.'

'I give up,' Nora said. Janet paused. Then she produced Clive the Rabbit from behind her back.

'Oh,' said Nora. She put down her biro, took the rabbit and gazed at it, for a long time, as if it might change into something else. She stroked the green satin.

'Weren't you going to give it to Daddy?' she said.

'No,' Janet said, and she felt tears coming into her eyes again.

'Don't cry,' said Nora. She put her arms around her, and they felt light and boney. And her hands, stroking her hair, felt heavy.

'I think you should give Daddy the rabbit,' she said.

Janet sniffed and looked at the patterns, close-up, on Nora's cardigan. Dark wool. Triangles and stars.

'It would make him happy,' Nora said.

And Janet pulled herself away. She brushed her hair out of her eyes.

'I'm going to go and find him,' she said. And she felt wild suddenly, bright, as if she had swallowed sunshine. She ran back to the door, then turned and looked at Aunt Nora, sitting at the desk, her hands folded in her lap.

'I can make you something too,' she said. She wasn't sure, but she thought perhaps it might make her happier.

Squid

THEY WERE IN Athens. They had been in Athens for three hours, looking for a hotel. They had not booked anywhere. It was much better, Alan said, to be spontaneous. You found better places like that. He was glancing back at Cathleen now, over his shoulder.

'Come on,' he said.

If she hadn't been watching him, Cathleen thought, she would have lost him by now. When Alan was unsure, he walked very fast. He was already halfway down another street. He had walked past two dogs, three people and a gallery before Cathleen had even reached them.

'Alan,' Cathleen called out, 'I need to sit down.'

'Come on,' Alan shouted over his shoulder, 'we can sit down in a while.'

'I need to sit down and eat,' she shouted. 'I need food.'

'Cathleen,' Alan said when she had caught up with him, 'we need to sort out somewhere to stay first. Why don't you have some of those toasted nuts?'

On almost every street corner, there were old men selling honey-coated peanuts. The smell was sweet and fragrant, and the old men smiled and waved the triangular peanut packets towards Cathleen. But she didn't stop.

Around two o'clock they turned a corner and saw a stone temple on a hill.

'Look,' said Alan. 'That could be the Parthenon.'

He stopped walking and began to look for the guide book in Cathleen's rucksack.

'Why did you have to pack it right at the bottom?' he said after a while, to the back of her head. Cathleen did not reply. She stood and looked at the wall of the building opposite. Things weren't the same as she remembered. She closed her eyes. Alan was sighing and pulling the shoulder-straps of the rucksack roughly against her neck. A single strand of hair got caught up in the buckle and pulled.

'Ow,' she said, and suddenly she hated Alan. She wondered how he could have become so rude. She touched her head, and then her neck. The sweat on her fingertips made her skin sting a little.

'Why did you have to pack so much stuff?' Alan said. Then he found the guide book, underneath some folded socks and the hairdryer.

'Here it is,' he said. He got it out and flicked to a chapter entitled 'The Ruins'. Cathleen stood a little distance away and folded her arms. She watched two young Athenians walking past, hand in hand. The traffic noise had stopped for a moment, making a little pool of quiet.

'It's not the Parthenon,' Alan said after a while, 'it's the Erechtheion,' and he began to read to her. 'An olive tree sprang from the ground here,' he read, 'at the touch of Athena's spear.'

'Really?' she said.

'Isn't that like something in the Bible? Someone touches something with a spear and water springs out.'

'Probably,' Cathleen said.

'The stunted olive tree in the precinct,' Alan read, 'was planted by an archaeologist in 1917.'

He put the book back in the rucksack and they carried on walking.

'Can't you walk any faster?' he asked.

'No,' said Cathleen.

She was thinking of the last time they were in Greece. Of visiting a village and meeting a fisherman who had looked so old and so

Greek, and she hadn't really believed that people like that – old Greek fishermen – still existed. He had looked as if he'd spent half his life in salt water. One evening, he had taken them out in his rowing boat, and they had just sat there, a few hundred yards out from the shore. The boat had rocked in the water and a warm breeze blew around their feet. The water had looked like quicksilver, thick and soft, and the sky was the purest black. Cathleen remembered looking up and seeing a whole sky full of stars.

Athens was different. It was noisy and full of diesel fumes. It was hotter and greyer than she remembered. But sometimes you could turn a corner and find yourself in the prettiest street, full of balconies and iron railings and geraniums. And there were still cats. They were all thin and white, or white with smudges of colour. Cathleen had taken half a roll of film already.

'We do have a cat at home,' Alan said. 'You can take pictures of him.'

'These are different cats.'

Alan sighed, but his sigh was drowned out by the sound of her stomach. It rumbled like a dog howling.

'Was that your stomach?' Alan asked. He looked shocked.

'It's because it's empty, Alan,' she said, 'completely hollow.'

They had walked past dozens of restaurants; past people sitting at tables, eating stuffed vine leaves and swordfish. But Alan had kept stomping past. And now, for some reason, just when they needed one, the restaurants had vanished. There were just streets full of shoe shops and offices.

'That street looks likely,' Alan said, and he pointed to another little lane. There was a sign on the wall which said ΤΟΥΡΙΣΤΙΚΗ ΑΣΤΥΝΟΜΙΑ. Cathleen had no idea what it meant. It was strange to be illiterate again. It made her feel cast adrift and somehow more aware of other things; of things that couldn't be read. She gazed at the white stone walls, which were very high, and at the sky, which appeared as a thin, blue strip above them. There was one small restaurant in the middle of the street, but it was closed. She could see a man inside, standing by the till, smoking. There were plants at the window, and a display of squid. Alan sighed.

'The thing is,' he said, 'we're not in the right part of Athens for restaurants.'

'Is that so?' said Cathleen.

'You're the one with the guide book,' Alan snapped. 'You're the one wearing the stupid sandals.'

'What?' she said. She stared at him. 'How can you blame my sandals for anything?'

'They're hardly walking shoes,' he said.

'I didn't imagine we'd be traipsing around Athens for five hours.'

'Bloody ridiculous sandals,' said Alan, and he began to walk away up the street, very fast and angry and sure of himself. Cathleen stood and watched him. *I could leave him right now,* she thought. *I could turn and leave him.*

There was a smell floating down the road, of burned peanuts and petrol and Lucky Strike cigarettes. It grated at the back of her throat. But it didn't make her feel less hungry. She turned and looked at the menu on the restaurant window. A plate of Greek salad was 900 drachmas. A plate of squid was 1,200 drachmas. When she looked over the top of the menu, the man by the till waved at her and a haze of smoke hovered over his head. He walked slowly across the restaurant and unlocked the door.

'We close for one hour,' he said quietly, holding one finger in the air. 'We open at three.'

Now he held three fingers up. Cathleen looked at her watch.

'Thank you,' she said in Greek. It was the only Greek word she knew. 'We will come back.'

'We have nice squid,' said the man. 'Very nice.'

'Thank you,' she said again. She didn't know what else to say. She smiled at the man and he smiled back. He was handsome. He had beautiful brown eyes.

She found Alan standing by a postcard rack outside a little tourist shop. From a distance, he looked so middle aged.

'What happened to you?' he asked.

'My stupid sandals,' she said. She stopped and adjusted the

strap of one of them; it had flopped over and was digging into her heel. 'Ow,' she said. Her heel was only at the sore stage; it was not bleeding yet.

Alan looked at her. Then he looked at the postcard in his hand: a picture of two Greek people in traditional costume. They were wearing shoes that had pink pom-poms on the toes. He smiled, and drew breath, as if he was about to say something.

'Well?' Cathleen said.

Alan looked at her. 'Nothing,' he said. He put the postcard back in the rack.

By the time they got back to the restaurant, the owner had switched on an electric fan and some balalaika music.

'You have come for squid,' he said.

'No,' said Alan, 'not me,' and when he said this, so rude and abrupt, Cathleen clenched her teeth.

'No?' said the man. 'No lovely squid? My brother gets them yesterday.'

'I don't eat fish,' said Alan and the man shrugged.

'Well,' he said, and he didn't say anything else. He seemed not to like Alan suddenly. He led the two of them to a small table near the toilets. The table was covered with a red cloth. On the wall there was a ceramic mask and a picture of a discus thrower.

'The best table for you,' said the man, and he pulled a chair out for Cathleen. When she sat down it was so comfortable, so perfect, with a real feather-cushion, that she started to smile. *I could stay here,* she thought, *in this restaurant. All I need is a chair and some food.*

'This is the first time I have sat down in Athens,' she said.

'Apart from on the bus,' said Alan, 'and the park bench.'

'Yes,' Cathleen said, 'apart from that, obviously.'

There were some water tumblers on the table, and the man turned them upright and poured iced water into them. He poured the water into Cathleen's glass first, and all the ice and the lime slices flopped into it. Alan didn't get any ice or lime slices.

'I bring the menus,' the man said, and he went away.

'It's alright in here,' Alan said. Sitting opposite him in dimmer light, Cathleen saw how tired he looked; tired and hot. His eyes were weary-looking and he had a grey mark across the side of his nose. He didn't know the mark was there. *Good*, Cathleen thought. She wondered what she looked like. She wouldn't know until they had found a hotel room and a mirror. She felt like an old carthorse that has just been allowed to stop for hay and water.

'Happy?' Alan asked her suddenly.

'I have been happier,' she said. She looked down at the tablecloth.

'Could I have one of your pieces of lime?' Alan asked.

'I suppose so.' She took one of the lime slices out of her glass and put it into his.

'Ice?' she said, the way she used to once, when she worked behind a bar and Alan came to visit her.

'If you can spare it,' said Alan.

'I can spare a cube,' she said in a small, sharp voice, and she dipped her fingers into the watertumbler and took an icecube out. But it slipped suddenly from her fingers and slid across the table and on to the floor.

'Oh,' said Alan. He looked disappointed. He bent, picked the icecube up and put it on to his side-plate.

'It's funny to be back in Greece,' Cathleen said.

'Yes,' said Alan.

Side one of the balalaika cassette ended, and the restaurant owner put on side two. After a while he came to their table and wrote their orders down in a small pink note-pad. Cathleen had been going to order a Greek salad, but at the last moment she changed her mind.

'I'll have the squid,' she said, pointing at the word on the menu. She had never eaten squid, but the last time they had been in Greece, she had always meant to try it. It was something she had thought she would eat, but she never had.

'Squid,' said the man, 'very good. The best for you.' He wrote something on his note-pad and walked back into the kitchen.

'Are you really going to eat squid?' Alan asked.

'Why not?'

'He probably just wants to get rid of them. They've probably been hanging around.'

'Why are you so rude?,' Cathleen asked, and she frowned at him.

'I'm not being rude,' said Alan. 'I just thought you might prefer something else.'

'I can make my own mind up,' said Cathleen.

'Well, I'm going to enjoy my vine leaves,' said Alan.

'Good for you,' said Cathleen, and she sat back, turned her head and stared at the plants in the window. She couldn't believe how quickly things went wrong.

'I only came here because you wanted something to eat,' said Alan. 'We could have been in a hotel by now.'

Cathleen did not reply.

When the man returned with their orders, the squid looked more alarming than she had expected. They looked rather rubbery and tragic. They were a very opaque white, and curled up like mythical beasts.

'Are you really going to eat those?' Alan asked, cutting a slice from one of his vine parcels.

Cathleen picked up her fork and pierced a squid. It was less yielding than she thought it would be. She sighed.

'Do you remember,' she said, 'when we went out in that boat? With that old man?'

Alan took a sip of water. 'What boat?' he said.

Cathleen looked at him.

'I hate you,' she said. And she opened her mouth suddenly and put a squid into it, whole. Her jaws froze. She chewed, three times, quickly, and swallowed. She took a large gulp of water. She couldn't quite believe what she had done. She shuddered. She was aware of a tiny haze of sweat on her forehead.

By the time they left the restaurant, the streets had become cooler and darker. There was another temple in the distance that could perhaps have been the Parthenon. But it was too dark to tell.

They carried on walking until they found a bench on the edge of a park.

'I don't think we're going to find a hotel now,' Alan said. 'I really don't.'

Cathleen did not reply.

There was a smell of drains. Children were chasing each other across the gravel, shouting incomprehensible things. White cats slunk and pounced on rats under the trees.

'I need to stop walking,' Cathleen said suddenly, and she sat down on the bench. She lifted her legs up on to the green-painted wood, stretched them out and unbuckled her sandals. There were pink marks pressed into her skin, around her ankles and on the tops of her feet. The whole impression of footwear – buckle-holes included – printed on to her feet. She held them with her hands and wondered if the marks would still be there the next morning.

'Cathleen,' Alan said, 'look at your feet.'

'I know,' said Cathleen.

Alan frowned. He put his hands in his pockets and started to walk about by the bench. He kicked at the gravel and cigarette butts, and cleared his throat. Cathleen closed her eyes and listened to the sound of his shoes on the gravel.

After a while, he stopped pacing and sat down. He put his hands under her calves, and rested her legs on his lap. His hands felt warm against her skin.

'I do remember being out in that boat,' he said. And he leaned his head back and looked up at the sky.

Watching *Dallas* with Jane

THE SUMMER HER father died Jane Winters seemed to be at Rebecca's house most weeks. Sometimes, she would take a pot of jam that her mother had made. Once, after Rebecca's parents had left to go to a restaurant, she brought out a box of chocolate liqueurs, slightly warm, from her green-plastic shoulder bag.

'Go on,' she said, holding out the box, 'have one,' and Rebecca took one, even though she didn't like chocolate liqueurs. It always seemed as if the sweets Jane offered her had come from somewhere slightly dubious, like a jumble sale or a drawer full of knickers.

'Thanks,' she said. She took the one she disliked least: the cherry one. 'Thanks,' she said again. Her parents had brought her up to be polite. She ate the sweet very quickly, in two bites, then rushed into the kitchen for a glass of water. Jane followed her. She wore anklets which clashed together when she walked.

'I was doing cartwheels today,' Rebecca told her. The taste of synthetic cherry was still in her mouth.

'Show me then,' said Jane, and Rebecca performed a stunt that, in her head, was magnificent, but in reality was crab-like.

'You didn't have your legs high enough in the air,' Jane said, and she stood on her hands in the middle of the kitchen floor, and showed her how you were meant to do a cartwheel, tall and straight. Coming down, she knocked the vegetable rack with her foot. 'Maybe we'd better not do this in here,' she said.

She would wander around the house some evenings, looking at things. She looked at the antiques in the corner cabinet, at the little china dishes and Staffordshire figures. She lifted them out of the cabinet, traced her fingers over the ceramic bouquets and put them back. Once, she poured old tea-water on to the house-plants, because she said it made them grow. Sometimes she would make a snack. She would open the fridge, get out some cheese, chutney and pickled gherkins, put it all on a tray and take it through to the living room with a tin of crackers. They would switch the television on and watch while they ate. There would often be some cop series involving cars – something like *Starsky and Hutch* – and on Saturday nights there was *The Generation Game.* Jane sat with their biscuit barrel on her lap, crunching Jacob's Crackers.

'What are these orange bits?' she asked Rebecca, holding up an olive.

'Pimentos. My parents are always eating them,' said Rebecca.

Jane took another biscuit out of the tin.

'Jacob's crackers,' she said. 'Do you get it, "Jacob is crackers"?'

Jane was always talking and investigating. She was always prizing things apart to see how they worked – olives, plant-sprayers, puzzle-games. But when the television was on she stopped fidgeting and concentrated hard. She was always shouting during *The Generation Game*, when contestants forgot what had been on the conveyor belt.

'Vacuum cleaner!' she shouted, crackers breaking in her hands.

There might be some drama then, or something romantic, or *Dallas.* Jane got out her makeup bag when the Dallas music started, and selected cuticle remover, nail varnish and handcream.

'Can I watch till the end?' Rebecca said. There was something about being up, with the sky black outside, with Jane sitting there on the couch, painting her nails and making jokes about *Dallas.* There was something about it. 'Please can I stay up?' Rebecca said, and sometimes, depending on the mood she was in, Jane said yes.

* * *

Rebecca was going to confirmation classes. These took place on Saturday mornings in Reverend Ferris's bungalow, which was right next door to the Methodist church. Reverend Ferris seemed to dislike the Methodist church. 'An ugly building,' he said. There was a sign on the church wall that you could see from his living room. It said: '*The Word of the Lord will be spoken here on the Lord's Day at 5pm, the Lord willing.*' 'The Lord hasn't been willing for a long time,' said Reverend Ferris, chuckling and drawing his curtains. On Saturdays, Jane had to sit at Reverend Ferris's vinyl-covered table for two hours. The time between nine thirty to eleven thirty was so long that she felt like crying. Apart from her there were two other girls: Lynne and April-May. They all had to write about different aspects of the Bible, and read them out.

'Psalms,' Rebecca read. 'Psalms are songs and poems that praise God, such as "The Lord is my Shepherd".'

'U-huh,' Reverend Ferris said, nodding, 'U-huh. And how does that go?'

> *'The Lord is my shepherd. I shall not want.*
> *He leadeth me to lie down in green pastures:*
> *He leadeth me beside the still waters . . .'*

'U-huh,' said Reverend Ferris. He talked about someone called Jacob at one class, and it made Rebecca think of Jane and the Jacob's crackers. Halfway through the classes, Reverend Ferris's wife Beatrice would come in, floral-dressed and smelling of washing powder. She would be carrying a silver tray of coffee and biscuits wrapped in green foil. Lynne didn't take any biscuits because her mother said she was allergic to chocolate. April-May always took two.

'How about you, Rebecca?' Mrs Ferris said.

'Thank you,' said Rebecca, and Mrs Ferris smiled.

'What a polite girl,' she said.

While Mrs Ferris was in the room, she and her husband would make secret jokes.

'Would you like a little top up?,' she would ask Reverend Ferris quietly. She stood behind Rebecca with the teapot.

‘A little top up would be dandy . . .,’ said Reverend Ferris, and Mrs Ferris giggled. The confirmation class girls sat around the vinyl-covered table and stared at them. After Mrs Ferris had left the room, Reverend Ferris would stop laughing and say ‘Now Rebecca, what do you imagine when someone talks about God?’

And Rebecca would begin to talk about God, about how she wasn’t sure about Jesus being the only way to God, and halfway through her sentence, Reverend Ferris would say ‘Uh-huh’ and make a snorting sound through his nose. He was still thinking about Beatrice.

‘But you know, the Christian way is to believe in Jesus, who was the Son of God,’ said Reverend Ferris. He clasped his hands together into a little knot of fingers.

‘Do you have to believe that to be a Christian?’ Rebecca said. She had talked about this with Jane Winters. Jane didn’t believe in Jesus either.

‘Well, yes,’ said Reverend Ferris. ‘That is what Christianity is about.’

He looked at her. Then he asked April-May what she imagined God to be.

‘I used to think of a man with a beard sitting on a cloud,’ said April-May, ‘but now I think of nature. You know, wind and water and stuff. And mountains.’

‘Well . . .,’ said Reverend Ferris. He reached forward for another biscuit. Outside the window, Beatrice waved at him. Then she started up a strimming machine and began attacking the edges of the lawn with it.

Reverend Ferris sent circular letters to his parishioners twice a year – at Christmas and when he and Beatrice came back from their holidays.

Dear Friends,
Beatrice and I have just enjoyed two weeks in Ibiza, soaking up the sun and trying out the local cuisine.

'Who bloody cares?' said Jane Winter. Jane did not believe in Jesus or God or Reverend Ferris. Sometimes, she described the occasions when she and her mother were invited to the Ferris's bungalow for lunch. The Ferris's invited the gypsy women round every summer; Mr Ferris wrote about it in the *Parish News. 'This year, as usual,'* he wrote, *'during the hop-picking season we are inviting our travelling friends to the rectory . . .'* Sometimes Rebecca would read the *Parish News* and it was always the same; hand-typed by Beatrice, and all about charity galas with floats and people dressing up, and vegetable-growing competitions and bell-ringing rotas and church flower-arranging. The names that appeared at the front of the *Parish News* were always the same names.

When Jane Winters came round one evening she described the Ferris lunches.

'Mrs Ferris is always in the kitchen chopping up vegetables,' she said, 'and we have to go and sit in the living room. Then Mr Ferris comes in and pours my mum this tiny glass of sherry. Then he goes away again, and we can hear them snogging.'

They sat and squirmed at the idea of Reverend Ferris kissing Beatrice. 'And sometimes he calls her, Bea-trichay,' said Jane, 'Bea-trichay.' They laughed until there were tears in their eyes, the way Rebecca had seen older girls laughing, until it hurt the insides of her ribcage and she could hardly breathe. She imagined Jane and her mother in the Ferris's living room, looking at the hunting scenes on the walls and the pile of knitted squares that Beatrice was always making and turning into blankets. Just before Reverend Ferris came back into the room, Jane said, her mother would top up her sherry and finish it in big gulps. 'She gets really drunk,' she said, and Rebecca held her sides and breathed in. She imagined them sitting at the vinyl-covered table at lunch, eating lamb and mint sauce. 'Gravy, anyone?' Mrs Ferris would say, holding up the gravy boat, catching a drip with a teaspoon.

'Have you ever eaten poached rabbit, Mrs Ferris?' Jane's mother would say. 'I like a nice bit of poached rabbit.'

Mrs Ferris would pretend not to hear.

In June there was a horse fair that none of the villagers went to.

They all discussed it in the village shops and then they ran home and locked their doors while the gypsies drove the horses on to the green. There was always a lot of shouting and drinking and wirey men with big eyebrows and black hair, men that the children were told to beware of, and in the morning there would be horse manure and empty cigarette packets and beer bottles on the grass. Every year, it took the villagers a week to get over the shock. Then, after the grass had recovered, Reverend Ferris would organise a fête. That summer, he asked Mrs Winters if she would run a stall to raise money for a donkey sanctuary. Rebecca had overheard him saying, during a confirmation class one Saturday, that running a stall would help take Mrs Winters's mind off her husband's death. Because it had been a very shocking death. Mr Winters had been found dead one morning, under a tree, and nobody really knew what had happened. People didn't talk about it, but Rebecca had heard a village lady saying there had been some fight over a horse. Rebecca had met him just once, the year before, and he had been very quiet and kind. He had had black eyes in a small, pale face. He had shown her a magic trick with a coin.

On the day of the fête, Mrs Winters stood for hours behind the trestle table, behind the home-made jam and the falling-apart cakes, but no one came to visit. No one came. Jane and Rebecca stood with her some of the time, but mainly they walked around the fête, trying out the lucky dip and the buzzing, electric maze. They stood and threw wet sponges at the church organist. They watched a man with bright, bloodshot eyes smashing up a piano with a sledge-hammer. Then they returned to Mrs Winters's stall. Rebecca looked at the things on the trestle table – a jumble of things – a little wooden horse, knitted toys, cat food, bath cubes and biscuits. 'Have you sold much, Mum?' Jane asked. 'Not much,' said her mother. The village ladies ignored her stall. They made direct routes to the stalls that belonged to their friends, that held fruit cake wrapped in plastic bags, and strawberry plants in tiny terracotta pots.

The strange, old, village men would shuffle up intermittently to Mrs Winters's stall and prod things with their fingers. 'How much?' they asked.

'Too expensive for you,' said Mrs Winters. Rebecca wondered if she wanted to raise any money for the donkeys. She just stood there, smiling, and supporting her bust with her folded arms. Sometimes, she would stand with her hands on her hips, and Rebecca noticed that she had hair under her arms, dark and fine. It was curious to see a woman with hair under her arms; it seemed abnormal. A few times, Mrs Winters wrote 'CLOSED' on a scrap of cardboard and propped it up against one of the jars of jam. Then she wandered around the stalls with Jane and Rebecca. She bought a strawberry plant from one of the village ladies, and a silk scarf. It was July but she was dressed in black: a long black skirt and a black embroidered vest and black high-heeled shoes that made little holes in the grass. Rebecca wondered if it was because she was mourning her husband. The village ladies were all wearing pale spriggy blouses and pleated skirts that swang like bells from their hips. They were all wearing low, rubber-soled pumps.

'Let's go into the tea tent,' Mrs Winters said.

Beatrice Ferris was in the tea tent, standing behind a huge urn of boiling water. Her dress was pale blue with sprigs.

'Hallo, Rebecca,' she said, fingering the flounces of her collar., 'Welcome to the marquee.' She didn't look at Jane or Mrs Winters.

'Can we have some tea, Mrs Ferris?' Jane asked.

Beatrice Ferris looked very slightly stung, as if she had been bitten by a mosquito.

'Yes, Jane,' she said, 'if you have the money you may have some tea.'

She picked up the battered metal teapot and poured tea into three depressing-looking green cups.

'Milk?'

'Yes, please.'

'That's £1.20,' Mrs Ferris said. She pushed their tea cups forward and looked over their heads. She looked slightly alarmed, as if she was in some big, deep lake and needed pulling out.

'This cup's chipped, Mrs Ferris,' Jane said.

'A hairline crack,' said Mrs Ferris quietly, and she began fiddling with a tap on the urn. Then she turned away and began opening some steamed-up bags of muffins.

There were raffle tickets for sale in the marquee, and Mrs Winters bought five. 'I'm feeling lucky today,' she said. The prizes were written up on a blackboard and propped against an oak tree. First prize was a coach trip to London with spending money. The other prizes were set up on a table which was covered, Rebecca noticed, with the Ferris's tablecloth. Mrs Ferris had secured the cloth to the table with plastic clothes-pegs. There was a hamper of groceries, a hairdryer, a cut-glass bowl, a bottle of champagne, two bottles of wine. There was also a bird cage.

'It's like *The Generation Game*,' said Jane.

Jane showed Rebecca how to improve her cartwheels while they waited for the prize draw. She tucked her skirt into her knickers and took running jumps, circling over and over, her painted toenails a blur of crimson. Rebecca always started well, but it felt frightening halfway up, as if she might fall and break her neck.

'There's no point being scared,' Jane said, 'you're only falling on grass, aren't you?'

Mrs Winter went back to her stall while the raffle tickets were sorted out. In an hour she sold one thing: a tin of cat food to an old man. She gave away a few of the other things to children passing the stall. She gave the wooden horse to a little girl. 'I want you to take good care of him,' she said, putting the horse into a patterned cardboard box. 'Keep him safe in here. This is where he sleeps. Put him in this box at night to keep him safe.' The little girl looked at her. 'Do you know what horses like to sleep on best?' Mrs Winters asked her, and the little girl shook her head. 'Straw,' said Mrs Winters, 'Mr Winters always gave them straw to sleep on. But if you haven't got any straw you can lie him on some grass.' The little girl took the horse and the cardboard box and ran away.

By five o'clock the fête was over. The only people left on the green were the ones who had bought tickets. It was cold. Reverend Ferris stood on a chair underneath the biggest oak tree, a little breeze blowing his hair and his black shirt. Beatrice Ferris stood on another chair and rummaged about in the top-hat he was holding, stirring the tickets with her hand.

'Going in reverse order,' she shouted into the wind, and there was a little pause. 'The prize of the bird cage,' she shouted, 'goes to red ticket 106.'

'That's me,' Jane's mother shouted. She waved her ticket. 'Look at this,' she said, coming back across the grass with it. 'We'll have to get a canary now.' She winked at Rebecca.

Beatrice Ferris kept pulling out tickets that Mrs Winters had bought.

'Oh dear,' she said, wobbling a little on her chair, rain beginning to flick onto her face, 'this is quite uncanny.'

'It's rigged,' someone shouted.

By the end of the draw, Jane's mother had won the bird cage, the cut-glass trifle bowl and the trip to London. 'I had a feeling in my bones,' she said. People started to complain. They said that two of the tickets should be put back and re-drawn. 'Bloody didds,' said a man, the one who had been smashing the piano, 'Bloody diddicoys.'

Rebecca was confirmed in August, but she still didn't believe in Jesus. April-May still felt that God was a man sitting on a cloud. None of them went to Reverend Ferris's bungalow again. None of them ever went to church.

Jane and her mother went to London soon after that, with their spending money and their bird cage and their cut-glass bowl. They went to Oxford Street and they never came back. Rebecca thought Jane would write – she said she would write – but she never heard from her.

'Well,' Beatrice Ferris said, smiling at her, 'the Winters were travellers, weren't they? They were travelling people, dear.'

Before she left, Jane had given Rebecca a tin box that she had filled full of bottles of nail varnish, and on Saturdays, when her parents went out, Rebecca used to sit watching *The Generation*

Game and *Dallas* by herself, eating crackers and painting her nails. She chose all sorts of colours: fuchsia, damson, grass-green. The smell of the acetate was wonderful and alien to the house.

Pearl

HER CAT PEARL had died – knocked down by a car that hadn't even stopped – and it was not easy to talk about. People were fine; they were very kind, but Lillian felt that if she mentioned it once more, they would say 'But, you know, Pearl was a cat, not a person.' And they were right. There was no comparison between people and cats.

But sometimes a friendship with a cat could work a lot better. It could be sweet and simple; it operated on a level which didn't need words. And Lillian missed her cat more than she had ever missed anything. She wondered if there was something wrong with her, to mourn a cat so much. Maybe, she thought, if she talked about Pearl any longer, she would lose all her friends. Maybe Bernard would start to come home later, and leave for work earlier. So she stopped talking about her. After a while she had to; she had to wrap the sadness up very tight and hide it somewhere. She hoovered the cat hair from the sofa, threw away the cat bowl and the leaflets from the vet's that said 'Hints for a Happy Life Together,' and 'Fleas: The Facts'. She threw them away because, after fourteen years, she wasn't a cat owner any more. She threw them away so she could pretend that she was coping.

She was half-awake on Monday morning when the alarm clock rang. She didn't get up. She just lay there.

'Go on,' said Bernard. He pushed Lillian's ankle with his toes; his toenails were as sharp as rabbit's claws. 'Go on,' he said.

Lillian rolled over and sat up, on the edge of the bed. She looked down at the patterns in the carpet. Sometimes, if she saw something out of the corner of her eye, something dark, like a pair of shoes, for a moment she thought it was Pearl. Cats have a way of just sitting. She stood up, walked across the room and switched off the alarm clock. She found her slippers under the bed and put them on.

After she had brushed her hair she went into the kitchen. She sat at the table and ate breakfast, staring at the taps. At half past eight she went back into the bedroom and got dressed. It was cold. She put the same clothes on as the day before because they were lying there, on the floor. Then she sighed, leaned forward and kissed Bernard.

'Don't forget the plumber's coming today,' she said. A few days earlier, she had dropped a perfume bottle into the basin and cracked the porcelain. She couldn't believe it; that it was the basin that had broken and not her bottle of Blue Grass.

Bernard turned over on to his back. 'I won't forget,' he said.

Before she left, she went back into the kitchen and got out a jar of coffee. She put it on a tray, beside a mug, a box of teabags and a bowl of sugar.

'He can help himself to tea or coffee,' she called out to Bernard. 'There's milk in the fridge.' She didn't often say things like that; it made it sound as if her life was calm and ordered.

She hated cars now. She hated all cars and car drivers. And men. She felt sure the car driver had been a man.

The café where she worked was in the centre of town, at the back of a small natural-history museum. The walls were decorated with posters of interesting artefacts. Kettles, motorbike engines and seagulls. Theodolites and harvest mice, swaying on ears of corn. People brought their children in at teatime, and the decibel levels hit 120. Sometimes it was noisier in there than an aeroplane taking off.

At nine thirty Lillian walked through the glass doorway, past the entrance desk and the potted plants. She walked through the empty café and into the staff room. She put her bag in her locker, said hallo to her colleagues Zoe and Clare, and took her apron off the peg. She went back into the café, took the bowls of salad out of the fridge, stirred them around a bit and put them in the display counter. Then she stood behind the cake display and thought of Pearl. She thought of her green eyes, and the way she had greeted her at the door, like a dog, when she came home from work. She thought of the way she used to chase bluebottles, and hide shrews in her slippers, like tiny, strange Christmas presents. She wondered if she would ever stop thinking about her.

Mid-morning, making coffee for people, her hands kept getting sprayed by tiny spears of boiling water. Her face, reflected in the urn, was pink and dark-eyed. A little boy stood by the till and stared up at her.

'What's wrong with the lady?' he asked his mother.

His mother frowned at Lillian as if she might be delinquent. A delinquent catering assistant. She whisked a flapjack off the pile and on to a side-plate. She did not reply.

'Are you all right?' Zoe asked her at lunchtime, and Lillian started to cry.

'Come on,' Zoe said, and she touched her wrist. Then she sent her off into the staff room; she scooped a big heap of moussaka on to a plate for her, added some of the green salad that no-one ever ate, and told her to have a break. Lillian sat under the clock in the staff room and looked at the moussaka for three-quarters of an hour.

The afternoon was better. It was sunny; through the café windows she could see tree branches waving in the sunlight, and she was thinking of colourful things: buying a new shirt and getting her hair cut into a bouncier shape; making a chocolate cake; buying some flowers. But at teatime, just as Deirdre the café manager walked in, she hit all the wrong buttons on the till and handed a woman a receipt for £120.

'I only had a cheese roll,' the woman said. She showed Lillian the receipt and laughed. 'Expensive place, this,' she said.

'Sorry about that,' Lillian said.

She looked at the curl of till roll, aware of a sound, an almost imperceptible sound, of people looking up. Parents turning a little in their seats. Children putting down their plastic trucks and sitting, open-mouthed. The world seemed very unfriendly. Very hard and unkind. Deirdre the café manager raised her eyebrows and plastered a smile on to her face. She was standing in the queue behind an old man who couldn't decide whether to have ham or egg sandwiches. 'Ham?' he was saying. 'Or egg? Ham or egg?' and Deirdre pushed him almost imperceptibly with her tray. When the old man had decided finally on ham and paid for it, Deirdre slammed her lunch on to her tray – a bowl of pasta salad, a tuna roll squashed beneath cling film, and an apricot pastry. She pushed it up to the till and handed Lillian a £5 note.

'What's got into you, Lillian?' she said.

'I'm just having a bad day,' said Lillian.

'More like a bad fortnight,' Deirdre said, and she stalked off to find a table.

Zoe stood at the till and breathed in. 'Silly cow,' she said.

'Look at her now,' said Clare. 'Packing her face with pastries'

'She'll forget about the over-ring,' Zoe said. 'We'll sort it out.'

These were meant to be soothing comments, to make Lillian feel stronger. But she didn't. Happiness was very vulnerable.

At teatime, she went to the little grey phone booth outside the Chinese porcelain room, and phoned Bernard. Sometimes she needed to speak to him even though she had nothing to say.

'Hallo,' she said, 'How are you?'

'Alright. How are you?'

'Alright. Did you let the plumber in?'

'Yes.'

'Well,' said Lillian. She pressed her thumbnail against the plastic curl of the telephone flex.

'How's work going?' Bernard asked.

'OK,' she said. She didn't mention over-ringing the till. Sometimes, she thought, Bernard was less patient with her life than with his own.

'Shall we go to the cinema tonight?' she said. 'I could get some tickets on the way home.'

'Is there anything worth seeing?'

'I'm not sure. I'm not sure what's on.'

'Hmm,' said Bernard.

She stood in the little oval of the phone booth and stared at an advert: 'Precious Things: Glass, China and Porcelain Of the Eighteenth Century'.

'So,' she said. Her eyes began to fill with tears.

A school party rushed past in red uniforms; their teacher was yelling something about Byzantium: 'the trading empire of the ancient world,' she was screaming. Lillian held the receiver a little closer.

'So do you want to go to the cinema?' she said.

'I don't know,' said Bernard. He sounded far away and annoyed. Lillian could hear him tapping instructions on to some computer in his office.

'It's just a suggestion,' she said, her voice beginning to wobble.

'Lil,' said Bernard, 'can we talk about it later?'

'No,' she said, 'don't bother.'

She put the phone down. Sometimes they were worse than strangers. After fifteen years they still did not know how to talk to each other.

On her way home, she walked past a small black cat drinking rainwater from a puddle on the street. It made her think of Pearl – the way she used to drink water out of flower vases; she had always done that, even though Lillian left her fresh water in a bowl every morning. She was not like other cats. Pearl had been a funny cat. She had been unique.

She got back at six and the plumber was still in their bathroom. She had forgotten about him. She been planning to run herself a bath and put some of her Blue Grass bath gel in it. But the plumber was still there. He was lying on the floor underneath the new basin, tightening pipes with a spanner. He was wearing a pair of bright-blue overalls. The mug she had left out for him was sitting, half-full, on the edge of the bath. It was a little thing, a very little thing, but the sight of it pleased her.

'Still here, I'm afraid,' the plumber said.

'Yes.'

The plumber pushed himself a bit further under the basin.

'I just keep losing things,' he said. 'I've been praying to St Anthony all day.'

'Who?' asked Lillian.

'The saint of lost things.'

'That sounds like a nice saint,' she said.

The plumber crawled out from under the basin. He stood up, wiped his hands on his overalls and ran the taps.

'There,' he said, 'better than new.'

He switched off the radio and took it back into the kitchen along with the mug, rinsed the mug under the tap and put it in the drainer. Lillian wrote him a cheque, waited until he had been gone for a while and was not likely to return for something he'd forgotten, and then ran herself a bath. She poured her Blue Grass bath gel into it and lay there, with her eyes closed, trying not to think.

When Bernard came home he gave her a bunch of flowers: irises, yellow and blue.

'I thought they were quite nice,' he said. 'I found them in that little shop.'

He kissed her. His face was kind; sweet, the way it could be. He smiled at Lillian but she shrugged him off. She was angry with him after the phone call. She was angry with everything. Everything. So Bernard poured himself a whisky, went into the living room and switched the television on, and she could hear a games show. He was sitting on the couch, watching people answering very easy questions. He was sitting on the cushion that Pearl used to lie on, curled up, soft and calming, like a piece of soap-stone.

When she looked out of the window the sky was almost dark. They should have been eating supper but she didn't feel hungry and didn't want to cook. She went into the bedroom, opened the wardrobe and got her slippers out. And something made her throat catch. She just missed so many things. So many little things.

She put her slippers on, went back into the kitchen and stood by the cooker. She was standing by the cooker, just standing there, when Bernard walked in.

'We could see a film if you like,' he said.

'Yeah,' she said, 'maybe.'

She didn't look up. She didn't move. It was strange in the kitchen; there was a curious kind of silence. Bernard walked to the table and sat down. He leant his elbows on the table-top and looked at the irises that Lilian had put there in a vase, in Pearl's vase.

'I miss her,' he said. 'I miss her too.'

And Lillian looked up through the window. Outside, all the lights of the tenements were on; little squares of light.

'Did you know there's a saint of lost things?' she said, holding her voice steady, keeping it low. There was something in telling him that, she thought; somewhere they could start.

These are all Signs

HE STEPPED INTO the house and it was Christmas again. The same decorations were hanging around.

'John,' said his mother. 'You're late. Have a mince pie.'

The sight of the green wicker sofa made his legs ache. His father was standing in front of the television, with his hands behind his back.

'We have had lunch,' he said. 'We thought you would be here at one o'clock so that is when we ate.'

John did not reply. He sat down and tried to lean back on the sofa but the wicker jutted out at odd angles. His mother was walking slowly towards him with a plate of mince pies. He was about to say something about the M8 and tailbacks, but in the end he said nothing. He had no strength to form sentences. He just closed his eyes for a minute, and when he opened them again his father had left the room.

'It would have been a good idea to phone us,' his mother was saying. Her hair had become blacker since he had last seen her, and she was peering at him, as if she had forgotten what he looked like. 'Your father . . .' she said, but she didn't finish her sentence, she just bent and picked a piece of cotton off the carpet.

'Well,' said John, 'it's nice to be here.'

'It's a pity Karen couldn't come this year,' said his mother.

'Catherine.'

'Catherine,' said his mother. 'Yes. They sound so alike, don't they, those names?'

'Yep,' he said. He didn't answer back any more, the way he used to.

Looking around the room, he saw that there was still a lot of pottery on the shelves: still the two old shire horses, the wizened goblin, the blue-tit and the ceramic basket containing one very shiny green apple. And there was the plastic tree, still hanging on to its needles.

'So . . .,' he said. 'So . . .'

'Would you like a drink?' said his father, walking back into the room and making him jump. He was holding a dark-green bottle. 'I have some mature port.'

'Port would be very nice, Dad,' said John, suddenly touched. His father must have gone to gnash his teeth in the kitchen for a while, then shaken himself and returned, pleasant, to the living room.

John drank the port in the kitchen, while his mother took things out of the oven. Roast beef and vegetables.

'We ate the Yorkshire pudding or it would have gone flabby,' said his father.

'How's Catherine's little job, dear?' asked his mother as she spooned carrots on to his plate.

John gulped. 'It's not a *little* job, Mum,' he said, 'it's just a job.'

'Yes,' said his mother, hanging on to the serving spoon.

Catherine had left him two months ago. He decided not to tell them; it would unsettle them. The subject would revolve around the walls of the house, getting into everything; he would open cupboard doors and there it would be, hiding behind the toothpaste and shaving brush: *Oh, but we thought you would get married.*

Last Christmas, Catherine had sat on the chair where his father was now sitting. She had worn something she called her 'sexy frock,' and had realised too late how inappropriate it was, as his father cleared his throat and his mother shovelled vegetables out of the floral china. They had laughed about it later; it had been a little thing, but something that held them together. When they went to bed in his parents' house, they would lie there, listening to the floorboards creak as his father stood outside their door, just outside, perusing the bookcase for something to read. 'Why doesn't he come in and join us?' Catherine had whispered.

There were more mince pies for pudding.

'I expect you're tired of mince pies,' said his mother, putting three in his bowl.

'Actually, yours are the first I have eaten this Christmas,' he said.

'Well, Catherine *isn't* a cook, is she?' said his mother. 'She's too intelligent to spend her time *cooking*.'

The pies were crumbly and difficult to swallow but he got through them, all three of them. While he ate, he stared through the window at a small bird that was standing on a branch of the apple tree. It was just standing there. Nothing moved in the garden, not even this bird.

'Still, today, isn't it?' he said.

'Yes,' said his father, pushing pastry crumbs into a little triangle on the tablecloth. 'The wind speed is only Force 1.'

'Really?' said John.

'Funnily enough,' his father continued, 'we have a friend coming round this afternoon who is a meteorologist. We thought you might rather like him.'

'Well,' said his mother, 'he is a dentist actually, but he is also good at forecasting the weather.'

'Yes,' said his father, 'a dentist and a meteorologist!'

Washing up, they stood together in the small kitchen, staring through the window and listening to a radio production of *The Winter's Tale.*

'*Worthy Camillo*,' a man was saying in a strangely choked voice, '*what colour for my visitation shall I hold up before him?*' but before Camillo could reply, John's mother poured more hot water into the bowl and drowned him out.

'They can be very good, these plays,' she said.

'Yes,' said his father. 'We heard a good one yesterday, didn't we? About a man who had lost his memory.'

'Yes,' said his mother, 'a thriller, wasn't it?'

'More of a mystery story,' said his father.

'Was it?' said his mother. 'Do you think so?'

Out of the corner of his eye, John could see the telephone, hanging on the wall, next to the calendar depicting *Beautiful Perthshire*. He wanted to phone someone up, to transport his mind somewhere else, but he couldn't think who to call. Catherine – he didn't know where she would be anymore. He hung the damp teatowel over the raeburn and said, 'I'll just have a look at the garden.'

'Yes,' said his father, pleased. 'Go and look at the new gravel.'

John opened the back door and walked quickly down the path to the bottom of the garden. As he walked he put his hand in his pocket and checked that his cigarette packet was still there. The shape of it calmed him; it was like some small, square genie. When he reached the end of the garden, he sneaked behind the shed, got out a cigarette, lit it and breathed in the smoke. But it didn't taste the way it usually did. Standing there, behind creosoted planks of wood, he just felt like a haggard eight-year-old. After two drags, he stubbed the cigarette out and threw it over the fence. There were some mints in his other pocket. He put one in his mouth then stood, numb on the cold grass, just staring at the shed wall and listening to a woman singing somewhere. He breathed in through his nose and out through his mouth and felt a huge ache, somewhere around his heart.

After a polite interval, there was the sound of the back door opening, and footsteps.

'Have you seen the gravel?' his father shouted.

'Not yet,' John said. 'I was just investigating the . . .,' he looked around quickly, '. . . the mole-hills.'

'Damn things,' said his father, appearing round the shed. 'One surfaced right in front of me the other day. Your mother thought it looked quite intelligent.'

He sighed and pushed earth around with his slippers. 'Damn things,' he said. 'At least they won't get through the gravel.'

It grew cold as they stood there; frost crystals were beginning to form in the grass. John was about to suggest that they went back indoors when his father sighed and started to point out new features on the back wall of the house. 'The guttering's new,' he said. 'And look at the replacement window.' They turned and looked at the replacement window. 'You can swivel it inwards when you want to clean it,' said his father. 'I see,' said John, and as he looked he was aware of some movement behind the glass. His mother was standing in the living room, offering mince pies to a strange man. For a moment, John was shocked. He watched their mouths moving silently, curling into smiles, and after a while the man reached forward and took a mince pie off the plate. This man had obviously eaten many mince pies in his life. A paisley waistcoat was stretched across his stomach, and the buttons seemed to be hanging on across an impossible divide.

'Hi,' said the man as they walked back into the sitting room. He stood in front of the Christmas-card display, laughing with rounded lips and breathing pastry crumbs asthmatically into the air. John's mother was smiling and talking about the man's waistcoat. 'What an interesting pattern' she was saying, anxiously.

'So,' said the man with the waistcoat, 'this is John.'

'Yes, this is our son John,' said his mother. 'John, this is Mr Mackenzie.'

'Call me Dex,' said Mr Mackenzie.

'Hallo, Dex,' said John, shaking the man's fat white hand. People called Dex were normally lithe and cleft-chinned, and broke in horses.

'So,' said Dex, and there was a little pause as the Santa Claus mobile spiralled on a tiny breeze, then span back in the opposite direction.

John cleared his throat. 'I hear that you forecast the weather,' he said.

'That's right,' said Dex. 'It's going to snow this afternoon.'

He blinked and stared through the window. The sky was a pure, blank white.

'You can tell it's going to snow when the sky is like that,' said Dex, after a while. 'When it's completely white.'

'Really?' said John's mother, struggling to achieve a look of surprise. She glanced nervously at his father.

'Let's go outside and I'll show you some other signs,' said Dex, and he led them all out into the front garden, John's father still in his slippers. The sky was turning from white to dark, and in the twilight, the pile of gravel on the front lawn looked like a tiny slag heap.

'Look,' said John's father, 'this is the gravel.'

'So I see,' said John.

'I'm going to spread it around the drive,' said his father.

'It's going to look nice,' said his mother.

'I hate gravel,' said Dex, unexpectedly, and everyone stared at him. 'I just hate that crunching sound,' he said. 'It's like walking over Grape-nuts.'

His voice was very loud in the small garden. In the half-light, the whites and yellows of his paisley waistcoat stood out, like tiny creatures.

'Oh,' said John's mother, and suddenly she started to laugh. She dug her teeth into her lower lip, but something was dissolving all at once, like sugar in hot coffee, and she opened her mouth and shrieked.

'I think gravel makes a rather classy sound, actually,' said John's father in a small voice, and she laughed even louder. She stood in the garden in her blue dress and shook, her mouth wide open, holding on to her sides.

'It hurts,' she said. 'My sides hurt. It's just so funny.'

'Caroline,' said his father, and the name sounded strange. John could not remember the last time his father had used it.

'Well,' said Dex. He looked at John's mother and fingered one of his waistcoat buttons. 'I'll show you some other things,' and he took them on a tour of the garden. He found a frog by the pond and told them not to touch it; he pointed out the way the birds were singing. 'Hear that?' he said. 'That means there's a weather change'; he knelt to feel how frozen the ground was.

‘Iron hard,’ he said. ‘These are all signs,’ and John’s father nodded solemnly, politely, and sometimes looked across at his wife, who was still standing by the front door, wrapping her arms around herself and laughing.

Mabbo

Jane went to primary school with a boy called Sean Mabb. His friends called him Mabbo. He was a tall boy with muscles and a big head, and one of his favourite pasttimes was to pick Jane up and drop her. He did this three or four times a term for several years; he would wrap his big boy's hands around her ribcage, lift her a couple of feet off the playground, tilt her at an angle and let her go. And Jane fell, swift and painfully. She knew what it was like to have the breath knocked out of her. But she never got used to it. She would lie on her back, gasping for air like a fish, and Sean Mabb would laugh and walk away.

After a while her friends would come and pick her up and walk her slowly away, like soldiers in the trenches. They took her into the girls' toilets and sat her on the lid of one of the little lavatories. They looked at the bruises appearing on her back. Then they dampened grey paper towels at the basin, and applied them, pulpy and dismal, to her forehead. Her friends had decided that they wanted to become doctors, and Jane was good practice.

'Shouldn't you put them on the bruises?' Jane asked.

'No,' her friends said, 'you need to cool down because of the shock.'

Jane sat and waited while they looked at her back and tutted.

'You ought to tell your mum,' they said.

'I will,' said Jane, but she never told anyone.

When she left primary school, she didn't see Sean Mabb for a while. He had gone to a different school. Some people said he had gone mad. They said he had jumped out of a tree and fallen on his head. They said he couldn't tell the difference between a *d* and a *b*, so he wrote his own surname wrong. 'Sean Madd,' they said. 'Mad Mabbo.' Some people said he had gone to a lunatic asylum.

But then, in the middle of the second year, he turned up at Jane's secondary school. He was wearing the school uniform, with the wild boar badge and the motto 'Strive to be wise'. He was going to be there for six years. Jane couldn't believe it. She was studying *Dr Faustus* in English at the time, and his appearance made her think of Mephistopheles, and Dr Faustus being dragged off to hell. At primary school, the only thing that had been nice about Sean Mabb was his wavy, golden hair. It had made him look like a lion, like the lion on the Lyle's Golden Syrup tins with the strange little motto underneath it: 'Out Of The Strong Came Forth Sweetness.' And now he had had his hair cut half an inch high all the way around his head. He was taller than ever and his hair made him look more frightening. He didn't seem to have friends any more, just boys who were scared of him.

For a few days Jane was worried he might start picking her up and dropping her again, but he ignored her completely. He looked at her as if he had never seen her before. At lunchtime he stalked the school playground with his bullet-headed acquaintances. In chemistry lessons, he stole sulphur and potassium nitrate and made bombs. Since Jane had last seen him, his voice had broken and he had a strange, crow-like guffaw.

In the third year, Jane's class began to study German. Their teacher, Mrs Buick, gave everyone German names because she thought it would make the lessons more fun.

'Du heisst Rosanna,' she said to Jane, placing her right index finger on top of Jane's head as she walked past. Jane could feel Mrs Buick's fingerprint on her scalp for minutes afterwards. It felt authoritative and irritating. But she was pleased with her new name. Most of the others got short, barking names like Gaby and Klaus, but *Rosanna* was pretty and romantic. It made her feel like Heidi. She would sit in the corner by the window, practising a Rosanna-type pout.

Their first exercise was to write something about the weather and read it out. Jane chose snow.

'Es scheit im Januar,' she read. 'Es scheit auch im Februar.'

There was a little silence. Then people started to snigger. Jane could hear Sean Mabb's guffaw from the back row.

'You have left out one very important letter, Rosanna,' said Mrs Buick, smiling grimly and hovering by the blackboard. 'There is a big difference between scheit and schneit.'

'What does scheit mean then, Mrs Buick?' asked Klaus, alias Sean Mabb.

'You know very well, Sean,' said Mrs Buick.

'My name's Klaus,' said Sean.

He sat very straight in his chair and stared at her with blank, brown eyes. Mrs Buick's eyes, when they gazed back, were small and curiously timid.

Their new names made the lesson fun in a way that Mrs Buick had not envisaged. People began to ignore her when she called out their real names. They only answered to the German ones. Mrs Buick had made herself a name-chart which she kept in her desk; she would open the desk lid and refer to it when pupils got out of hand. But it seemed unnecessarily complicated.

One Friday, Mrs Buick came into the classroom with a strange young woman.

'This is Fraulein Richter,' she said. 'She is going to be leading your conversation groups this term.'

'Hallo,' said Fraulein Richter. She stood by Mrs Buick's desk, gripping a curious, white handbag. She was wearing a white, angora cardigan that looked hand-knitted. Nobody said hallo. They just sat in their chairs and looked at her.

'Say "Guten Tag, Fraulein Richter",' said Mrs Buick.

'Guten Tag, Fraulein Richter,' droned the class, and a small, unfathomable smile flickered over Fraulein Richter's face. Mrs Buick always wore very tight tweed suits which made her look like a travelling sofa. Compared to her, Frauleuin Richter was very willowy and elegant.

Before the beginning of the lesson, the two women turned

towards each other and spoke in German, in low voices. Then Fraulein Richter left the room. Jane watched her through the window. She walked quickly across the playground and disappeared through the double set of doors at the far corner. Maybe she went to the staff room to check her timetable. Or maybe, Jane thought, she was rushing away down the school drive as quickly as possible.

By the middle of the first term, Jane discovered that she was good at German. She could say 'Ich' when most people said 'Ick'. People said it was an ugly language, but she liked the sound of it. French was beautiful and changing, like melting ice, but German was dependable, like something made from wood. It was constant. Her favourite German word was *Eichhornchen.* It meant 'squirrel.' At home, her little sister said 'Say squirrel,' and when Jane said *Eichhornchen,* with all the *ch's* at the back of her throat, it made her crease up with laughter.

Conversation classes took place in the most unprivate part of the school. This was a carpeted expanse known as the Resource Area. It was in the middle of a building called the Language Block, and it reminded Jane of an enormous waiting room. There were dying cheese plants propped up in corners, and curious little formica islands reserved for the sixth formers. The formica islands bore kettles and instant soup-mix packets. People rambled through the Resource Area, chatting and carrying books, and then they would turn and stare at Fraulein Richter and her little group sitting miserable and hunched behind a small, blue screen. Fraulein Richter didn't seem to mind the lack of privacy. She gave Jane and her group A4 sheets, with pictures on them of German teenagers waiting for buses and going shopping. There were bubbles coming out of the teenagers' mouths.

'Guten Tag, Sonja!' said the boy teenager on Sheet 1A, 'Wie geht's?'

'Es geht mir gut, Klaus!' said the girl teenager.

'That's my name,' said Sean. Sean had been put into Jane's conversation group.

Fraulein Richter looked up. 'Your name is Sean,' she said, 'not

Klaus.' She didn't go along with Mrs Buick's name-game. 'And please do not speak English,' she said. Sean scowled and looked down at his shoes. There weren't any other boys in the group. There was nobody to call him Mabbo. He sighed and folded his arms. It was strange; he skived nearly everything else, but he was always there when Jane arrived at the Language Block, sitting, over-tall and awkward in a plastic chair. He would be looking intently at the sheets of paper, mouthing through the speech bubbles. He never looked up when she sat beside him.

Fraulein Richter had a huge number of cardigans, and they were all knitted from different shades of angora wool. The angora haze stood out around them like a kind of halo. At the next conversation class, she told the group that her hobby was knitting.

'A very peaceful occupation,' she said. 'Sehr ruhig.'

She smiled, clasped her hands together and rested them on her knees.

'Let's talk about hobbies now,' she said, 'Celia, what is your hobby?'

'Cooking and photography,' said Celia, blandly.

'Very good. And Wendy?'

'Walking and music.'

'U-huh, and Sean, what is your hobby?'

'I haven't got a hobby,' said Sean.

'Everyone should have a hobby, Sean,' said Fraulein Richter, and she repeated this in German to the rest of the group. She always pronounced Sean's name 'See-anne,' and Jane saw a ripple of irritation cross Sean's forehead every time she said it.

There was something fascinating about Sean Mabb; all that picking up and dropping that had gone on for years. All the bruises he had given her. Some weeks, she had turned and peered at her back in the bathroom mirror and counted seven or eight. She used to wonder if they would ever go away. They went through so many colours, from purple to green to yellow. At mealtimes, she would sit very straight in her chair, hardly ever leaning back because it hurt too much, and the teachers commended her for her good deportment. Bruising had been Sean's hobby, his favourite pasttime, and now he pretended it had never happened. He had left primary school and grown taller and worse, and the only thing that seemed to frighten him was Jane. She was like some dreadful secret. If she passed him in a corridor, he looked shifty and embarrassed. He could never look her in the eye.

Towards the end of the summer term, Fraulein Richter gave them an exercise to do. They had to fill in gaps in the sentences and hand them in for her to look at.

Do you like tennis?
Yes, I like tennis.
No, I do not like tennis.

You could qualify how much you liked tennis with adverbs.

The group sat in silence for ten minutes, while Fraulein Richter sat back and read a magazine called *Prima!* It had a picture on the front of a woman wearing too much pink lipstick.

Out of the corner of her eye, Jane could see Sean Mabb chewing his biro and bouncing one shoe against the floor, very fast. He put his biro against the paper, hesitated and then lifted it off again. He looked oddly lost. Sad. Sometimes, Jane could hardly believe how unkind he had been.

Jane turned back to her exercise. 'I do not like tennis much,' she wrote, 'but I like swimming in the sea.'

She looked at it. 'There,' she said.

It took Fraulein Richter a few minutes to look through the exercises. She read through them while the girls talked and Sean Mabb sat silent, staring at the wall. Then she handed them back.

'Sea-anne,' she said, 'you are a very negative boy. You do not like anything.'

'So?' said Sean.

'You must like to do something.'

'I don't like tennis,' said Sean. 'I don't like gardening. I don't like discos.'

'I know what Sean likes doing,' said Jane. She just said it, suddenly.

'What is that, Jane?' Fraulein Richter asked, and, as Jane looked at him, Sean started to blush. The blush began at his hairline and travelled slowly, like a cloud, across his face. It was amazing; his face had always seemed so set and unmoved, and now he was sitting there, with sweat on his forehead and his cheeks the deepest red. He moved the heel of one foot, very fast, against the floor.

'Tell us, Jane,' Fraulein Richter said, and everyone shuffled forward a little in their seats and grinned at her.

'Well . . .,' said Jane, and she paused. They all had such eager, open-mouthed faces it was quite disconcerting. She had never felt so popular. 'Well,' she said again, and she looked at Sean, at Mad Mabbo, sitting there like something vulnerable. She wondered what she would say. The trick was not to feel for him.

Staircase

Coming up the stairs, I meet Miss Brasso. My flatmate calls her that. He mentioned her the day I moved in.

'Watch out for Miss Brasso,' he said, 'she's always polishing her letterbox.'

Miss Brasso stops polishing as I walk past.

'You people never do any work,' she says. 'You just laze around all day.'

I can't think of anything to say. So I don't say anything. I carry on walking with my shopping: a packet of oatcakes and a banana from the cornershop. On my way up I glance through the bannisters at Miss Brasso's pink, fur-trimmed slippers. Through the open front door I can see her little white Scotty dog, Andrew, Andrew Brasso, sitting on the red, swirling hall carpet. He just sits there, with his head to one side, looking at her. From here, Miss Brasso's hallway looks very neat and homely. A home. Not like my flat: a collection of odd furniture and a flatmate who steals my food. I can hear a radio in the kitchen. It is tuned to a quiz programme. There is a smell of casserole. There are shiny ornaments on the hall table, and a shiny clock on the wall.

I have just reached the third landing when Miss Brasso says 'Anyway. Thanks for the card.' She stops polishing the brass, straightens up and peers through the bannisters at me.

'That's all right,' I say.

'Nice of you,' says Miss Brasso, grimly. She smiles a strange, brief smile.

'That's allright,' I say, and I continue up the steps, two at a time.

'You're next on the stair-cleaning rota,' Miss Brasso shouts. She can't resist it. Even now, she can't let it drop.

The flat is empty and it makes me shiver; the loneliness of a big flat on a Wednesday afternoon. I open the fridge door and look inside. There is a margarine tub but Graham has only left a few scrapings of margarine around the sides. In the cupboard there are pickled onions, lentils, flour and cinnamon sticks. I have a lot of teabags though.

The tap drips. When I have filled the kettle up and turned the tap off, the water still wells up and drips on to the stainless steel. Above the sink there is a spider hanging from a thread. Beneath the spider there is a gap in the window, with a draught blowing through it and rotten wood around it. I look through the window. Four flights down, a child is screaming in the drying green. Another one is blowing notes on a recorder.

This flat is – how would you describe it? Not homely yet. Not home.

I have lived here for six weeks, and there are still things that surprise me. The height. The draughts. The fridge. The doorbell is also very loud and it makes me jump. And the neighbourhood: it is taking me a while to get used to it. Last week, I was making supper in the kitchen, and when I looked up through the window I could see little squares of yellow light outside, all around the drying green. And in the squares of light, I could see people. Dozens of them. It was pretty, like an advent calendar. All these people, cooking in the sky. But then I thought 'They can see me. They can see me standing here, in my plastic apron.' So I went to Ali's Cave and bought some bamboo blinds. They have a label on them saying 'Cheap and Cheerful', and it describes them perfectly. If I pull the little ropes too hard they fall down. Graham thinks blinds are unnecessary, because our tenement stands on the seafront. He says there is nothing between us and Norway. But he is never in, anyway. And I think the blinds look nice in the evenings, with pot plants in front of them. Almost Mediterranean.

The doorbell rings and makes me jump.

When I open the door, there is a short, ginger-haired man standing on the doormat. He is wearing overalls – blue with clips.

'I've come to measure your floor,' he says. 'I'm from Hasties Property.'

'Oh,' I say, 'good.'

The man takes a laminated card out of his top pocket, shows it to me and grins. On the card there is a little photo of him, also grinning.

'Can't be too careful these days,' he says, 'particularly an attractive young lady like yourself.'

He scrapes his shoes against the doormat. I open the door wider and he walks in.

It is two in the afternoon. Outside, it has begun to rain. I can see two seagulls flying above the sea.

'Nippy today,' says the man, rubbing his hands together.

'Yes,' I say.

I lead the man silently through the flat and show him the kitchen floor, where the lino is coming up at the corners. Graham and I trip over it at least once a day.

The man bends and peers at the lino.

'Aye,' he says.

Then he takes the top off his biro and begins to write on a notepad.

'Lino cracked and unhygienic,' he says, slowly, as if he is chanting a mantra.

'What are you going to do?' I ask him.

The man stops writing and puts the lid back on his biro. He looks at me.

'I'm going to report it,' he says.

'Aren't you going to fix it?'

'Not for the moment, no,' he says. He stands there. 'Although I am a fittings and fixtures man,' he says, and he winks. He doesn't move.

I put my packet of oatcakes and banana on to the kitchen table.

'Lunch, is it?' the man asks.

'Yes,' I say.

'You'll be on the dole, then?' he says. The fridge clicks.

'Yes,' I say.

'And have you got a date?' he asks.

'Sorry?'

'A date. A boyfriend.'

'Not at the moment.'

'But I'm sure you get plenty of offers.'

He winks again.

'Thank you for looking at the floor,' I say. 'I have some work to do now.'

'Work?' says the man. 'Work?'

He starts to laugh. I don't reply. I turn and walk out of the kitchen, and he follows me towards the front door.

'So, Miss Connor,' he says at the door, 'where's your local? Maybe we could meet up for a drink.'

'I don't have a local,' I say. 'I have only just moved here.'

'I don't believe that for a minute,' says the man, and he folds his arms and grins at me again. There is a sudden waft of aftershave. It smells like Jif lemons.

I look back at the man, but then I think that looking at him might make him think I am interested. So I look away, quickly, at the metal wind-chimes that Graham pinned to one of the architraves. There is a draught in the hall, but for some reasons the wind-chimes never move. They never make a sound. They just hang there.

I put my hand up to the doorlatch.

'Bye then,' I say, but the man doesn't move. He just stands and looks at me. He looks down, and then up.

'Bye,' I say again. My voice sounds abrupt and high. I can hear a bus changing gear four flights down, and wish the man was in it. I turn the doorlatch.

'I have to do some work now,' I say. 'Please leave.'

I have never asked anyone to leave before. It sounds odd; blank, like a martian request.

'No need to be unfriendly,' the man says. He walks forward and smiles. He opens his mouth as if he is about to say something else. He moves his hands towards me.

And the doorbell rings.

I jump.

'Whoops,' I say.

I open the door, and there is Miss Brasso, standing there in her pink slippers. Andrew the dog is sitting by her feet.

'Hello,' says Miss Brasso. She looks at the man and the man stops smiling. He picks up his bag suddenly, looks at the carpet and shuffles through the doorway.

'I'll get those details to property services,' he mumbles. He does not look at me. He walks out on to the landing and scampers down the stairs, businesslike, in a hurry, with his head bent. His footsteps scrape against the stone.

Miss Brasso clears her throat. She looks at me.

'Well,' she says, ignoring the man's existence, 'this is just a little card,' and she hands me a white envelope.

'Thank you,' I say. My heart is thumping suddenly; sounding in my ears. I take the envelope and start to open it but my hands are shaking. The whole of me is shaking. I get the envelope open finally, and pull out the card. It is a picture of two Scotty dogs in tartan jackets, and some Christmas-tree baubles, covered in glitter. Some of the glitter comes off on my hands.

'Thank you,' I say, and I want to cry.

There is writing in the card. 'Happy Xmas,' it says, 'from 2FR.'

At the bottom of the card it says 'Your turn to clean the stairs.' 'Just a reminder,' says Miss Brasso, and she turns and starts to walk away, down the stairs, with her dog following her, and I say 'I'll do it now,' because I feel like it, suddenly; going out on to the stairway and scrubbing every step clean, until I am pleased with it; until it feels like mine.

Margarita Weather

SHE KEPT BUYING things. That day she had a bag containing new shoes; they were black patent leather with little Cuban heels and straps across the arch. They had been in a sale because they were glamorous-looking and nobody seemed to want them. But she liked glamorous shoes. She normally had to wear squishy soled things because she was standing up all day.

After work, Maureen went to the grocer's. She looked at washing powder, then she went to the back of the shop and looked at orange-juice cartons. There was a big selection. She counted five different designs. Stuck to one was a star-shaped label that said '79p Only!' and she picked that one up.

She couldn't find the baked beans or the tinned tomatoes, and had to ask the shopkeeper where they were.

'I'm a bit lost today,' she said.

'But my smile is always here,' said the shopkeeper. He smiled. 'See?' he said.

When she got back, her husband Alistair was already at home. He was sitting on a kitchen chair in the garden, drinking beer.

'Maur,' he said, 'hallo.'

'Hallo,' she said, 'I've been shopping.'

She went into the kitchen and put away the groceries. Then she walked through to the bedroom and hid the shoes, still in their box, underneath the bed. She didn't know when she would tell Alistair about them.

'Did you have a good day at work?' she asked when she went back outside. The sun was hot, even at six in the evening.

'It was OK,' Alistair said. 'Nothing happened.'

Alistair worked at the station. He had a metal badge that said 'Alistair Bell: Station Staff.' He had been there for nine years, and he kept saying he was going to give up and find something better, but it was one of those jobs that wasn't quite bad enough; it was gently bad, like something unwinding slowly, so he hadn't moved on. Maureen worked in a department store, selling fabric. She measured yards of different fabrics every day, silks and rayons and linens and cotton. 'This is a beautiful fabric,' she would say. 'Are you making a dress? Something for an occasion?' She had to be pleasant all the time, and she only ever sat down for half an hour at lunchtime. Sometimes, hidden behind huge rolls of tweed and poplin, she thought about buying the most expensive silk and making herself something sensational.

It was heartening, at the end of the day, to buy things; to be on the other side of counters. She would go into Boots and buy shampoo even though she had bottles of it already; on her way home, she would walk into department stores and buy stationery and boxes of soap, as if one more thing, one addition to what she had, would alter her in some good and subtle way.

There were bees in the honeysuckle. Three pigeons, sitting on the window ledges of the flats above them, were crooning a round.

'What shall we have for supper?' Alistair asked.

'I bought some bacon,' she said. 'I thought we could have bacon and eggs.'

'What about scrambled eggs?' Alistair asked.

'What about them?'

Alistair finished his beer. 'We could have scrambled eggs,' he said.

'We could,' said Maureen, and Alistair closed his eyes and smiled. 'Friday,' he said, and he breathed in, slowly, and then out.

Maureen didn't reply. She sat in the warmth. She listened to the pigeons and the sound of their neighbours' voices. After a few minutes, the man next door stepped outside into his garden with a kitchen chair. He positioned it so it didn't wobble in the grass, and went back indoors again. He came out again with a second chair. Then his wife emerged. 'How nice,' his wife said, and she sat down. 'Evening,' Maureen said to them, but they didn't seem to hear her. Now the man was bringing things out to eat while his wife sat there. He brought out a bowl of salad, another of bread and a bottle of wine. He got a little green barbecue set out of the shed, filled it with charcoal and firelighters, and lit it with a cigarette lighter. His wife sat, shielding her eyes from the sun, and watched him.

'Alistair . . .,' Maureen said. She was in the mood for telling him about her shoes – she wanted to put them on and emerge into the garden with them, smart and flamenco-looking – but she had bought so many things recently that she thought he might be annoyed.

'Supper,' she said. She put her hands flat down on her knees and looked at them.

While she was cutting the bread she thought about the grocer, and the strange thing he had said, about his smile. She buttered the bread slices and put them on a plate. Then she looked in the fridge for the milk, bending down, her hands on her knees. She picked up the carton and shook it. It was almost empty. Alistair must have been there earlier. He was always doing that; drinking milk straight out of the carton. She sighed. Then she walked into the hallway and picked up her purse.

She was about to open the front door but she suddenly changed her mind, turned and walked into the bedroom instead. She crouched down, pulled the shoebox out from under the bed, took her new shoes out and looked at them. They had patent-leather uppers, leather soles and pale leather linings. And they had a name, a silly shoename: 'Desire.' But they supported her instep perfectly. And they were a good height; they looked elegant. But they didn't go with her work clothes so after she had put them on she had to change completely. She opened the wardrobe and took out her new palazzo pants and her new silk blouse. Then she stood at the mirror and clipped her silver locket around her neck. She stared at her reflection. She always looked slightly different in the mirror from the way she hoped. Alistair hadn't seen any of the clothes yet, only the locket. He'd given that to her. Inside it she kept a little picture of him. She'd had to cut the picture into an oval shape with her nail scissors to fit it in, and his face, filling the whole frame, always reminded her of a spaceman behind a visor.

In the summer, the sun always shone right into the bedroom. The room became bright yellow, and the brightness of it reminded her of holidays they had had in Spain. It was the perfect weather for shoes like her new ones. Salsa weather. Margarita weather. She walked to the back door and leaned against the door-frame. She just needed a rose and castanets.

'Look,' she said, 'look, Alistair,' but Alistair didn't look. The neighbours looked up though, very briefly, and then looked away. 'Great,' said Maureen. She stood on the step, hesitating in her new clothes and her new shoes. Then she walked quickly back into the flat.

When she got to the grocer's the man was unpacking apricots.

'Back so soon?' he said.

'Yes,' she said. 'I just forgot a pint of milk.'

'And I thought it was because I was irresistible,' said the man.

He went to the fridge, opened the door and took a carton out for her. 'Anything else?' he asked. Maureen shook her head and got some change out of her purse.

'Are you going out tonight?' the man asked. 'You're looking very nice.'

Maureen blushed. 'Some friends have invited us round for a barbecue,' she said. 'We're having margaritas.'

'Alright for some,' said the man. 'Whose in the locket? Will you put my picture in it?'

'The space is already taken, I'm afraid,' Maureen said, and suddenly the tone of her voice went all flat and snappy. She looked away. She was no good at flirting.

'Shame,' said the man, and he handed her the milk.

* * *

When she got back, Alistair was still sitting in the sunshine. Two gardens away, an old woman was digging, and the sound of the spade in the earth was like a teaspoon in a sugar bowl. Maureen went into the kitchen and put the milk in the fridge. Then she went to the back door again. She walked quickly down the steps and across the grass, and stood in front of Alistair.

'Alistair,' she said, and after a moment he opened his eyes and looked at her.

'You don't know how lucky you are,' she said, 'to have me.' And she walked away again, beautiful in her flamenco shoes.

We Love Bulldogs

THE CARPENTERS HAD two bulldogs. They had brought them in their car.

'They can stay in the car,' Frank Carpenter said when they arrived. 'We'll leave a window open.'

'No, it's fine,' said Colin. He was nice to guests, even to bulldogs. 'They can come in,' he said.

'We'll put them in your outhouse,' said Frank Carpenter, and he whistled them out of the car.

They were the ugliest dogs Rachel had ever seen. They flopped out of the car and shuffled along the path, their nippled bellies swaying. The edges of their mouths were rubbery, dark purple and wet with saliva. One of the dogs kept sneezing.

'Hallo Ruby and Garnet,' Rachel said.

She stooped and patted Ruby on the back, and the dog turned round and snuffled at her hand. Its tongue left a wet mark across her knuckles. Rachel stood up and wiped the back of her hand on her skirt.

'You don't often see bulldogs these days,' she said.

'They're getting quite uncommon,' said Frank. He stood and leaned his hand against the wall of the house. 'They're not cheap,' he said.

'But that's not why we got them,' Sheila Carpenter said. Everyone looked at her and her face became pink and she stopped talking.

The dogs waddled into the outhouse and sat down next to each other on the tiles, panting. Their coats were dense and the colour of pale sand, swirling snugly over their backs. The colour of their coats, Rachel thought, was the only beautiful thing about them.

'How old are they?' she asked.

'Six,' said Sheila. 'Frank wanted to call them Winston and Churchill. But he couldn't because they're female.'

Colin and Rachel laughed and looked down at the pebbles in the path.

'Did I tell you I've been brewing my own beer, Frank?' Colin said. 'I'll show you.'

They walked indoors, leaving Rachel to put the dogs in the outhouse. She closed the door and looked through the glass at them. They sat, wrinkled and panting and staring into each other's watery eyes. She could almost see how people grew fond of ugly dogs.

'Hallo, doggies,' she called through the glass, and they turned their big, confused heads and looked at her.

After a while, she heard Colin and Frank walking down to the cellar to look at the beer, and she went into the kitchen. Sheila was standing by the dishwasher.

'So,' she said, 'is the beer ready for drinking yet?' She cleared her throat and touched the washing machine's control-dials with her pink fingernails.

'Not yet. This is the first batch,' Rachel said. 'I hope that demijohn doesn't explode.'

Sheila smiled. 'It's nice that Colin's interested in it, though,' she said.

'Colin enjoys himself, bless him,' said Rachel. Sometimes she found herself saying things like that. Wifely, ironic things, because she loved him.

Over supper, things kept falling apart. The seat flipped out of Frank Carpenter's chair, then the handle dropped off the fondue pan, and the ice-cream scoop exploded into pieces of coil and metal. But Rachel was standing in the corner when that happened, and only Sheila noticed.

'What do you do, Sheila?' Rachel asked while they ate. She had a curious feeling that she had met Sheila before.

She picked up a large piece of green pepper and wondered whether to put it, whole, into her mouth. 'That's an awful question, isn't it?' she said. But she couldn't think what else to ask.

'I'm studying part time,' Sheila said.

'Sheila's temporarily between jobs,' said Frank. He turned 'temporarily' into five slow syllables. He laughed and patted Sheila on the knee.

When Rachel had seen Sheila before, she had been happier-looking. She had an impression of sitting opposite her somewhere; Sheila had been laughing and talking to a man, and wearing a green dress. Rachel remembered the dress, because it had been a dull day, and the dress was so bright-looking.

But it was tiring to try and get to know her while the men talked about work. Sheila was very quiet. During the fondue, which Rachel had thought might be a 'fun thing,' she had sunk into silence. From time to time they looked at each other and smiled.

'It's funny,' said Rachel, 'but I'm sure I've seen you before.'

'Really?' said Sheila. The mushroom fell off her fork and into the fondue.

'Oops,' Frank said, breaking off his sentence. 'Anyone who drops their vegetable has to pay the price,' he said.

'Do I really?' Sheila sighed, although she looked quite pleased when he said this; she became slightly pink and seemed about to stand up. But no one was paying attention now; Frank and Colin's conversation continued, and the forfeit was forgotten about. Sheila stared into the cheese sauce as if it was a lake.

'This is a fractal,' Frank Carpenter said suddenly, stabbing a piece of cauliflower with his fondue fork. He waved it in front of Rachel. 'A cauliflower,' he said, 'is an example of a fractal.'

'Wheels within wheels,' said Sheila Carpenter blandly.

'Whirls within whirls,' said Frank.

He dipped the cauliflower into the fondue, put it in his mouth and crunched.

Sheila looked at the vase of red roses that Rachel had put in the middle of the table.

'What a beautiful scent,' she said. 'Is a rose an example of a fractal?' she asked Frank, but her voice was quiet and he didn't reply.

After dinner, Colin suggested they played a game. 'My parents gave us Trivial Pursuits at Christmas,' he said. He went to the drinks cupboard in the living room and took out the box.

'Trivial Pursuits goes on an awful long time, Colin,' Rachel said.

'There's four of us,' Colin said. He looked at her and raised his eyebrows. 'It'll go quicker,' he said.

He set the board up on the coffee table and took the plastic pieces out of the little bag. 'Shall we pair up?' he said. Frank said that if they paired up with each other's partners, it might be a bit too much like wife-swapping.

'I think the girlies should play against the men,' he said.

Rachel was thirty-five. She could not remember the last time she'd been called a girly.

'You girlies will have an advantage on the arty questions,' Frank said.

Sitting on the sofa, she tried to think where she had met Sheila before. It was disconcerting; a feeling of walking around a room in the dark. And it was such a clear picture she had of her, looking happy.

Trivial Pursuits lasted for two and three-quarter hours. Frank and Colin won by two squares.

'I know a lot more than I thought,' said Frank.

'You always do,' said Sheila.

'Another game?' Colin asked.

'I think that's enough,' Rachel said. Colin looked across the table at her and she looked back. She wished that Frank and Sheila would leave. She stood up, flattening her new long skirt against her legs. She was aware that she was slightly drunk; she had been drinking glass-fulls of red wine to try and calm herself.

'Would anyone like a coffee?' she said. Her words were beginning to slur.

'That would be lovely,' Sheila said. 'Can I give you a hand?'

'I said that once, to a one-handed man,' said Frank. He smiled and looked up. 'I said, "Can I give you a hand"?'

Everyone looked at him.

'He was trying to hammer a nail into the wall,' said Frank. 'And I said "Can I give you a hand"?' It's just a natural question, isn't it? "Can I give you a hand"?'

He looked at them.

Sheila did not say anything. She just picked up her wine glass. Then she turned and followed Rachel out of the room.

When they got into the kitchen there was a smell of burning.

'Oh God,' said Rachel. She ran to the oven, opened the door with a teatowel and pulled a tray of apples out. Smoke rose out of the oven and she had to shut the door quickly, before the smoke detector started. The apples were burned black; there were blackened sultanas stuck to the tin.

'They were supposed to go with the sorbet,' she said. Then she thought of the ice cream-scoop that she'd broken into dozens of little pieces.

'What a disaster,' she said.

Sheila smiled and fingered her necklace. 'They'll probably taste alright,' she said. 'They'll taste better than they look.'

'Hmm,' said Rachel. She got a serving spoon out of the drawer and put the apples into some bowls. She covered them with sorbet and put them on a tray with the mugs and the cafetiere. Then the two of them walked back into the living room.

Frank and Colin were sitting, side by side, arms folded, on the sofa. They seemed to have run out of conversation. They were listening to a CD of Roy Orbison. 'I hear the sound . . .,' Roy Orbison was singing, '. . . of distant drums . . .'

'Pudding,' said Rachel brightly, like someone dispensing food in a soup kitchen. She had put the sound into her voice that people described as 'breezy'. She bent and placed the tray on the coffee table.

'I didn't know we were having pudding,' said Colin.

'Well, now you know,' she said. She felt exhausted. She realised her teeth were fixed into an unnecessarily wide smile.

'Is it baked apples?' Colin asked.

'Caramelised,' said Rachel.

'A-hah,' said Frank, and he sat up, suddenly focused, like a man coming out of a trance. He sat on the edge of the sofa and looked at the pudding bowls. Then the four of them picked up their spoons and began to eat. It tasted awful. The skin was impossible to break; the sultanas were bitter and hard.

After a few moments Frank shuddered suddenly and put his spoon down. Rachel noticed Sheila frowning.

'This is nice, Rachel,' she said. She put a spoonful of apple into her mouth.

'You don't have to finish it,' said Rachel, 'honestly.'

'They are a little burnt,' said Colin.

Roy Orbison began to sing another song: 'I was alright for a while,' he sang, 'I could smile for a while . . .' It was 11.20. It had become dark.

After a while, Rachel got up and went to close the curtains. When she looked through the window she saw that the door of the outhouse was wide open and swinging slightly. The bulldogs had gone. 'No,' she thought. She couldn't believe it. She stood behind the curtains for a moment and wondered what to say. There was no sign of them. They could have been gone for hours; they could be waddling down the dual carriageway, padding along the tarmac. They could be dead.

'Excuse me,' she said, and she left the room. She walked through the kitchen and outside into the back yard.

'Ruby,' she whispered, 'Garnet.'

But she was not used to this; her voice, in the darkness, was small and unconvinced. She did not have the authority of a dog-owner. She did not know the right way to whistle. Ruby and Garnet were pretty, tinkling names that you couldn't call out commandingly. She looked up at Colin and the Carpenters sitting in the living room, in the orange light. Sheila was putting her mug down on the table, getting up and walking out of the room. She was at the kitchen door in seconds.

'What are you doing?' she asked Rachel.

'I'm really sorry,' Rachel said, 'but your dogs have escaped'.

Sheila looked at her and smiled.

'They're always escaping,' she said. 'They won't be far.'

She went out into the garden and said 'Ruby! Garnet!' The names of precious gems floated across the suburbs. There was a pause, then the noise of creatures rustling through flower beds.

'Here they are,' Sheila said. The bulldogs swayed up to her, panting and wheezing, and she knelt and put her arms around them.

'Silly things,' she said.

'I thought they might be on the dual carriageway by now,' Rachel said. One of the dogs put its tongue against Sheila's face, and licked.

'They're quite sensible really,' Sheila said. 'They know how to look after themselves.'

She stood up. 'I think we'll be setting off soon,' she said. 'That was a lovely meal.'

'No, it wasn't.'

'Yes it was. It was lovely.'

'I know where I saw you,' Rachel said suddenly. 'On that train to London. We were sitting opposite each other. About a month ago.'

Sheila looked at Rachel quickly, blushed, and looked away.

'Really?' she said. 'How funny.'

Then she put two fingers underneath each of the dogs' collars and walked them to the car.

Just before midnight the Carpenters drove home. The bulldogs were stowed away behind the backseat, and they stood by the glass, looking out. There was a sticker on the car window that said 'We love bulldogs'. The dogs hung their purple tongues out and panted goodbye.

Colin smiled and waved to the Carpenters. 'I hope we won't have to do that again,' he said.

'Yes,' Rachel said, and she looked at the roses in the vase; at the dark petals curling around each other.

'I know something,' she said.

'What?' said Colin.

Rachel paused. 'It's a secret,' she said, and she walked across the room and kissed him.

Friend of the Befriender

ANGELA'S PHYSIOTHERAPIST IS a kind person, with warm, massaging hands. 'You must relearn how to sit,' she says, rubbing the ache in Angela's back. 'Children have such wonderful postures, and then they grow up and start slouching.'

Sitting down, on buses, on theatre seats, Angela thinks of that. Whenever she remembers it, she sits up, straight as a toddler.

She spends a lot of her time sitting. She works for an organisation called Friends In Need, which involves sitting down a lot with an old lady called Elsie. Elsie is her particular Friend in Need. She has a low income and no close family, so she falls into the right categories. Twice a week they sit in her house, or they go out for day trips and sit down when they get there.

Elsie's house is on an estate of newish bungalows. On Saturday afternoons, Angela goes round to pick her up for their weekly excursion. She rings the doorbell and calls 'It's Angela,' and her voice bounces, unconvinced, around Elsie's porch. Elsie keeps an electric shopping buggy in the porch, beside a ceramic boot filled with ceramic flowers, and occasionally Angela looks at these things and feels she shouldn't be there, intruding. Some evenings she feels too reprehensible to take old ladies out for day trips.

After a while she can hear slow footsteps coming down the hall. She can see a short, lumpy shape behind the bobbles in the glass doorway. Then Elsie opens the door.

'Come through,' she says, and she leads her down the hallway. There is a smell of an overheating electric fire, and doors leading off the hallway into small, beigely decorated rooms. They progress slowly down the hall into the living room. There is a television, a fireplace and a three-piece suite. On the walls there is a picture of African elephants in the sunset and framed photographs of brown-haired, distant grandchildren. Elsie lowers herself into her armchair, pulls at the arms and suddenly the chair shoots out at a different angle.

'All set?' Angela asks.

'There's plenty of time,' says Elsie.

'Yes, but we'll need to get there, and park, and find our seats. It starts in less than an hour.'

'There's plenty of time,' says Elsie again. 'Don't fret.' She leans forward and picks up a dish of pan-drops. 'Would you like one?' she asks.

This evening they are watching *Cats.*

The woman on the stage is about to sing 'Midnight'; Angela can tell. She is roaming about, mumbling something to do with longing and love. Beside Angela, Elsie has taken her glasses off. She is polishing the lenses with a small chamois leather. Now she puts them back on again. This is the fourth time she has seen this production.

The people on stage don't look like real cats, but from the Upper Circle, everything is blurred anyway. The rows are steep, and the seats are small and hard. Angela is not really sitting; just perched, conscious of her hurting back and her posture. On her left is a man in a tweed jacket whose right elbow is encroaching over the seat-arm. He is breathing loudly and eating Chewits. On her right is Elsie. Elsie is sitting forward, her back humped, her eyes focused on the singer. She opens her handbag without taking her eyes off the stage.

During the interval, Elsie and Angela drag themselves out of their seats and make their way to the Upper Circle bar. Angela buys a tub of vanilla ice cream and Elsie orders half a pint of Guinness.

'This is pleasant,' Elsie says. Then she sighs, leans back against the maroon leather bar seat and starts to talk. She talks a lot. There never seems to be much order to her sentences; it all just jumbles out together, with no full stops. Some people can do that; it's a skill.

'That fishmonger's across the road from here does very nice, fresh haddock,' she says, looking through the window. 'I like a bit of haddock.'

'Yes,' says Angela.

'My mother always used to say that fish made your hair curl, but it never did that with mine. I don't have naturally curly hair; it's still very thick for my age, but I have to get it waved every week by my hairdresser. That fooled you, didn't it?

'Yes.'

'The hairdresser comes to my house; she's a nice girl is Morag; she has a hairdressing business called Hairizons; everything comes to me on wheels.'

Elsie stops talking and takes another sip of Guinness. She smiles. Then she is quiet. Angela sits, eating her ice cream. These days, it is easiest if she blanks things from her mind. Just to sit and not feel bad. The seats in the bar are very comfortable; they seem almost kind.

'How is your husband?' Elsie asks her suddenly.

'He's left me,' Angela says. 'I told you last week.'

'So you did,' says Elsie. 'That's a shame.'

'Yes.'

'You had a falling-out, did you?'

'You could say that.'

Elsie thinks for a moment. She glances up at somebody walking past.

'Did you . . .' she begins.

'I met a man at work,' Angela says.

'And what's his name?' says Elsie, interested.

'Look, Elsie, if you don't mind, I'd rather not talk about it.'

'Sorry,' she says, 'sorry, darling.'

Angela feels her eyes watering. She can't remember the last time somebody called her 'darling'.

The theatre bell sounds and Elsie swigs back the last of her Guinness. 'Round Two,' she says, and she puts her hands flat on the wobbly little bar table, leans her weight on it and stands up. Her hands are pale. The skin is thin and white.

She and Elsie both have bad backs, which used to make Angela's husband laugh. He used to find most things about Angela very sweet and amusing. Then, suddenly, he stopped finding her sweet and amusing, and began saying that she wasn't earning enough money. There were dodgy people behind the scenes where she worked, he said, raking in the cash. He was always talking about dodgy people behind the scenes.

He left her twice. The first time, he went away, abroad, for four months. He phoned her sometimes, mostly when his company was paying for the phone bill, and said how much he missed her. 'I miss you, too,' Angela said. She did. They had been together for five years.

While he was gone, she imagined herself doing something pure and creative with her evenings, like painting or tapestry; she saw herself sitting in the living room with a canvas or a cloth. But she tried it for a fortnight, and her mind started to wander. She was meant to be doing a beautiful tapestry of birds and trees, to put on the wall. But she ended up going out instead, to parties and films and exhibitions. She had never had so much fun. She became friends with a man she worked with. Tom Sands. Big, comfy Tom. Tom used to massage her back for her.

The second month David was away, Angela and Tom started going to the cinema. They sat and watched a lot of adverts and trailers and dark, French films. Then, after a few weeks, they started going out for meals, and then back to each other's flats, where they would talk and listen to music. She was not in love with Tom. She just liked to be with him. She liked the romance and the warmth of it. And when she got home in the evenings, she would lie under her duvet, cold and alone, like some sea-creature.

Cats does not finish until eleven twenty-five. Angela feels completely drained. Outside, snow has started to fall: February snow, cold and slight and beautiful. She thinks: *My husband has gone. I am standing in the snow with an 84-year-old woman.* Some days she can't help thinking about all the bad choices she has made.

They walk back to the car and Angela helps Elsie into the passenger seat. She leans across her to do up the seatbelt.

'I can manage,' says Elsie.

'Sorry.'

'That's alright.'

They drive home in silence. Angela feels depressed by all the songs. She glances at Elsie, and sees she is smiling.

'Wasn't that big ginger cat handsome?'

'I couldn't see much. I didn't have my glasses on.'

'Next time we come to a musical, darling, bring your glasses.'

At this time of night, all the lights look very pretty; the yellows from the chip-shop windows; the reds and ambers and greens of the traffic lights. The lights shine very beautifully against the snow.

Deportment is not a word she comes across very often. It sounds like a cross, she thinks, between Important and Depart.

At her next physiotherapy session, Angela is given a grey walking stick. The therapist thinks it will help her walk better. 'Really?' says Angela.

'It might give you more confidence,' says the therapist, doubtfully, 'particularly on icy pavements.'

Angela practises walking with it and feels a curious pride of ownership. She can't think why, but she is so excited to own a walking stick that she rushes home with it on the bus and writes David a postcard.

'I have been given a walking stick!' she writes.

She doesn't know what else to say. That's about the only news she has. David doesn't want to speak to her in any case. He doesn't want to see her.

'Anyway,' she writes, 'hope to see you at some point.'

There is a little printed instruction at the edge of the postcard. It says 'PLEASE DO NOT WRITE BELOW THIS LINE.'

'Why not?,' she writes, and then she wishes she hadn't written it. So she scrubs the words out with black biro. Now it looks a mess. She looks at the card for a moment. Then she tears it into six pieces. She puts the pieces in the bin.

They don't always go to musicals. On the first Friday in February they go to Sainsbury's to get Elsie's weekly shopping.

It takes a while to walk there from the car park. They totter across the road and along the icy pavements, like damaged eagles on a thermal breeze. Angela has only had her walking stick for five days but she is already beginning to rely on it. She doesn't know whether to offer Elsie her arm; she is more likely to fall over than Elsie. If David could see us now, she thinks, he would have hysterics. He would say the whole situation summed her up. Now Elsie is veering slightly to one side.

'OK there, Elsie?' she asks, which sounds like an appropriate Friend In Need kind of question, when Elsie suddenly stops sharp. She points at the sign on the edge of the path.

'Pedestrian Footway!' she says. 'What's wrong with the word pavement?'

'I don't know.'

They continue, a short distance apart.

Sainsbury's doors open automatically and their hair is blown around by hot air. The store is filled with an unearthly white light. Before they can get to the food they have to traipse past all kinds of things Angela would never think of as groceries. Blouses, shoes, saucepans, lampshades. She is suspicious of supermarkets that sell things like that.

Three trolleys are ganged up in the pet-food aisle, forming a kind of wall, and it is difficult to get round them. Angela moves one of the trollies slightly, and suddenly a woman appears at her side. She is holding three packets of Schmackos dog treats.

'That's my trolley,' she says.

'I was just moving it a bit.'

The woman glares, and Angela glares back.

'Angela,' Elsie calls, from the cat-food shelves, and she leaves the woman and limps across. She feels so angry with people these days. Anger and regret follow her around like naughty twins.

'Some people are so aggressive,' she mutters, but Elsie is not listening. She asks Angela to reach up for a bumper packet of Friskies cat biscuits. 'My cat likes these,' she says.

'I didn't know you had a cat.'

'She's white. She's difficult to see in the snow.'

On top of everything else, David would say, Elsie owns an imaginary cat.

They decide to go for a coffee in the Country Kitchen café. Stevie Wonder is singing 'I Just Called To Say I Love You', and waitresses are walking around in pink, puff-sleeved uniforms. Fluorescent tubes light up the potato mayonnaise and pickled gherkins, and it's almost horrifying. Angela feels like dropping everything and rushing out. She feels that her life, everything that her life has been, is collapsing into a heap. A huge board at the café's entrance says 'Please Wait Here To Be Seated', so they stand, with their hurting backs, and wait. Elsie wobbles a little, and Angela holds on to her arm.

After a while a waitress leads thems to a table. It is situated next to an automated kiddy-plane.

'Alright?' says the waitress, and she takes their order. Elsie orders a pear tart and a coffee. Angela just orders a coffee.

'Nothing to eat?' Elsie asks. 'Look at you, thin as a rake. No wonder you need a walking stick.'

'No thanks, Elsie.'

Every few minutes the kiddy-plane rocks from side to side. 'Jump in,' says a voice, 'and we'll take to the skies.'

'Jesus,' says Elsie.

After a while another waitress appears. She is wearing a paper hat. One of her eyes wanders in a different direction from the other one.

'Today we are doing a Special Promotion,' she says. She shows them a laminated menu which has glossy pictures of peas and steak on it.

'For just £1.99,' she says, 'you can have a main meal with a free cup of tea or coffee.'

'I think we're OK,' Angela says. She didn't realise it was afternoon already. Time is passing her by. Panic is beginning to creep in.

'You don't want a main meal, do you, Elsie?' she asks.

'Heavens, no,' says Elsie.

'It's up to you,' says the waitress, 'It *is* lunchtime,' and she stomps away.

There are parents and children everywhere, sitting at tables, eating chips. A young man feeds a baby some mixture from a plastic bowl. 'BIG spoon,' the man is saying to the baby, 'BIG spoon'. The baby looks at him.

'Have you seen much of your new young man?' Elsie asks.

'He is not my new young man, Elsie. No. I haven't.'

'Plenty of time,' says Elsie.

The first waitress brings the coffee and pear tart over. The coffee is in cups with individual plastic filters. Elsie lifts her filter up and puts it down on to the table, and coffee continues to run through it. The coffee forms a little pool, then a slanting rivulet. They watch it trickle across the table and drip on to the floor.

'I think you're meant to put it the other way up,' Angela says, 'in that little plastic tray.'

Elsie looks up and tries to peer through the window but all there is is the reflection of the salad bar, and people eating.

'BIG spoon,' says the baby's father at the table opposite.

'Oh for God's sake, James,' says the baby's mother.

Angela is thinking, *this is the store I used to go to with David.*

They used to have fun, buying packets of coffee and jars of

pesto. He had a penchant for pickled onions. The jars of pickled onions make her think of him.

Her back has begun to hurt more. Sometimes, she wonder if it's psychosomatic. But her physiotherapist says it is entirely physical. She has referred her to the Spinal Injuries Unit for X-rays, to make sure, she says, that there isn't some underlying problem. Angela wonders what she means by underlying problem. She will be at hospital for a day and a half. When she gets there on Saturday afternoon and looks up at the hospital signs, she keeps misreading Spinal as Spiral. She keeps thinking of snails and winding staircases.

She hobbles through the automatic doors and approaches a desk marked 'Enquiries'. The hospital was revamped a few years ago, and everything is polished and discreet. There is a young man sitting behind a vase of yellow chrysanthemums. That is all. It is like a temple. All the computers and bits of paper are hidden in a little recess below the desktop.

'I've come to check in,' Angela says to the man at reception, and he looks down at a sheet of paper and tells her she must go and speak to the staff nurse on Ward 18.

She clanks up all the corridors with her walking stick, and the base of her spine twists and hurts. It hurts so much that she wants to lie flat on her back in the middle of the corridor. But she limps on, past the gift shop and the café that smells horribly of soup, and the WRVS shop. She finds a lift and presses a button. The doors open. There is a doctor in the lift, frowning and wearing a white coat. He looks like a doctor in a medical drama.

At Level 5 the lift doors open again, and she shuffles out. She walks along another corridor, past the flowery-curtained windows of the private wards and up to another desk that says 'Staff Nurse'. The staff nurse is very busy. Angela introduces herself and she glances at her, stands up and starts to walk away very quickly. Angela ends up a long way behind her.

'This is where you'll be,' the staff nurse says, when Angela catches up. She is standing beside a very high, white bed.

'You can change into your nightie through here, pet,' she says, opening a door.

Angela walks into the room, puts her overnight bag on the sparkly hospital floor and sits down. She straightens her spine, remembering what her physiotherapist told her, about the wonderful deportment of children. She starts to unbutton her clothes, and thinks of Tom. She and Tom never got as far as unbuttoning each other's clothes. But sometimes she thinks they might as well have done. She thinks it might have been good.

There's a lot of activity in her ward. Orderlies wheeling stainless-steel trollies with tubes flopping from them. People coming to visit friends and relatives. The young woman in the bed next to Angela's has three separate groups coming to see her. They are all men. At one point, there are twelve men surrounding her bed, like disciples.

Angela sits in her bed. It is nice to sit in a bed that someone else has made, the sheets heavy and starched. It is like sitting on a train, travelling from A to B. And all the time you are sitting there, you are not responsible. You are in someone else's hands.

But after a while it is like being stuck in a siding; in the snow, outside Crewe station, with the heating broken. Nothing happens. Nobody appears. You wonder if anybody is going to announce anything. Angela sits in her bed for one and three-quarter hours and wonders if there has been some mistake; if, maybe, she shouldn't be there at all.

At teatime she gets out of bed, puts her clothes back on in the little room, picks up her walking stick and walks down all the corridors again. She goes to the WRVS café to get a roll.

'One cheese roll, please,' she says to the woman at the counter.

'All the rolls are frozen, dear,' says the woman.

'But it's nearly four o'clock. Shouldn't you have some unfrozen rolls?'

'One of our ladies forgot to take them out of the freezer,' says the woman. 'How about a scone?'

'No, it's alright thanks,' Angela snaps. 'I don't want a scone.'

She puts her money back into her purse and leaves the café. *I don't want to be here,* she thinks. *I don't want to be doing this.*

On her way back to Level 5, she sees a phone booth. She hesitates for a moment, then leans her walking stick against the wall and takes her purse out of her pocket. She dials the number of the flat David is staying in, and waits for his voice.

He answers after the fourth ring.

'Hallo,' he says. He has his happy, capable phone voice.

'It's me.'

'Oh.' Now his voice becomes smaller and more closed off.

'I'm phoning from hospital,' she says. This is a cheap trick to make him worry about her. But it doesn't seem to work.

'I'm in the middle of something,' he says. 'I'm just about to go out.'

'Oh. Well. I just thought I'd phone to say hallo.'

'I see.'

'For goodness sake, David,' she says, pressing the receiver so close to her head that she can feel all the bones in her ear, 'I didn't sleep with Tom. We just went out a few times. We just went to a couple of films. For goodness sake.'

A man in overalls walks past the phone booth. He looks at Angela out of the corner of his eye. He is wheeling a trolley containing cellophane-wrapped rolls.

'I haven't got time for this,' says David's voice, and then Angela thinks she can hear another voice in the background, a woman's voice, low and soft – the biblical definition of a good woman's voice. Then there is the sound of David sighing, swearing and putting down the receiver. A clunking sound, like the sound of a walking stick falling on to a linoleum floor. Angela stands and holds on to the receiver.

She spends the evening watching *To Have And Have Not* on the big overhead television, and reading magazines which all have the same articles in them. They all say the same thing: 'Take Control!' 'Sort Out Your Life!'

In the evening a nurse brings her a tray of food. Curry and peas. Angela dodges around the curry and eats the peas. Just after ten o'clock, she puts the magazine on her bedside table, switches off her little nightlight and goes to sleep. She sleeps deeply, flat out, right through till eight in the morning. Maybe, she thinks, the peas were drugged. At nine fifteen she is led to a room which has a yellow sign on the door saying 'Hazard – Radiation' and has the base of her spine X-rayed four times. Then she is told to lie in a machine which is very close and white and lonely, like an igloo. The machine does something called a CAT scan. It makes her think of cats and Elsie and Andrew Lloyd Webber musicals. The thoughts you can have when you are lying in a machine.

She has to wait a while for the CAT scan results, but the X-rays show nothing wrong. No more than a slight misalignment.

'Carry on with the physiotherapy,' says the spinal specialist, who is the medical-drama doctor she saw the day before in the lift. As she is putting her shirt back on he leans over a table and writes some notes very quickly with a green pen.

'You need to relearn good posture,' he says, looking up briefly at her shirt-collar, and looking down again.

'I know,' she says.

'And you don't need that walking stick,' he says, a look of mild scorn on his face.

'No. I never thought I did.'

She walks out of hospital, with thoughts in her head of poised people. Ballerinas, gymnasts, Victorian children learning deportment. People who have been left; who have been left and must continue alone, head high. And she is shuffling across to the bus stop, and the wind is snarling around the corners of the hospital, when she sees Tom, standing beside the little forsythia at the corner of the car park. He stands awkwardly, badly, his weight on one leg, his arms folded. She feels blood colouring her face. *How does he know I am here?*, she thinks. *How does he know? Look at me, my hair needs a wash.*

Elsie. Elsie must have told him. She must have done, because she is standing just behind him, like an ancient Cupid, holding on to her black handbag. And her face is arranged into an expression Angela hasn't seen before. Concern. Relief. But mainly she looks pleased. Because they have become friends, at such an odd moment in her life. 'We were coming to visit,' she says.

And Angela stands, straight and poised. She puts on a smile, and makes her way towards them.

Pink Liquorice

DUSTIN HAS HAIRY legs. He is standing by the kitchen door, wearing boxer shorts.

'Am I indecent?' he says. 'Am I underdressed?'

'Yes,' says Karen.

Dustin blinks. But he does not go upstairs to put on a pair of trousers. He sits down at the breakfast table and spoons jam on to a roll.

'So,' he says, 'here we are. Eating breakfast in France.'

Karen ignores him. She starts to wash up the plates. She scoops coffee grounds out of the jug and swishes water around.

We bumped into him near the St Michel metro station. It was our third day in Paris. Karen said, 'See that man by the fountain? He looks just like Dustin.'

'Hey,' Dustin shouted, waving and picking up his guitar case.

Now he is staying with us, in our house, because he has nowhere else to go.

We planned this holiday months ago. We had everything sorted out: money, clothes, novels. And the house we are renting is beautiful; it is simple and civilised, like something in a magazine. It is an hour away from Paris on the RER. It has a garden with roses, and a cellar where we can store our bottles of wine. There is white china in the kitchen and white linen in the airing cupboard. 'Beautiful,' said Dustin when we showed him around, then he went to sleep for nine hours on the living-room sofa. We had to creep around him. When he woke up he had a cold. 'Flying does things to your immune system,' he said.

Karen finishes the washing-up and raises one eyebrow at me. I hang the teatowel over the back of a chair and we go through to the living room. We shut the door but the door is see-through. From here I can see Dustin adding more jam to his bread roll. He is framed behind rose decorations in the lace curtains.

'I can't believe how much he's changed,' says Karen.

It is already sunny in this room; the leaves outside are making deep-green shadows; patterns on the walls.

'We're going to be stuck with him for the rest of the fortnight,' says Karen.

We turn and watch Dustin get up from the table. He walks to the kitchen window and looks out.

At five in the morning a cockerel flies up to the roof above my head and starts to crow. This is the first time I have been woken by the sound of a single bird. At home, it is a chorus of them. An owl also hoots outside this house, donkeys bray, dogs bark and crickets chirp.

It is Wednesday. After breakfast, we visit the local market. It is described in our guide book as 'historic, with 14th-century fort'. Dustin follows at a slight distance. He has put on a pair of shorts, and a straw hat. 'Bonjour,' he says to the stall-holders. He stops at a fish stall decorated with bay leaves and takes a photograph. Karen frowns. She does not stop to take pictures. She rushes around the square, prodding fruit as if she's in a competition. By the time I catch up with her she has put her thumb through an over-ripe melon.

'I can't believe how much Dustin's hair has receded,' she says.

Before I can answer, there is a shuffle of sandals and the whirring sound of a camera. Dustin has a sudden way of taking pictures.

After the market we go into the church and sit on one of the pews. Dustin finds details about the church in English, stuck to a board that looks like a wooden tennis racket.

'It says here,' he says, 'that the Earl of Shropshire came here in the thirteenth century.'

'Really,' says Karen.

It is very cool in here. There is a smell of damp stone. An old man is playing complicated fugues on the church organ. A woman walks in with her three children, kneels and crosses herself. Then they sit down beside us to listen to the music. Another woman is arranging flowers in the font. Occasionally she glances across at us and frowns. No one talks apart from Dustin.

'Shh,' Karen says.

Outside, Dustin takes a picture of us in front of the church.

'Three beautiful things,' he says, rewinding the film.

We return to our house on the train. Inside there are signs that say 'Ne pas se pencher au dehors.' 'Look at the sunflowers,' says Dustin. He leans through an open window and takes a picture of the passing fields. The train slows down, stops, we get out. There is another field of sunflowers beyond the platform, a bright-yellow rectangle. I have never seen sunflowers growing like that before. Neither has Dustin. Karen says she has seen them plenty of times. Karen can be a show-off; I had forgotten that. We have not been on holiday together for fifteen years, not since a school exchange. We went to Boulogne and spent most of the time in a supermarket. Karen bought a small round box of Pont L'Évêque, and I bought a small round box of Camembert. Outside, we got flashed at by a man who had been lurking around the trolley park. We talked about it all the way back on the ferry.

Now Karen and I have reached the age of being polite. I never imagined I would be polite to Karen – it always seemed to be something very old women in eau de Nil dresses did, saying things like 'No, I insist,' kissing each other and smelling of mints and handbags. So far, Karen has only been rude once, about the state I left the bathroom in. 'It looks like Waterworld,' she said. 'Look at the towels,' and she tutted. Then she turned and walked into her room, one sandal making a sticking noise against the hall tiles.

On Thursday morning, Dustin steps on a cricket in the hall. There is an awful crunching sound. 'Oh oh,' says Dustin. He lifts his foot up and looks down. The cricket is bright green and squashed. 'Oh,' says Dustin, 'oh, that's a terrible thing to have done. Like Pinocchio. Look,' he says, 'what a beautiful colour it was.' Karen looks at the cricket. Then she looks at him.

'You've only been here a day and a half,' she says, 'and you're already killing insects.'

Karen and Dustin met in San Francisco, five years ago. She used to write to me about him, and I felt a tiny bit jealous. Dustin was great, she said. Funny and sweet. She was working in a coffee shop and he used to come in and chat. He was small and bright and sweet-looking and he talked about people's relationships. 'He is such a nice guy,' Karen wrote. For a while, Dustin was her best friend. They used to talk about her lovelife. Sometimes, they would go to the cinema together and sit in the dark, eating pink liquorice. When she first came back to Britain she used to go to Woolworths and buy bags of pink liquorice to remind her of those days. 'Good old Dustin,' she said. She would sigh, and sit, chewing pink liquorice, in front of the television.

'Do you ever hear from Patrick these days?' Dustin asks Karen while we are unpacking the shopping. He still talks about relationships but something has changed. His hair is receding and sometimes he gets a baseball cap out of his bag and puts it on the wrong way round. Karen pretends she has not heard him. He looks at her for a second as if he is expecting an answer. Then he says 'Oh,' very quietly. His eyes seem to twinkle. After a while he looks at me.

'How long are you staying here?' he asks.

'A fortnight.'

'But nothing lasts a fortnight.'

On Friday evening we decide to stay in and drink some wine. Karen bought six cheap cartons of wine the day before in the supermarket. 'It's how they drink it in France,' she said, 'in cartons. It's local. It's much better wine.' We open a carton and pour some wine into three glasses. 'Cheers,' we say, and we drink. The wine tastes acrid; almost like vinegar. It tastes sharp against the side of my tongue. We sip in silence for a while. Then Dustin says 'I don't think I can drink this.' He goes down to the cellar and comes back up the stairs a few minutes later with two bottles of Cabernet Sauvignon. It tastes much nicer.

When we have refilled our glasses I get out my book and my packet of Gitanes, then I go into the living room and sit on the floor. Dustin follows me. He sits on the leather pouf by the open back door, and strums chords on his guitar. He plays and sings at the same time. 'Hotel California'. 'Ruby Tuesday'. 'While My Guitar Gently Weeps'.

He stops for a while as if he's listening to something, some noise I can't hear, and then he starts strumming again.

'Karen,' he shouts, 'are you coming through?'

'No,' Karen shouts back. She stays in the kitchen. She sits cross-legged on the table, reading her novel and grinding her fists into her cheekbones. She is smoking Gauloise cigarettes. We decided to get different types. Under the central light, she looks green. She has put a teatowel over the washing-up, to keep the flies off.

At ten o'clock Dustin stops playing and sighs. 'What an evening,' he says.

He looks out across the grass. There is a thick cupressus hedge in the garden. You can't see anything through it but you can hear the neighbours shouting at each other. None of us understands French well enough to know what's going on. Occasionally, there is the noise of a toddler, zooming past on a tricycle. But after a while the toddler goes indoors. Now, the adults are eating. There is the sound of glasses clinking, voices and the rasp of a match against the side of a matchbox. Now that Dustin has stopped strumming chords, I'm sure I can hear mortadella being prised off a plate.

Dustin sighs again. Then he gets up and scrapes the pouf along the path, so that he can rest his feet against the balcony railings. Now we can both see Karen: just a silhouette. She looks scary from here, with the smoke.

'Karen has changed,' Dustin says. 'She knows what she wants.'

Just when I think he might be OK he says something like that.

* * *

Karen and I have been here for five days now. We have nine days to go. We talk all the time to fill in the gaps and at the end of the day I have a headache. It is so bad that it is painful to stand up straight. In the evenings I bend into bed. We have discussed friends and enemies and work, but we can't find anything new to talk about. Nothing that will sustain itself. 'Well,' we say. Then we sit, sipping fruit infusion from our aesthetic French bowls.

But now we have something else to talk about. We can talk about Dustin. We don't just have to reminisce.

'He was different in San Francisco,' says Karen.

We sit in her room to talk about Dustin. We sit, putting on her moisturising cream. Karen is browner than me; she wears less suntan lotion and stays out longer, reading her novel. She has brought with her a piece of material some man bought for her in Africa. It is stripey and she lies on it, getting browner and browner.

'Why don't we go to Paris tomorrow?' she says. 'Maybe we could lose Dustin in the crowd.'

'We could,' I say.

At the moment Paris is not a good place to be. There are policemen who walk around in threes with expressions that could kill you. It is August so everyone is suspicious; everyone is a tourist. We walk around with thin, expensive baguettes and fizzy drinks. We clutch our 'petits plans de Paris' and try to look as if we live there. Karen knows the city better than me; she walks ahead of me into stations and directs me into trains which rush us, always, to the right location. 'Let's go to that little café on rue Poissonière,' she says, using her good French accent. It is a much better accent than mine. The consonants fall out of her mouth and disappear.

'We could,' I say. But sometimes, I would like to be here by myself. I would like to sit down, without Karen, in a square.

At about eleven o'clock on the sixth day, just as I'm about to go to bed, Karen yawns and says 'Have you seen the donkeys in the field?'

'No,' I say, 'not close up.'

It's beginning to get dark, but we all troop off to look at the donkeys. Dustin comes too, with a bag of stale bread.

'They're not ducks, Dustin,' says Karen.

'Who said they were?' says Dustin. 'Stale bread is not restricted to aquatic life.'

Karen is silent.

There are five donkeys. They are standing at various points in the field, leaning over dock leaves. When they see Dustin with the bag of bread they come over to the fence.

'Aren't they lovely?' says Karen. 'Hallo, donkeys.'

'How do you feed donkeys?' Dustin asks. He edges forward with half a baguette in his hand.

'Honestly,' says Karen, and she tells him he needs to break the bread up and hold it flat, so the donkeys don't chew his fingers.

'And I thought they were vegetarians,' says Dustin, and he glances quickly at Karen. He has a habit of doing that after he's spoken, looking for a smile. He always looks miserable when there isn't one.

It's getting colder; everything that was green in daylight looks blue now. We stroke the donkeys' noses for a while; white and cool as chilled winceyette. Swallows catch flies above our heads, and the donkeys move the grass with their hooves, kicking up a sharp smell of broken clover.

And suddenly there is a sparking noise; a kind of buzzing, like a bluebottle flying too close. It's a tiny sound, but the night is so silent that it carries all the way across the field, into the darkness. A second later, Dustin opens his mouth and gives out a loud cry, and it makes me shiver. It is a cry of pain. Undisguised and loud. All the donkeys jump back in fright, toss their heads and canter away.

'Electric fence,' says Dustin, rubbing his arm. 'That was weird. It hurt but it didn't hurt, you know what I mean?'

He has dropped the bread on the grass, and now he bends to pick it up.

'Are you OK?' I say.

'I think so,' says Dustin. 'That was weird.'

'What a girly scream,' says Karen. 'I don't think the donkeys will come back now'.

We walk back up the lane. Dustin is pale. The tarmac is black and hard, like frozen lava.

Dustin goes and sits in the living room when we get back, but Karen and I stay in the kitchen. We sit down at the table. We sit as if we are waiting for something.

This evening is a little cooler so I boil some milk and make some hot chocolate. We drink it out of our French bowls. Our 'bols de café'. Karen calls them 'bols de café,' but the first time he saw them Dustin said they looked like ordinary soup bowls to him. You could get bowls like that in Woolworths. Just because we're in France, he said, we don't have to think everything is so wonderful.

Before I go to bed I look for Dustin, to say goodnight. He is still in the living room, sitting on the floor, reading a laminated brochure that he found under the television. There are pictures in it of waiters in white aprons, and cantering horse statues and fountains, and it all looks very expensive. It is called *Paris: The Romantic City*. Karen and I have already looked at it.

I sit down on the carpet, beside Dustin.

'Are you OK?' I say.

'Yeah.' He turns a page.

'Are you going to Paris with Karen tomorrow?' I say.

'Paris would be good.'

'I think I might just stay here,' I say. 'I think I'd rather sit in a field.'

'That would be good too.'

'I've had enough of looking at statues.'

Dustin twists his mouth into a little upside-down smile. 'Yes,' he says. 'Those statues can get you down.'

We look at each other, in the dark room, for half a second. We are so close we almost kiss. A kiss of recognition.

'So,' I say, and I get up and step over the door-lintel into the garden. There is an olive tree at one end of the lawn, and dried-out geraniums in the flower beds. Behind the cupressus hedge I can hear the owl hooting. At night the house feels big and lonely, surrounded by trees and dark fields. The living room is the only thing illuminated, a bright-yellow square with Dustin in it, reading *Paris: The Romantic City*. It is one o'clock. In a few hours the cockerel will stand on the roof and start crowing. I step back indoors and close the shutters.

'Sleep well,' says Dustin. He puts the brochure away and leaves the room.

In the morning we will find some crumpled francs on the table, and a note. Karen will read it out.

'I've decided to go on to Italy, so am taking an early train . . .'

She will stop and look at me.

'Typical! He was always pissing off like that.'

'But I thought he'd changed.'

'I never said that.'

'Yes you did.'

'No I didn't.'

We will glare at each other.

'Anyway,' Karen will say, and she will sit down with her coffee bowl and take a sip. I will sit down too, after a while. I will have a few sentences in my head, to do with coffee and Paris and shopping trips. But I won't say them. Karen will sip. The lace curtains will hang. There will be a Dustin-shaped absence in the room.

You Don't Know What You're Missing

THERE WAS A bead curtain separating the kitchen from the rest of their house. Bead curtains were popular in town, Esther had noticed, but mainly with butchers and greengrocers, and sometimes she would watch these people as they walked through their curtains, carrying one long swathe of beads on the tops of their heads, all the way into the room, until the length of it would run out and go swaying back into place. Her mother never did that: she parted the curtain neatly with her hands and let the beads clash back together.

Esther was making herself a dress for the summer. It was complicated, with hundreds of little pleats, like something an Elizabethan would have worn. She stood on a kitchen chair while her mother pinned up the hem.

'I hope you're not going to go off this,' her mother said. 'It looks like the kind of style you'll go off any minute.'

'I won't,' Esther said. 'It's classic, mother. I will always wear it.'

She looked down and admired the way the dress gave her a tiny, sexy cleavage.

'It'll trail,' her mother said, 'and pick everything up off the floor.'

'No it won't. I'm going to wear heels.'

'Oh, are you?' said her mother, and she sighed.

Esther was already as tall as her mother; they sometimes measured themselves at weekends, back to back, Esther skimming her hand across the tops of their heads. Her hair was coarser and darker than her mother's. These days, everything about her seemed coarser. She looked out through the glass panes of the kitchen door. There was a little wire milk stand on the step that said 'One silver top today, please, Milkman'. It always said that: the arrow was rusted at that phrase.

Their house was in the middle of a row of three. On the left was Mr Fowler's house. It was exactly like theirs but without the concrete driveway, and the front door was a kind of nectarine colour. Mr Fowler was ancient. He kept hens. Esther would look through the kitchen window and think 'There are Fowler's Fowls'. Her father used to say that. It was one of the things she remembered.

On the right was the Costellos' house. Mrs Costello was a teacher at Esther's school and it was embarrassing to live next door to them, but, worse, Esther's mother went there twice a week to do the cleaning. She said she enjoyed cleaning their house, because of the things in it. They were elegant and you felt like keeping them dust-free. The Costellos' kitchen had a real fireplace and a huge oak table and curtains which weren't just lined; they had an inner lining, blanket-thick, and when you pulled them they swished like something opulent.

'I ought to make curtains with inner linings,' Esther's mother said.

'Why?' said Esther.

'They're just . . . grand,' said her mother.

As well as cleaning, Esther's mother prepared vegetables for them. The Costellos got through a lot of potatoes. She had to peel twenty every week, and leave them soaking in a bucket of salted water. 'You shouldn't have to peel potatoes for them, mother,' said Esther. Sometimes, she said things like that; things that maybe her father would have said. Sometimes she felt responsible for her mother. She felt potato-peeling should not be part of cleaning a house.

* * *

Mrs Costello worked in the school library. But she wasn't fusty. She would stride into rooms and pin poems to the walls. 'Read and consider,' she would say, and then she would stride out again. She looked like an old flamenco dancer. She had curly black hair and when she screwed up her eyes, you could see exactly how her wrinkles had formed. Sometimes, at home, she read Tarot cards for Esther's mother. 'You are about to begin a new phase,' she would say, turning the pictures over. 'You are on the cusp of something new'. 'Really?' said Esther's mother. 'Do you think so?'

There were three Costellos but normally only Mr and Mrs lived next door; the son, Gideon, had gone away to boarding school. Gideon was two years older than Esther. She hardly ever saw him any more, but sometimes she would sit in his room when her mother went round to do the cleaning; she would lie flat on his bed, listening to his record collection. Gideon's room was dark and full of things he had grown out of: plastic aeroplanes and strange, collapsable aliens. The air in the room had a certain smell, of carpet tiles and plasticine and pine furniture. She could spend an hour in there without realising it, until she heard her mother and Mrs Costello talking downstairs. They would talk while Mrs Costello smoked and drank Martini, and then there would be the sudden, jolting sound of the hoover being switched on. While her mother hoovered, Esther would read Gideon Costello's Spiderman comics and listen to his out-of-date records. She almost felt as if she owned his room. Sometimes, she picked up some of the things lying around on the carpet and wondered what it was like to be him: older and a boy and somewhere else. Once, she had written him a letter – it had been a friendly letter – she had wanted to reassure him that she was not in love with him. So she had filled it full of dull statements. She had described what the weather was like and told him that she had finally managed to pick the brick up from the bottom of the school swimming pool, surfacing to sea a watery image of Mrs Johnson standing on the tiles shouting 'You have a lot of catching up to do.' But Gideon had never written back. These days, she left his door slightly ajar when she went round, so it didn't look as if she was stealing things.

One afternoon, as Esther was creeping downstairs from Gideon's room, Mrs Costello looked up and frowned. 'What have you been up to?' she said, sharply.

'Esther was just helping me dust', said her mother.

'Poor Esther,' said Mrs Costello, 'you'd much rather read than dust, wouldn't you?' and she looked over her mother's head and winked. She walked to the window and looked out at Mr Fowler feeding his chickens in the yard. 'That man is mad,' she announced. Then she turned from the window and watched Esther's mother as she bent and put all the cleaning things back into the cupboard under the stairs. 'Vim,' she said, suddenly loud. 'What a funny name! Like a Greek god.' And Esther's mother stood up abruptly and banged her head against the door lintel.

On summer evenings, Esther would sit at the very end of their garden, in the long grass near the compost heap. Mr Fowler's hens were only a few yards away from her there, on the other side of the fence. She sat and watched their scaly, colourless legs, and sometimes she would look up at the clear, blue sky. She missed her father sometimes. Occasionally she took her diary with her and wrote for twenty minutes or so, pressing the biro hard against the paper until it formed thick impressions when she turned the page.

I saw John Kenison on the bus again today, she wrote.

He has really brown eyes. He sat opposite me and I think he was looking at me surreptitiously. Unfortunately, when he got off the bus he hit me on the head with his hockey stick. I know it was an accident, but it really hurt. I think I have lost a lot of brain cells.

She stopped writing and watched Mr Fowler walking out of his kitchen, stooping, and pulling up a few weeds before disappearing into his greenhouse.

In the last week of the summer term, Mrs Costello asked Esther's mother if she would keep an eye on the house while they were away. They were going to Canada, and she invited them both round to supper, to talk things over. They all sat around the oak table, eating fish soup. Prawns kept somehow surfacing in Esther's spoon, and she didn't know what to do about them. She kept putting them back in her bowl until it was full of nothing but prawns.

'Don't you like seafood, Esther?' Mrs Costello asked. 'You don't know what you're missing my love.'

She put a prawn in her mouth and crunched it.

'What is there to tell you?' she said to Esther's mother. There was a bit of prawn-anatomy stuck between her teeth which Esther tried not to look at. Instead she looked around the kitchen. It was big but full of little things. There was a rubber lizard on the window-sill, and a plastic bag with some soil in it that said 'Congratulations! You now own a piece of Tasmania'.

'We'll be away for four weeks,' said fat Mr Costello, who was bubbling away at the corner of the table like an old hookah. 'Feel free to sit in the garden. No parties though. Ha. Ha. Ha.'

Mrs Costello looked at her husband and smiled.

'Ha,' said Mr Costello. He bit a prawn and stroked the cat at the same time. He was a big man, sociable, but there was something alarming about his fleshy face and his laugh.

'Do you want us to do any gardening?' Esther's mother asked. It was strange, Esther thought, to see her, sitting there, eating soup. Not to be cleaning. Esther noticed that she had hidden a number of prawns underneath her spoon.

'Well, if it's hot,' Mrs Costello said, 'the garden will need the odd water with the sprinkler so it doesn't dry out. Just the odd water, now and then.'

'Right,' said Esther's mother. The cat came and jumped on her lap, and began to pierce her thighs with its claws.

'And please feel free to eat anything from the freezer that's nearing its use-by date,' said Mrs Costello, 'it would only go off.'

'Lenny has half a tin of food a day, morning and evening,' Mr Costello barked suddenly.

'Where are you off to again?' said Esther's mother.

'Canada,' said Mrs Costello.

'Niagara Falls' said Mr Costello.

'We're staying in the Rainbow Hotel,' said Mrs Costello. 'Isn't that a wonderful name?'

For the last week of term, Esther's school was airless and full of big insects trying to fly straight through the window panes. It was as dust-spinning and dismal as a forest pond. Pupils started to return to the school library, requesting books for projects they should have finished two months before, and Mrs Costello smiled behind the lending desk, her teeth glinting in the sad, afternoon sunlight, and said 'I am sorry, child, but we have nothing on the Aztecs. All those Aztec books have been taken out.' Then she went away and started to take the poems off the walls.

On the last day of term, the day before the Costellos left for Canada, the pupils were allowed to wear anything they liked. Nearly all the girls wore patterned tights, and some people's legs came out in rashes because of the heat of the sun. Esther put on her new dress, hoping that John Kenison would notice her figure and the way the blue of the fabric made her hair look darker, but when she got on the bus in the morning, she realised that his school must have finished a day earlier than all the others. She felt a sudden, stupid sense of loss. She walked up the school drive and felt inappropriate. 'How charming,' said the teachers about her dress. 'How bizarre,' said the girls wearing patterned tights. At lunch she spilled tomato sauce on her dress's pleated front. She splashed the front of the dress with cold water from the drinking fountain but the tomato stain didn't come out; the water just created a huge damp circle on top of it.

During the final lesson, when they usually had Library Hour, they played a quiz devised by Mrs Costello. She sat on the lending desk and asked questions. Hardly anyone knew the answers. 'Where did the Aztecs live?' she asked. 'Come on now. This is not difficult'. Nobody seemed to know. Esther found some pink tacking stitches in one of her sleeves, and it made her think of her mother, sitting in the kitchen. She might be drinking tea, and listening to the radio.

'Where are the Niagara Falls?' asked Mrs Costello.

'Canada,' said Esther, 'And the United States. They're in both.'

'Well done, Esther,' said Mrs Costello. 'A moment of rare inspiration.'

Walking down the school drive at the end of the day, something happened. Three sixth-form boys were waiting behind the trees.

'You can't get past unless you give us a kiss,' said one of the boys, and suddenly they were ambushing Esther and her friends, holding on to their arms. The tallest one, the one with the palest face, held Esther round the waist. His face zoomed up white and close and his eyes were suddenly so near that they were dark and out of focus, like strange bees, and he put his lips against hers and kissed. His lips were warm and tasted of black jacks.

'Nice tits,' he said, and suddenly he unwrapped his arms and took his lips away from hers and all three boys disappeared; they evaporated silently into the trees, leaving Esther and Jane Moody and Eleanor Cave puce in the face and exhilarated.

When Esther got home she rang the doorbell but her mother didn't appear. So she waited, standing on the path. The afternoon was still and hot, and she felt the sun dazing her, beating against her head, and summer stretching, spiralling, from July to September. I have been kissed, she thought, I have been kissed. After a while she went round to the back door and found that it was unlocked. She walked through the bead curtain and into the kitchen, calling out. But there was no answer; the house was quiet; just a wave of ordered silence. She went upstairs to her room, opened her money box and counted the coins in it. There seemed to be an extra £1 note in there. I have been kissed, she thought. She picked up her diary and went back into the garden. She sat in her usual place, in the long grass and looked through the fence at Mr Fowler's hens. They were pecking at feed in the shade.

She picked up her biro and wrote

Last day of term

and couldn't think how to describe it. She tore a piece of paper out of her diary and wrote

Dear Gideon

and then she tried out her signature, six times, with and without her middle initial.

Dear Gideon, she wrote again, *Dear Gideon, Dear Gideon,* until the words became meaningless, a scrawl, lines. She stood up, dizzy, wondering where her mother was. She walked around the garden, looking for her, and then, after a while she walked down the path and along the road to the Costellos' house. Her mother had put the sprinkler on in the garden. Esther could see water dancing against the trees and forming little rainbows in the sunlight. And she was surprised because it was the wrong time of day – her mother was always telling her not to water plants until the evening, but the lawn already looked waterlogged, as if the sprinkler had been on for hours.

'Hallo,' she called, because from the gateway, she could see her mother, standing in the Costello's conservatory. She was holding up the lid of the freezer, and moving plastic tubs around. Esther watched as she brushed a strand of hair behind her ear, reached out and put one of the plastic tubs into a large cardboard box.

Esther walked down the path. 'Mum,' she called, but her mother didn't reply. When she knocked on the window, her mother didn't move for a moment, and then she looked up, blushed, walked slowly to the conservatory door and opened it.

'Hallo, sweetheart,' she said, 'four o'clock already?'

'School finished early. It's the last day of term.'

'Of course it is. I forgot.'

She picked up one of the tupperware boxes and looked at the label. Then she looked back at Esther. She looked at the tomato stain on her dress, but didn't say anything.

'What are you doing?' Esther asked.

'I was just seeing what needed eating,' her mother said. 'There's some casserole in here . . .,' and she held up another box in the afternoon light of the conservatory. It was dated July, two years back, when Esther's father was still with them; when things were much simpler.

'Aren't freezers strange?' her mother said. 'You put something in them, and you take them out two years later and your life is completely different.'

Esther looked at her. And for a while she felt as old as her mother; aware of the world, and what it could do.

Masterclass

RACHEL GOES INTO the living room, lies on the carpet and switches on the television. It is the time of day for school broadcasts, and there is a programme about parabolas. A man is standing in a tight suit, in front of a curve and an equation.

She looks around the living room and wonders if it is the right kind of place for an English lesson. It is neat, but it doesn't look intellectual. Her son has left his black sports bag in the corner of the room. It has 'Head' written on it. Why? Why call a sports bag 'Head'? It makes no sense. She can see her son's football boots in the bag, heavy and ugly as dogfish. Next to the bag there is her husband's guitar in its case, which he hasn't played for about two years, and several cardboard folders filled with papers that need sorting out. Underneath the television there is a basket of white knitting wool with needles stuffed into it. The wool and needles look like a long-legged little sheep. Above the television, the picture that her husband put up is at a slight slant. She has always disliked that picture. It is a picture of nothing in a plastic frame; it is just a whole lot of different, jangling colours. Her husband liked it, so he bought it and stuck it above the mantelpiece. That was all.

Her new student is ten minutes late, and she is beginning to wonder whether he will turn up, whether she should breathe a sigh of relief and make some tea when the doorbell rings. She leaps to her feet and snaps the schools programme off. There are pieces of carpet-fluff attached to her jumper. She brushes at the fluff, and goes to the front door.

Her student is taller and plumper than she expected. He is holding an umbrella and a blue plastic wallet. His anorak is covered in rain-splashes.

'Hallo,' says Rachel. 'You must be Mr Lee.'

'Hallo,' says Mr Lee. He is already halfway down the corridor. It is a very long, narrow corridor.

'The living room is on the left,' Rachel says, but Mr Lee continues to walk down the corridor until he is almost in the kitchen, where her son is skulking.

'This way,' Rachel says. The lesson is going wrong already. She almost runs into the living room. From there, she hears Mr Lee stop walking. Then there is the sound of shoe leather turning on floor tiles.

The teaching area of the room looks quite composed. She has pushed the table up to the window, and on it she has placed a vase of yellow chrysanthemums, pens, notepaper and an exercise book. The exercise book is called *Masterclass.*

'Have a seat,' she says. She gestures at the chairs.

'Thank you,' says Mr Lee. His voice is clear and low. He sits down on one of the little balloon-back chairs, still clutching the blue plastic wallet, still wearing his anorak.

'Oh,' says Rachel, 'I should take your coat.'

Mr Lee smiles. 'It is cold today,' he says. Rachel sits down.

Almost a year ago, she had gone to the university campus and put an advertisement in the postgraduate union. It had been a warm day, full of birds singing, and she had been feeling capable and clear-headed. The advertisement said: 'English Lessons: Individual help with grammar and conversation. £8 per hour.'

She had included her name and phone number but no one had phoned. No one had responded for ten months and very quickly she had forgotten about being an English teacher. Then, in December, Mr Lee rang.

'I am Lee,' he said.

'I think you have the wrong number,' said Rachel.

There was a pause, then Mr Lee began to speak again. It

sounded as if he might be reading something from a piece of paper.

'You teach English,' he said.

'Sorry?' she said, and then she remembered her advertisement.

'One hour, eight pounds,' said Mr Lee.

The day before, she came home from work early to prepare the lesson. She bought an exercise book, and drew a timetable in it.

11.00 – General chat
11.10 – Suggest what we will do
11.20 – Ask him things – what is he doing here etc.

But she is not sure how many words he has for a general chat. She hadn't thought about that. They will have to skip that and go straight on to the suggestions.

'Would you like a cup of tea?' she asks.

'Yes,' Mr Lee says. 'Thank you.'

'Milk? Sugar?'

'Sugar,' says Mr Lee.

'OK,' she says. She smiles. Then she gets up and scampers away into the kitchen. Waiting on the sideboard is a kettle-full of recently-boiled water, and some teabags in mugs. They are her favourite mugs, with pictures of loopy-looking farm animals.

Her son is sitting at the kitchen table. These days her son is known as Baker. That is what his schoolfriends call him. It is startling, to hear his friends barking out 'Baker' when it is her own surname. Baker Junior is sitting at the table, drinking Pepsi and eating a peanut-butter sandwich. He is wearing his mad head T-shirt.

'How long are you going to be?' he asks in a morose, cracking voice.

'An hour,' Rachel says.

'But I wanted to watch telly,' he says.

'There's nowhere else we can go,' she says. 'Why don't you go and watch it at Ian's?'

She misses one of the mugs and pours water over the sideboard.

'Ian's not even there,' says her son. 'He's in the bloody Pentlands.' He picks up another piece of bread and walks into his room. He slams the door.

Mr Lee is emptying the plastic wallet when she returns. On the table he has placed several sheets of printed paper.

Rachel smiles and says 'Here we are.' She wonders if that is a good phrase to use; maybe it is too meaningless.

'Thank you,' says Mr Lee. He looks at the farm animals on the mug and takes a sip of tea. 'Nice,' he says.

'Mm,' says Rachel.

She is about to ask him some of the questions she has prepared, *What are you doing here? Where do you come from?*, when he says 'Please say these sounds,' and he shows her one of the sheets of paper. Rachel looks at the paper and feels her heart flip with anxiety. It is not what she had planned to do. There are printed words, placed into different sections. *Rake, bake, make. Snow, cow, wow!* It is not something you can talk about.

'Please,' says Mr Lee, and he points to *wow!*

'Wow!' says Rachel.

'Wow! says Mr Lee.

'Snow,' says Rachel.

'Snow,' says Mr Lee.

He moves his head to one side and breathes through his teeth. 'Why are they different?' he asks.

'I don't know.'

Mr Lee frowns. 'It is important,' he says, 'to know.'

'Yes,' says Rachel, hopelessly. She grips her mug of tea and tries to explain the difference between wow and snow. She had not anticipated having to do this. She had thought they would have some kind of chat.

'How,' says Mr Lee. He leans forward in his chair and it creaks.

'At the moment . . .,' Rachel says, and she pauses, wondering how to retrieve the lesson.

'Tell me,' she says, 'are you a student? Do you study?'

'Yes,' says Mr Lee, 'I study memetic algorithms.'

'Oh,' Rachel says. She does not know what memetic algorithms are. She looks at the jangling picture on the wall, and her mind feels blank.

'How long are you here for?' she asks.

'One week ago.'

'Do you have a family?'

'A wife and daughters. My daughters are one and three.'

'Does your wife study?'

'At the moment my wife is in the house. She speaks no English.'

Mr Lee stares at the chrysanthemums. 'Korean flowers,' he says. 'You are kind.'

'Oh,' says Rachel, pleased.

The door opens, making Mr Lee jump and spill a little tea, and her son shuffles in. He mumbles something. He has put on his incoherent voice. He looks at Rachel and then at Mr Lee. He mumbles again. He stomps towards the piano, picks up his magazine about amplifiers and stomps out again. He does not close the door properly.

'Sorry,' says Rachel.

'Your son,' says Mr Lee.

'Yes,' says Rachel. She does not want to talk about her son.

'How old?' says Mr Lee.

'Nearly fourteen.'

'A bad age for boys. Your husband works?'

'Yes. He works late. He works too hard.'

'Ah,' says Mr Lee. He nods, gulps and looks out of the window at the rain.

'In Korea we have four seasons,' he says. 'They are all different.'

Halfway through the lesson she does not know what to say any more. Her mind is exhausted. They have gone through more words: *Glad, Lad, Had. Rake, Make, Bake. Sky, High, Why,* and after that she started to talk, fast, hysterically, about anything that came into her head. But suddenly she can't think of anything else. She has gone all the way through British customs, from Valentine's Day to Christmas, and now she has run out.

Mr Lee sits and looks at her. He smiles.

'Your country has many traditions,' he says.

'Yes,' she says. She feels she has been lying to him, cramming ideas into his head about April Fools and mistletoe.

'Your husband' Mr Lee says. 'When . . .'

'When does he come back?' Rachel says. 'Late. After I'm asleep. He is working a late shift tonight.'

Mr Lee nods.

'Here is my family,' he says, and he takes a photograph out of his wallet and shows it to her. It is a small picture of his wife and children, sitting in a wood. His wife is reading a book, with the baby on her lap, and the toddler is walking the length of a fallen tree. They have a picnic with them; things in plastic pots, and a bag of fruit. They are surrounded by blue flowers.

'How nice that looks,' Rachel says.

'A place in Korea,' Mr Lee says.

'It looks beautiful.'

'Yes.'

It doesn't look the way she imagined a Korean wood to look. She thought there might have been blossom or bamboo.

'Tell me about your country,' she says.

'I think there is no time,' Mr Lee says.

He shows her his watch. It is five to four.

'Oh God,' says Rachel. She has been talking, non-stop, for nearly an hour.

Mr Lee puts his papers back in the plastic wallet and zips up his anorak. Then he gets up and walks towards the picture on the wall.

'Nice,' he says.

'My husband put that up,' Rachel says. She stares at her Masterclass book. She can't believe how she has wasted the whole lesson.

Mr Lee does not reply. He points to a little square in the picture. 'Is this blue or green?' he asks.

Rachel looks up. Then she gets up from the table, walks over and peers at the picture.

'It's turquoise,' she says after a while. 'Or some people might call it aquamarine. Or duck-egg blue.' She pauses, wondering if there are any other colours she could teach him. She has never stood so close to the picture, not since the night her husband bought it and put it on the wall, and they had a row about it. Their first row of the year. She has hardly looked at it since then. But he is right about the colours – the colours, in fact, are beautiful.

'Duck-egg blue,' she says.

'Very nice,' says Mr Lee. 'Very nice.'

He goes back to the table and picks up his notes and starts to walk towards the door, and Rachel has an urge suddenly, a strong urge to run and put her arms around him; to stop him for a moment, so she can thank him, for pointing that out.

We must be the Misfits

TODAY, I CAN'T get my boyfriend out of my head. I am thinking of him on the day he proposed to me, and on the day he left; of standing at the train station one afternoon last November and watching his lips forming words, but not hearing them because there was an announcement for someone called *Hugh Brain* over the PA system: 'Would passenger Hugh Brain please report to the Information Desk.'

'Phone me,' I said to my boyfriend. 'Write to me,' but he didn't reply. He picked up his suitcase and got on to the train.

I walked out of the station and went home on a 44 bus. I didn't feel heartbroken, as I had expected; just stunned because something had failed; something had not worked. A woman in a headscarf sat down beside me, and I could feel the warmth of her through her coat. 'Look at that rain,' said the woman. Opposite us, a boy with flashing red lights in his trainers was reading the bus map and breathing through his mouth.

'Those bus steps are too high. And I've just had a knee operation,' the woman said.

'Oh dear,' I said.

But I didn't want to talk. So I turned and looked out through the bus window at the buildings and the streets; at the whole city without my boyfriend in it.

I'm thinking of him today because I am at a wedding reception; I am here to be merry, to sing merrily, with my guitar. The reception is fifteen miles away from the church, and I am the first to arrive, apart from the vicar. He is standing in the little white porch, watching the wind blow the chestnut trees about.

'Hallo,' the vicar shouts when I get out of the taxi. 'All on your own?'

'Yes. Just me and the old guitar.'

The vicar smiles and looks uncomprehending.

'Some of the guests appear to have taken the wrong turning,' he says. He pulls at a rose leaf. 'Are you with the bride or the groom?'

'I am just here to play the guitar,' I say. The vicar's smile becomes a little more fixed and no less uncomprehending.

'I hope they haven't all ended up in Rickmansworth,' he says. 'Once you are in Rickmansworth it is very difficult to get out.'

He chews a tiny bit of the rose leaf. Then he goes indoors and speaks to a woman who is pulling cling film off a plate of cheese.

Slowly, people begin to appear. Estate cars roll up the drive, and I can see faces composing themselves behind the windscreen of each car. People putting smiles on. People finishing their arguments. A man in a silvery suit jumps out of a car and starts to run around by the rhododendron bushes, telling people where to park. He stands in empty spaces and points. He claps his hands together and shouts.

'There is room here if everyone moves up,' he shouts. He steps back into a small group of daffodils and looks down. Then he looks up, sees me watching him, and winks.

'Someone has to take charge,' he shouts into the wind. I look away.

People slide out of their cars, looking crumpled and oddly dressed for one in the afternoon. There is a lot of yellow and white, and the wind blows it around. The bridesmaids stand by the pebbledashed walls, chilled and long-faced, holding lillies and roses. But nobody is allowed into the Reception Suite. The woman with the cling film tells us that we can't come in for another five minutes. 'No,' she says, glaring at us, 'it is not one fifteen yet.' She shuts the door and walks away into the dining room, and all the wedding guests loom up to the glass and watch her. Through the panoramic window, we can see her arranging table napkins.

Nobody speaks. We are like sheep hesitating in front of a pen.

After a while the man in the silvery suit says 'It's freezing out here. Oi.' He knocks on the glass.

I couldn't see myself being married to this boyfriend I had. 'Let's just stay the way we are,' I said, and when I said that, after a short while, a couple of weeks, in fact, he went off in the train. He went to Basingstoke and I have never heard from him again. I had picked a traditionalist, disguised as a radical. It still amazes me. I was fooled for three years.

In my right hand is my guitar case. In my left hand I am holding the *Order Of Service*. It is printed on cream-coloured paper, embossed with doves, and it has a white ribbon running down the spine. There are two hymns printed in it: 'At the Name Of Jesus' and 'All Things Bright and Beautiful.' The bride's name used to be Sarah McKenzie. It is now Sarah Cowe. Her husband's name is Russell Cowe.

'Look at Sarah,' whispers a woman in a very wide, white hat. 'Where did Sarah get that tiny waist?' and before anyone can answer, the woman with the cling film comes and opens the door and we all squash in; a half-polite scrum. Somebody treads on the edge of my shoe and leaves a dusty footprint. A man puts his hand on my shoulder and leaves it there slightly too long. Sarah and Russell Cowe have to elbow their way to the front to get there in time to greet everyone. But it becomes more orderly after a while; an intuitive kind of queue forms.

When it is my turn to speak to Sarah Cowe, I don't know what to say. We have never met before. We are the same height in our slightly elevated shoes, but my shoes are black and come from the bottom of the wardrobe. Sarah Cowe's shoes are pearly white and brand new. I am wearing my old white blouse and the kilt I've had since I was sixteen. Sarah's dress has hundreds of little pearls sewn on to it.

'Well done,' I say to her.

Sarah Cowe looks at me. A tiny sound emerges from her mouth, which could be 'Thank you,' and I sidle on towards Russell Cowe. Russell Cowe grabs my hand and squashes it hard.

'Thanks,' he says, before I have said anything. His face is bright pink.

'Congratulations,' I say, but he has already let go of my hand and is focusing on the next person in the line.

Now I am facing an elderly waitress. She is wearing a white blouse similar to mine, and holding a tray which contains champagne and small pieces of rolled-up bread.

'Bride or groom, Madam?' she asks.

'I am just here to play the guitar,' I say. 'Is there anywhere I can leave it?'

The waitress looks at my guitar case. There is a sticker on it that says 'It's Madness!' I stuck it there when I was fourteen.

'Oh,' says the waitress, 'that's different.' She thinks for a moment. 'It'll be safe behind the reception desk,' she says, and she puts the tray of champagne down on a little side-table and takes my guitar away. I feel a funny mixture of lightness and heaviness without the guitar, like a mother saying goodbye to a child. I pick up the fullest-looking champagne flute and walk into the dining room.

The wedding guests are arranged in groups around the tables, and the place-settings are all a little too close. Some people claim space with their elbows; others make themselves very narrow. In front of each guest there is a plate containing a pinkish pyramid surrounded by lettuce.

'This is salmon mousse,' says a woman in a pink sequinned top, and the table immediately falls silent.

Out of the corner of my eye, I notice the vicar scuttle into the room, whisper something to the new Mr and Mrs Cowe, and rush out. After a few minutes I see his small red car drive fast past the window.

Nobody knows whether to start eating; whether we should perhaps be waiting to drink champagne. But there is no announcement, no tapping of the side of a champagne flute, so we pick up our cutlery and begin. After a while, we start to introduce ourselves, groping for something that will connect us. The people on my table don't seem to be connected in any way.

'We must be the misfits,' says a man sitting beside me, the one in the silvery suit. 'The fifth wheels,' he says.

I clear my throat.

'It's quite a neat way to deal with us, though,' I say, 'sort of wholesale' and the man looks at me. He smiles. The silvery threads of his suit sparkle.

'Who do you know?' he asks.

'I don't know anyone,' I say. 'I'm just here to play the guitar.'

'Oh,' says the man, widening his eyes. I am shredding a corner of my napkin with my fingertips, and wondering how many more times I will say that sentence.

'How about castanets?' asks the man, cramming an over-large piece of lettuce into his mouth. 'Do you play the castanets? You look quite Spanish.'

I pretend I haven't heard. I feel like picking up my salmon mousse and throwing it at his horrible suit. My boyfriend always wore very nice suits. Nothing loud. He would never have worn something with silver threads. Sometimes I wonder what I have done. How I could have rejected a man who wore such stylish suits.

While we are eating the main course, the man picks a camera up from the table and takes a picture of me.

'Say cheese,' he says.

'Cheese,' I say. It occurs to me that the man will not know where to send the photo. One day he will look at a picture of a slightly uneasy girl eating roast beef, and wonder why it belongs to him.

'So,' the man says. 'Do you study music at college?'

He looks down and cuts a slice of beef in half. Then he puts it in his mouth and looks up at me again.

'No,' I say, once I have finished chewing a rather tough piece of beef. I put my glass to my lips and take a sip of water. Wedding receptions are always so awkward; you always end up having strangely-angled conversations with strangers. I turn a little in my chair. 'I've just played the guitar for a long time. Since I was nine.' I smile in a phoney kind of way and put my cutlery down.

And a waitress appears, suddenly, at my left shoulder, and takes away my plate.

'Oh,' I say. I look up and see the waitress walking away. 'Excuse me, I . . .,' I call after her, '. . . I hadn't quite finished.'

But the waitress doesn't seem to hear. She stomps into the distance with my plate, scrapes my lunch off it and puts it on a trolley.

'You're not English, are you?' says the man. 'You don't look English.'

'What?' I feel unsettled at the sudden removal of my lunch. 'Why not?'

'You look emotional,' says the man. He sits back a little, looks at me as if I am perhaps a painting or a bank statement, and then eats another piece of beef.

'Married?' he asks.

'No.'

'Not the marrying type? Or too young to settle down?'

'Both,' I snap. 'Both, probably.'

When the main course is over, the waitress returns, wheeling a dessert trolley, and everyone turns in their seats and looks at it. There are three desserts: fruit salad, raspberry pavlova and chocolate profiteroles.

'This all looks very tasty,' says the man. He pours more wine into his glass; a big glassful of it. Then he stops and thinks for a moment.

'I'll have the chocolate profiteroles,' he says to the waitress, and she picks up a white dish and spoons a few on to it.

'Cream?' she says.

'Please,' says the man.

The waitress picks up a silver jug and pours a little pool of cream over the profiteroles. Cholesterol, I think, cholesterol, and I put my hand up to my heart for a second, just to feel it ticking.

'I knew you would have that,' I say.

'Am I so transparent?' the man asks.

'You just look like the chocolate-profiterole type.'

The man looks rather sad when I say this. He slices a profiterole with the edge of his spoon and it sinks a little. These days I feel so mean – I can say mean, deflating things to people, especially middle-aged, traditional-looking men, and I don't care.

'Excuse me,' I say, and I get up. 'I'm just going to check on my guitar,' and I leave the man ploughing dismally through his profiteroles.

I walk out of the dining room, through the lobby and along a corridor. Fixed to the walls there are photographs of brides who have all had their receptions in the same place. They are all sitting in front of landscapes and smiling fearfully in soft focus. In some pictures, the husbands stand behind them, their hands placed, like oversized epaulettes, on their wives' shoulders. In others, the husbands adopt noble stances, one knee slightly bent, like monarchs of the glen.

There is a breeze in the corridor, and an unromantic smell of bacon and carpet freshener. Leaning against the wall there is a small, stained table with brochures on it of the local sights. It reminds me of hotels my boyfriend and I stayed in. In particular, of a hotel in Notting Hill. We stayed there for one night, a few weeks before he proposed to me, and sometimes, I wonder if he had planned to propose to me there. I imagine him saying something about tying the knot in Notting Hill. But the hotel had not been right. It had had earwigs and depressing lilac bedspreads and bad plumbing, and my boyfriend had stood at reception on the day we left, and demanded a discount. We had picked up our suitcases and left in a melodramatic rush.

When I reach the reception desk I crouch down beside the coats and open my guitar case. My guitar is covered by one of my boyfriend's T-shirts. It is a patchy blue; I dyed it blue by mistake when I washed it last summer. Before that it had been perfectly white, and I had ruined it. It was an expensive, designer T-shirt. I pick it up, put it to my face and breathe in. But the scent of him has gone.

The hotel is full of corridors, and I choose a different route back. When I get back to the hallway I can see Mr and Mrs Cowe roaming about, newly mature, at the far end of the dance hall, and I am heading towards them, to ask when they want me to start playing, when I notice a little room beside the staircase. There are people in it, and a table, covered with a white tablecloth. There are plates and dishes of cheese and grapes, and the cutlery is shining in the sun. There are three women in hats and the man with the silvery suit. Damn, I think, damn, and I quicken my pace. But the man sees me.

'Hey, pet,' he calls, 'come here a minute.'

'Oh,' I say, surprised, as if I've just noticed him, 'OK.' I can't think of an adequate excuse, so I walk in. I smile. It won't be long now, I think; soon I will be back in my flat, drinking tea.

'I'm just about to start playing actually,' I say.

'Right,' says the man, 'I see.' He looks a little disappointed. 'And how is your guitar?' he asks.

'It's fine.'

'Still in one piece? Good.'

It is cooler in the little room. Spring sunshine falls, pale and beautiful, through the window. The three women finish selecting their cheese and biscuits and walk out of the room, leaving behind the scent of three different perfumes. The man sighs, cuts a huge wedge of Stilton and puts it on his plate.

'I had an argument with my wife this morning,' he says, 'that's why I'm alone. That's why she's not here.'

'Weddings always bring out the worst in people,' I say. This sounds rather blunt. But it is true, as far as I'm concerned. The man sighs.

'Sometimes,' he says, 'sometimes . . .,' but he doesn't finish what he was going to say. He just looks at me, with his blue eyes – nice eyes, I notice, suddenly – kind eyes, and says 'Why don't you play me something?'

'What – here?'

'Yes,' says the man. 'Why not? Just quietly. Something jolly. Something happy.'

I can't think what to say. I stand and grip the neck of the guitar, feeling the strings, tied tight, tight as heartstrings, tight enough to snap, across the fingerboard. My boyfriend never asked me to play anything to him, not ever. He never made a request like that.

'Go on,' the man says, and so I move the guitar up into my arms and start to play something – a tune I learned years ago, a little tune of celebration that I've always loved; that I play sometimes, when I'm suddenly, unexpectedly, glad.

Foreign Music

IT IS A fast road, and there are squashed frogs on the tarmac. A car slows down and stops. In the heat-haze, it looks like a mirage. A boy selling watermelons by the side of the road runs over to it with a melon and a knife, and when he gets to the opened window, the driver turns to the people in the car.

'Fruit at knife-point,' he says. He laughs, revealing a gold tooth.

The car is so loaded with people that it is scraping against the road. There are three old fat women in the back, and a woman in the front with a gold necklace and a cigarette, and a baby on her lap. In the boot there is a child and a hairy dog.

'Give me a half,' the man says to the boy. He is wearing a gold chain, and a leather one beneath it.

'Half won't go very far,' says the boy. He likes haggling.

'These things are the size of a pig,' says the man. 'Half or nothing.'

'OK,' says the boy. The man is holding $1.50 in the air and the boy takes it and hands the melon through the window.

'Do we have a knife?' asks the woman in the front seat. But the man doesn't reply; he just drops the melon on her lap, narrowly missing the baby, and the car blasts away, covering the boy in dust. The dog stares through the back window, and the boy stares back. All the people's heads lean slightly as the car goes around the corner. The boy puts the money in his pocket. He walks down the road for a while, then he turns, walks back and sits down on one of the watermelons. There are twenty-eight of them. He just sits and watches the cars going past, and the sun getting higher. It is nine in the morning but still cold, and the sky is a pale-orange colour. It is not a good day for selling watermelons. The boy gets out his knife, cuts one in half and looks at the black seeds.

Behind him is a patch of wasteland and a little store. Cows graze on either side of the store; he can hear their tongues wrapping around the grass and pulling it up. In front of the store is a big, purple cow made out of fibreglass, and advertising chocolate. She leans, as if she is tired, against the door.

At about nine thirty two girls get off a bus on the other side of the road. They wait until there is a gap in the traffic, then they run across to the island in the middle. The boy watches them. Both girls are carrying bags of toy animals. They walk along the island a little way and then stop. One of the girls takes the toy animals out of the bags and piles them up on the ground. The other one puts up a small blackboard which says 'Toy Rabbits – just $10!'

'I'm here already,' the boy shouts, but the girls ignore him. They each pick up a rabbit and hold them up as cars drive past. Nothing stops. After a while, they throw the rabbits back on the pile, sit down and stare at the road.

The boy stands up because the melon he is sitting on is getting uncomfortable. It rolls around, like a circus ball. He takes a radio out of his pocket and switches it on, but the sound is very faint. It is fading away, like somebody walking into the distance. He takes one of the batteries out of the back and holds it against his tongue. His father told him you can check if batteries are new that way, but he isn't sure what batteries are meant to taste like.

By eleven o'clock he has sold three and a half watermelons. It is getting hot, and he goes and stands in the shade of the purple cow. There is a label around the cow's neck that says 'SILVIA'.

'How's business?' says the man in the store.

'Improving,' says the boy.

'Everyone wants iced drinks,' says the man, 'and the refrigerator is on the blink.'

The boy does not reply. He just stands and watches the traffic. There are Ford pick-ups and trucks with 'EXPLOSIVES' written on the back, and station-wagons. Cars being driven fast.

After a few minutes one of the girls with the toy rabbits runs across to them.

'Hi,' she says to the boy. She looks at him. 'My sister thinks you're nice,' she says.

'Oh,' says the boy.

'Your lucky day' says the store-man. He turns and kicks the refrigerator.

'You've sold all those watermelons and we haven't sold anything,' says the girl.

'There aren't enough kids on the motorway for toy rabbits,' says the store-man. 'Only big kids. Big kids in big cars.'

The boy touches the dollar bills in his pocket. 'Do you sell batteries?' he asks the man.

The man unfolds his arms, stretches up and lifts a pack of batteries off the shelf behind him. The pack is gold and black; exotic, like a new box of cigarettes.

'Where do you live?' the girl asks.

'Villa,' says the boy.

'Which side?'

'North.'

'That's the best side, isn't it?'

'Yep.'

On the north side of Villa, everyone has a television. And when they're not working, he and his father watch TV most of the time. They watch football, surrounded by a crowd of fruit: watermelons or pomegranites or nectarines.

When he has put the new batteries in, the radio is perfect. It sounds as if the station is just at the end of the freeway. The boy listens to FM radio. FM for Foreign Music.

By midday the sky is a bright, bright blue. The boy looks up at it. When there are no clouds, it is hard to tell how far away the sky is. It all looks the same distance. And when there is no traffic, the road is silent; there is not even the sound of crickets.

At one o'clock a man on a motorbike stops to buy a slice of melon. He eats it sitting on the bike with the engine still running, juice dripping on to the tassles of his jacket. He is wearing his crash helmet in a strange way, with the chin protector over his forehead. When he has finished eating, he throws the melon rind on the ground. 'Thanks,' he shouts, and he drives away.

The next car that stops is a Ford. The driver gets out, his stomach flopping over his waistband. He walks past the boy and into the store. He says something to the store-man and walks out again a few moments later carrying a burger. He does not look at the watermelons.

The boy takes out his packet of potato-chips. While he is eating them, a woman pulls up in a station-wagon and asks for a whole melon.

'Is this the kind you eat with ham?' she says.

'You can if you want' says the boy. He wipes the salt from his mouth with the back of his hand.

'Oh' says the woman. 'Well. Maybe I will.'

She squashes the sides of a change purse and it bulges out like a toad. She gives him $3 in small change.

'How old are you?' she asks.

'Eleven.'

'Do you live in Villa?'

'Yes.'

'I thought so,' says the woman.

'Why?' says the boy.

'I just thought you might,' says the woman. She smiles at him.

Mid-afternoon, a white coach stops at the traffic lights on the girls' side of the road. It has silver stripes and a palm tree painted on the side, and it makes a lot of noise, black smoke pouring out of the exhaust pipe. The girls run to one of the open windows at the back, where a woman is beckoning and calling out to them. The boy watches the youngest girl handing a pink rabbit up to the woman. Other people in the coach turn their heads and watch. The woman smiles and starts to look for her purse, but suddenly the coach has set off again, and the rabbit is inside it. The woman shouts 'Oh damn' through the window. But she does not throw the rabbit back. She waves and blows the girls a kiss.

When the boy walks across to the island, the youngest girl is crying.

'Poor rabbit,' she says, 'poor rabbit.'

The boy imagines the rabbit sitting on the coach, staring with its vacant, plastic eyes, up at the luggage racks. Chewing a plastic carrot. On its way to somewhere else.

'It's just . . .' he says, 'it's just gone somewhere with a beach.'

The older girl looks at him. 'Don't be ridiculous,' she says, and she goes and sits on the pile of rabbits. She crosses her arms.

'Do you want to hear some music?' the boy asks the youngest girl, and he switches on his radio. A man is singing a song about a woman.

'How much money have you made?' asks the girl after a while.

'$12,' says the boy. He is thinking he will have to hide his radio, or his father will make him listen to educational programmes. He will make him listen to some programme with people talking about measuring bookshelves.

'Where did you get the rabbits?' he asks.

'I'm not telling you.'

The girl puts her arms around one of them.

'I know this song,' she says, and she starts to sing. 'That's the way the heart aches . . .,' she sings, tunelessly.

'It's not "that's the way the heart aches", it's "dance away the heart ache",' says the older girl.

'Oh,' says the younger girl.

Her sister looks across the road, towards the store. 'You've still got twenty-four melons left,' she says to the boy.

'At least I haven't been giving them away.'

The younger girl starts to cry again. It makes him feel mean.

'Do you want a piece of melon?' he asks her, and she nods. So he runs back across the road, cuts three pieces of melon with his knife and runs back again. The three of them sit and eat in silence.

The watermelon is warm and sweet after the sun has been shining on it all day.

'We should sell fruit,' the older girl says.

'This is a good day for fruit' says the boy. 'It's not always like this.'

By five o'clock it is beginning to get cooler. There are fewer cars. The girls get up and pack away the rabbits.

'Bye then,' says the boy, and he sits and watches them walking to the bus stop. Then he switches on the radio again. He is wondering about his father; whether he has sold anything. Sometimes, his father sells fruit to canning factories but the canning factories don't always want it. They want different-shaped fruit. 'More elongated,' says the man at the factory, 'to fit the cans.'

Just before six, he sees his father's truck at the end of the road; a tiny dot getting bigger. He runs across the road and drags all the watermelons into a group. He arranges them so they look like a little crowd of people waiting for someone: a movie star or a president.

Hazy Daze

SITTING IN THE black slidey taxi, Jill had run out of things to say. She was just perched, staring ahead, like the queen of Egypt. The streets kept blurring and then being wiped clear again.

'Funny,' said the taxi driver, 'it always rains on Thursdays.'

'Does it?' said Jill. She looked into the oblong mirror that contained the driver's eyes, but the eyes did not look back; they just stared, wide and unfocused, at the road.

'Statistical fact,' said the driver.

They kept missing all the green lights, and every time they stopped, the driver began to scratch his head, fast, like a dog scratching, but he didn't use all his fingers, just the nail of his pinkie.

'Will we get there by 7.30?' Jill asked.

'People always ask me how long it's going to take,' said the taxi driver. He didn't say any more. He began to hum a little song.

'Oh,' said Jill.

It was a while since she had sat in a taxi. It felt glamorous. It had the smell of nights out: warm and rich.

She opened her bag and checked that her money and makeup bag were in there. Then she opened her makeup bag and checked that her mascara and lipstick were in it. She found her lipstick and twisted it up to check that it was the right colour. Hazy Daze. She never used to wear lipstick, but then she had found Hazy Daze in the chemist and she thought it made her face look more structured. More together. She put a little on, just a little on her bottom lip. Then she put the lipstick back in her makeup bag. She looked out of the window at a very fat woman who was checking her reflection in a shop window, adjusting the alignment of her breasts beneath her blouse.

'Off on holiday, then?' the taxi driver asked.

'I'm meeting my husband,' Jill said. 'He's been in Germany.'

'You don't look old enough to be married,' said the taxi driver in a loud voice, and he started to hum again. 'Do you know that song?' he asked, turning round to look at Jill. He hummed a little more. 'I am a rock,' he sang, 'I am an island'. His eyes looked enormous and flat behind his glasses. 'No?' he said. He turned back. 'Maybe it's before your time.'

It was January and dark. There was a low, white moon in the sky. Graham was coming back from two weeks in Germany, and she was going to hang around Terminal B until he arrived. She was going to sit waiting on an airport seat, her life temporarily on hold.

There were several people out on the tarmac, the wind blowing their clothes about. Just before she got out of the taxi, Jill saw two people she recognised. Their neighbours, Doug and Marleen Mackie. They were lurching across the car park with an empty trolley. She tried to scuttle inside quickly when she got out of the taxi, but they saw her. Doug began to shout. 'Jill,' he shouted across the car park.

'Oh,' said Jill. She arranged a surprised and delighted expression. 'Hallo,' she said.

'What are you doing here?' Marleen Mackie asked, trundling towards her with the trolley. It had a poster on it advertising J&B whisky.

'I'm meeting Graham,' said Jill.

'We're waiting for our son,' said Doug. 'He's been on a school exchange.'

'Is Graham on the Frankfurt flight?' Marleen asked.

'Yes,' said Jill.

'So's Jason,' said Marleen. 'Jason's on the Frankfurt flight. What a coincidence.'

'Yes,' said Jill.

When they got in to the arrivals lounge there were several taxi drivers standing by the sliding doors, holding up placards. One of them said 'Welcome, Wilt Party'.

'Oh look,' Jill said, 'isn't that funny?'

'What?' said Marleen.

'It's gone now,' said Jill.

She wanted to run and hide somewhere, to go into the tie boutique and hide behind the rainbow of silk cravats. She wanted to wait for Graham alone, like Anna Karenina on the train station, but now here she was, with Doug and Marleen Mackie.

They walked a little further into the hall and stood underneath the arrivals screen. Jill wondered why they always positioned the computer screens so high that you had to crane your neck to read them. She held her head back and looked for the number of Graham's plane. She had it written down on a slip of paper – BA463 – but for a moment she couldn't see it. A tiny feeling of fear slipped into her heart. It was not there. It was not there. And then she saw it. It was the last number on the screen, in a different colour from all the other numbers. Arrival time 19.30. Expected 20.05.

'Marvellous,' said Doug.

'We might as well go and get a coffee,' said Marleen.

'Good idea,' said Doug.

They walked to the coffee bar and dragged some chairs up to the counter. Jill had imagined herself doing this days ago, except in her mind she had been glamorous and alone. And she hadn't had one slightly bloodshot eye.

The chairs had small metal seats and were all a little too tall.

'Well,' said Marleen. She looked at Jill and smiled.

'I'm going to have an iced bun,' said Douglas. How about you, Marl?'

'I'll have a chicken tikka sandwich,' said Marleen.

'Jill?' said Doug.

'Nothing for me,' said Jill. 'I'll be back in a minute,' and before she had even really thought where she would go, she lowered herself off her metal chair again and walked away. She was aware of Doug and Marleen looking at her but she didn't look back.

There was a Ladies' toilet, illuminated with a green light at the far end of the hall, and she walked towards it, past all the check-in points and the stewardesses in their slim skirts and an old man with a small dog at the end of a lead, and parents waiting for the Frankfurt flight, in gloomy groups. On the door of the Ladies there was a picture of a very elegant woman, wearing a swishing kind of skirt. Jill pushed the door open and went in. Someone had put some pink roses on the shelf below the mirror, and she put her handbag next to the vase and looked at them. It seemed so thoughtful to put flowers in an airport toilet. They looked so pretty and so out of place, like a little memory of home when you weren't prepared for it.

She spent a long time in the Ladies. Her heart was thumping. She felt slightly sick. She put some more Hazy Daze on her lips and thought she looked more structured. More together. She wanted to look like a mysterious and beautiful wife. She wanted to look different from the other people, standing there in their sagging grey tracksuit trousers. She thought of Graham, sitting in the aeroplane, a few miles away from her and 35,000 feet up. It was strange, to have a husband flying through the air. A husband who had been to Germany for a fortnight, while she had been getting up and going on the bus to work, and coming home and going to bed. Something about the airport reminded her of the day they were married. The smell of floor polish, and the flowers, and the waiting.

Her lips looked too red now. She took a paper towel and wiped most of the lipstick off again. She didn't want to look over the top. She put the lipstick back in her make-up bag, stood for a moment and stared at herself in the mirror. Be calm, she thought, be calm. Then she walked back through the door. She could see

Douglas and Marleen in the distance, sitting, tiny at the other end of the hall, their reflection shining against the tiles. Douglas was eating a second iced bun.

While they were drinking coffee Douglas got out his cigarettes.

'I thought you were giving up,' said Marleen.

'No,' said Douglas. 'Since when did I say that?' He glared at her.

The old man with the dog came and sat with them for a while. He ordered a white coffee and started telling them about his life.

'I have two budgies, a dog, a hamster and a wife,' the old man said to Marleen. 'The wife is the most trouble.'

Marleen didn't reply. She turned away a little in her seat, pursed her lips and looked fixedly at the jars of coffee beans on the counter. The old man cackled and wandered off with his dog, towards the Viewing Lounge.

'Why didn't you drive here?' Doug asked Jill after a while.

'Because we don't have a car,' said Jill.

'We can give you a lift home,' said Doug. 'There's plenty of room in our car.'

'No, no,' said Jill, 'we'll get a taxi.'

'It's no problem, love,' said Douglas. 'Our car's better than a taxi. It's a Multi-Purpose Vehicle.'

'We could have brought you here and all, if we'd known,' Marleen said. She smiled, glanced at Douglas and winked. She had a little piece of bread on her cheek from the chicken tikka sandwich, and Jill was about to tell her. Then, at the last moment, she decided not to.

The plane touched down at 18.50. Somehow, it had speeded up at the last minute. She didn't think planes could do that. When she went to check the computer screen, there was a little sentence, flashing in yellow, saying 'ARRIVED', and it made her heart jump.

They went to join the other people, shambling around by the staircase. Marleen and Doug stood right at the foot of the stairs, and Jill retreated a little, into the crowd. She hoped she looked mysterious and slightly tragic. She leaned against a pillar and watched people appearing. All the businessmen first, young and pale and slightly overweight, and carrying expensive travel-cases. Graham had one the same, and she didn't like it. She thought it made him look dull and middle aged, and he was only twenty-four. She could imagine the young pale businessmen hanging their cases over the backs of their hotel doors, and looking in wardrobes for the courtesy trouser press. After the businessmen there was a little wave of older, German people. There was something neat and proud about them. They were sharp-looking and tucked-in, even after sitting for two hours in a pressurised cabin.

There was a little lull, and then a few solitary passengers, looking dark-eyed and slightly haunted. And then the school group. World-weary teenagers. Trendy and unjetlagged. Around them, parents began to call out the names of their children, like ewes bleating for their lambs. Jill saw Marleen and Doug's son approaching them. He didn't quite smile. He was wearing a T-shirt that said 'Ich bin ein Frankfurter.'

Graham was one of the last people to emerge. He stood at the top of the staircase and looked around. Then he saw Jill and waved. He walked down the stairs and navigated his way around the family groups.

'Hi,' he said. He never normally said 'Hi'. He was looking handsome and chewing gum.

'Hallo,' Jill said. Suddenly she felt shy. She was aware of her slightly bloodshot eye. She put her arms around him. After two weeks without him, she had forgotten how light and boney he was.

'What was it like?' she asked. 'Did you have a good time?'

'It was great,' said Graham. He had developed a strange, nonchalant drawl, as if he'd been in Texas for two months.

'I missed you,' Jill said, stiffly.

'I missed you too,' said Graham.

'I got your postcard this morning,' Jill said, but Graham had already turned away and was standing at the carousel, looking out for his travel-case.

'It should have appeared by now,' he was saying.

'It's probably last off the plane. Like you,' said Jill. She went to stand beside him.

'Where is it?' Graham said.

His travel-case was blue, with green zippers. It was unmissable. But it didn't appear. Every now and then, someone would step forward, pull a bag off the carousel and walk away, and Graham would sigh. After five minutes he folded his arms and stopped chewing gum. Jill glanced at him. Something, some exotic quality he'd had, was beginning to wear off. The longer he stood waiting, the more he looked like Graham.

By eight thirty the hall was almost empty. The businessmen and elderly Germans and teenagers had all got into cars and taxis and driven off. A young man appeared through a doorway and started to push a very wide and dirty-looking mop across the floor tiles. Out of the corner of her eye, Jill could see the Mackies, standing, talking in low voices by the closed bookshop.

The bags on the carousel had formed a pattern. There was a square, brown suitcase, then a little gap, then a cardboard tube with 'Fragile' written on it, then a very long gap, and then a tartan hold-all.

'Where is my bag?' Graham said.

Jill didn't reply. She wondered if Graham's bag was on a solitary journey to Prague or Florida. They stood and watched the cardboard tube disappearing through the rubber flanges again. Then the square brown suitcase emerged at the other end, like some jaded actor appearing from the wings.

'Graham . . .,' Jill said, but before she could say 'The Mackies are here,' they were walking towards them.

'All set?' said Doug.

Graham looked at Doug. 'Hallo, Doug,' he said.

'Bag not arrived?' said Doug.

'They'll put it on the next flight,' said Marleen. She was standing with her hand on her son's shoulder. Jason Mackie didn't speak. He was wearing a set of headphones. He glanced at Jill and Graham, and frowned.

The Mackies' Multi-Purpose Vehicle was huge and bright red, with enormous windows. It had three rows of seats. Doug and Marleen sat in the front, Jason in the middle and Graham and Jill at the back. They all put their seatbelts on and stared ahead, serious and awkward, like Lego people.

'By the time you get home,' Marleen said to Graham, 'they'll be couriering your bag out to you.'

'I hope so,' said Graham.

Doug turned the key in the ignition, and they lurched off, out of the car park and on to the road.

'So, Jason,' Doug said to his son. 'Did you learn lots of German?'

'Nope,' said Jason, staring out at the empty flowerbeds on the roundabout.

Jill looked at Graham and tried to catch his eye. But he was staring out of the window too.

'Your bag will probably be on the next flight,' she said quietly.

'Hmm,' said Graham. He sighed, and Jill moved away from him a fraction. She stared at the interior of the Mackies' car. It was like being in a minibus. Or a low-flying aeroplane. There was a fold-down table and places where you could put your mugs. She thought 'I have waited for this moment for two weeks.'

But it was at least quiet. The indicator clicked discretely. Jill looked at Graham again, and he looked back and smiled a tiny smile. He put his hand in hers for a moment. Then he took it away again and stared out of the window at the streets, at the second-hand shops and the bakery and the church.

'Did you get me those marzipan chocolates, Jason?' Marleen asked suddenly, from the front. There was a little silence. Marleen turned to look at her son.

'I'm going to be sick,' said Jason.

'Christ Almighty,' said Doug, and, almost at once, he swung the car dramatically off the main road, through an amber light and down a little lane. The car rumbled over stones and puddles for a few yards, and stopped.

'Are you sure, Jason?' Marleen asked, and Jason nodded. He had his hand over his mouth.

Marleen opened her door and got out. She ran around to Jason's side of the car and helped him out. Then they walked fast around a corner and out of sight.

'Marvellous,' said Doug. He sat and stared ahead, at a large pile of bricks in a builder's yard. The dashboard clock ticked very loud. 'At least the car seats won't get ruined,' he said.

They tried not to hear Jason Mackie being sick around the corner. But they did hear him. It was an extraordinary, animal sound. Jill tried to think of something to say, in a loud voice. But she couldn't think of anything, and after a few minutes, Marleen and Jason walked slowly back. Jill watched them through the enormous window. Marleen had her hand on her son's shoulder again. She had a little collection of lines on her forehead. She reached the car and opened the front passenger door.

'He's alright now,' she said. 'He's fine.'

But Jason looked dreadful. His skin was pale and sweaty. His T-shirt was ruffled like a bed that has been slept in for a fortnight. He crept silently into the car with a miserable expression on his face. He put his headphones back on, shuffled to the edge of his seat and closed his eyes.

'All set?' said Doug, brightly. He turned the key in the ignition and they glided off again. The engine hummed. Jill watched the streets rushing past Graham's profile. There were a few flakes of snow in the air; she could see them, beautiful crystals, in the headlights of other cars. And if they had been in a taxi, a big, glamorous taxi, it would have been different.

Every couple of minutes, Marleen turned round in her seat to look at Jason. 'Poor boy,' she said. Just before they got home, she stretched out her arm and brushed his hair back with her jewelled hand. 'Poor boy,' she said again, and Jason scowled and knocked her hand away. Marleen smiled, gazed at her hand for a moment, and then looked at Jill.

‘Homecomings never go quite right, do they?’ she said.

‘No,’ said Jill, turning to unbuckle her seatbelt. ‘Sometimes they’re not quite as wonderful as . . .,’ but she couldn’t find the catch, and she stopped talking and looked down. There was a little orange button that said ‘Press’. So she just pressed it, and waited to be released.

Manhattan Imagined

THE HOTEL ENTRANCE looks impressive; the front-door-handles are made of brass, and there are two little ficus trees in pots. But it gets worse. Inside, the lobby echoes. The walls are painted a pale, shining grey, and there is one picture, hanging at a slant, of a green-looking woman. The porter is always watching television. This evening, there is an infomercial about a porcelain doll.

'Look at the exquisite craftsmanship in the broderie anglaise,' a woman's voice is drawling. 'Look at the fine needlecraft.'

The porter stares at the screen, his mouth open.

'Hallo,' Robert says, and the porter ignores him.

Robert walks to the reception desk to pick up his key. There is a typed sign pinned underneath the counter. It says:

> *To all hotel staff; if* anyone *approaches you asking about the manager, please say you don't know who he is. WE ARE RUNNING A LEGITIMATE BUSINESS and have EVERY RIGHT TO REFUSE QUESTIONING BY THE POLICE.*

'What time is breakfast?' Robert asks the receptionist.

'We don't do breakfast,' says the receptionist. He looks at Paul. 'How old are you?' he asks.

'Twenty-three,' says Robert.

'Minors are not permitted to stay here unaccompanied,' says the receptionist.

'That's OK then,' says Robert.

In the morning, he gets the subway to Central Park, finds a large, grey rock near the entrance and sits down. He has brought a cinnamon bagel in a paper bag, and he takes it out. There is a little pot of cream cheese and another one of grape jelly, but he doesn't have a knife so he takes the lid off the cream cheese, bends it and uses it as a knife. The bagel is smooth and cold.

When he has eaten it he takes an apple out of the bag. It is a large, red apple and it cost a dollar. There is something about eating a big, overpriced apple in New York; if someone had been with him he would have made some comment about it. But he is alone, so he eats the apple without comment.

He always imagined Central Park to be an open place, with broad walkways and people taking quiet, intellectual strolls. But it is nothing like that; it is full of little slopes and rocks and congestion. Squirrels and strange blackbirds hop about like thieves. There is a stream of people coming from all directions. They travel in motorised buggies, in horse-drawn carts, on tandem bicycles. Some dance past and some appear, sudden and close, on roller blades. A little way off, two men are having a sword-fight. The silver blades shimmer and slice the air. Robert gets up from the rock and moves a little further off.

He finds another rock to sit on and takes a postcard out of his pocket. It has four views of New York: the Empire State Building, the Statue of Liberty, Wall Street and the Manhattan skyline. The little caption on it says: 'New York – City Of Wonders'. He plans to send it, with a short, ironic message, to a girl he knows.

There are two Manhattans in his head now: one imaginary and one real. The imaginary one has been there so long that it won't go away. It is full of witty coffee shop-owners and wise-cracking drivers. In the real Manhattan, the coffee shop-owners he has met seem rather silent. The taxi-cab drivers do not crack so many jokes. But they still yell at each other through their windows.

* * *

His brother said 'I'll meet you by the Walter Scott statue,' and Robert found the statue almost as soon as he arrived. It is impossible to get away from people like Walter Scott, even in Central Park.

He tries to lie down on the rock, but it is uneven and there is a big gap under his head, so he sits up again, too quickly, and white sparks whirl in front of his eyes. Sunlight is beginning to warm him. A blue jay hops a few feet away and pecks at a sandwich that someone has left in the grass.

At nine thirty he sees a young man walking up the path. He has untidy hair and his brother's pondering kind of walk. He is wearing a green coat that Paul might have chosen. But then the man stops resembling Paul and walks past. Waiting for Paul in Central Park feels like waiting for him, twelve years earlier, at football games. Sitting, ten years old, on a park bench, while Paul was kicking a ball around.

He doesn't notice the real Paul until he is right beside him.

'Robert,' Paul says.

Robert turns and has to squint against the sunlight.

'Hallo,' he says.

'You found Walter Scott then.'

'Yes.'

'So,' says Paul, and he frowns and looks at the grass. He is wearing a jacket that Robert has never seen before. He has had his hair cut very short. He has a nose-ring. He looks up at the statue. 'Does he make you feel at home?' he asks.

'No,' says Robert, 'I hate Walter Scott.'

'I just thought it would be a reasonable place to meet,' says Paul.

'It is perfectly reasonable,' says Robert. He feels annoyed suddenly. He gets up from the rock. The back of his coat, where he has been lying down, feels damp.

On the other side of the statue, an old man gets off his bicycle. He opens his bike-pannier and takes out a collection of metal baking trays: two large cake tins, a biscuit tray and a wire cooling rack. He puts them on the ground. Then he gets a pair of drumsticks out of his pocket, kneels down and starts banging the trays. It is a complicated beat. The cooling rack makes a sound like cymbals.

'People are bizarre here,' says Robert.

'Central Park is like that,' says Paul.

They decide to go the the Museum of Natural History. It seems a quieter place to talk. They have to pay $8 to get in but it seems worth it.

There is a café in the basement called the Diner Saurus. It is full of children and noise and electric light. They stand and hesitate in the entrance.

'This is like Forton Services,' says Robert.

'So it is. I'd forgotten about Forton Services,' says Paul, and when he says that, Robert feels a little stab of sadness. How could you forget Forton Services? he thinks. The walkway over the motorway. The spidery window frames.

They decide to try a café on a different floor. It is in the Ocean Life hall. They find a table covered in empty polystyrene beakers, and sit down. A blue whale floats above them, suspended from the ceiling by thin wire.

'I hope that whale is securely attached,' Paul says, looking up. Then he looks down again and drinks some of his coffee through a bendy straw.

'I'm sure they've fixed it with the right stuff,' says Robert, 'trip-wire or something.'

'Hmm,' says Paul.

Paul has developed very faint worry-lines while he's been in America. It is odd to have a younger brother with lines on his forehead. Robert had forgotten how much he worries. He used to worry about all kinds of things: insects on the pavement; school; dying.

The lighting in the Ocean Life hall is very dim. People huddle together, eating hotdogs in the semi-dark.

'Strange café, this,' says Robert.

'One of the things I miss most about Scotland,' says Paul, 'is the plates. They're china. They don't get thrown away.'

'You don't miss the people, then,' says Robert. At odd moments he feels so angry that he just wants to get up and run, fast, straight through the doorway, past the lumps of quartz and the dinosaur skeletons and on to the Manhattan streets. But he doesn't even know what he is angry with: Paul or New York.

'Weird pickles,' says Paul, frowning at the contents of his hotdog. Then he bites into it, and pieces of gherkin fall out.

Robert ignores him.

'See that woman over there?' Paul says after a moment. 'She's just going to that bin and throwing everything in there. That's what I mean about the china plates. That would never happen with china plates.'

'I thought you might have got used to waste by now,' Robert says.

Paul shrugs. The blue whale moves, very gently, in the breeze.

'So,' Robert says, 'do you like living here?'

'Yes,' says Paul, 'it's great.' He picks up his coffee beaker again.

'Have you got a girlfriend?' Robert says. He almost shouts.

'Yes. Her name's Deborah. She's studying journalism.'

'Oh,' says Robert. He stares at his brother's nose-ring and thinks it looks stupid.

'How's your lovelife?' Paul asks. He smiles as if he finds the idea strange, or embarrassing.

'It's fine,' Robert says, and he stops talking. *I am three years older than you,* he thinks.

'Right,' says Paul. 'Good.'

Robert looks at the museum floor-plan he picked up, and reads what is on Floor One.

'Molluscs and Our World,' he says. 'You've always liked molluscs.'

'Yeah,' says Paul.

Robert remembers Paul following him around when he was little, peering at the snails on the garden path. He would pick them up sometimes and show them to him. He would show him their strange, gentle eyes on stalks.

'So. Where are you staying?' Paul asks.

'Quite a grim hotel on the East Side, actually,' Robert snaps.

'Why didn't you stay with us?' says Paul.

'I didn't think I could just turn up. At such short notice.'

'Of course you could. Some parts of town are kind of weird.'

The way Paul speaks has changed. He has become blasé, and he runs a lot of his consonants together. Nearly all his sentences seem to have the word 'weird' in them. He doesn't speak the way he used to. He finishes the last of his coffee and wipes his mouth on the paper napkin. There is a picture of a dinosaur on it.

Robert looks at him.

'You disappeared for nearly a year,' he says.

'No I didn't,' says Paul. 'You had my address.' He says *add*ress.

'Not for six months.'

'No?' says Paul. 'Sorry about that. Things were a bit hectic for a while'.

'Well, how exciting for you.'

When they have finished coffee, they go for a look around the museum. They go to look at Molluscs and Our World, and then to a section called 'Biology and Evolution'. There are glass cases with models of primitive humans. In one there is a small hairy man and woman, less than five feet tall. They are standing in a sandy landscape, with an artificial sea in the background. The man is spearing a fish and the woman is scraping something with a piece of flint.

'She looks like Mum,' says Paul. 'There'll be a thermos flask in that tent, and some salmon sandwiches.'

He touches the glass case with his index finger.

'You ought to get in touch with them,' Robert says.

'Yes,' says Paul.

'You ought to get in touch with me,' Robert says, and he strides off fast, his heart beating, to look into the next glass case; another small hairy man and woman, a few thousand years more advanced. These ones are wearing clothes and shouting at each other.

At the subway entrance, there is a man sellotaping himself to a broken chair. He has a very earnest expression on his face.

'New York is full of weird people,' Robert says, as they get into the train. Now he's using the word.

'No more than anywhere,' says Paul.

The carriage empties after a couple of stops, and they sit down.

'Well,' says Paul, addressing his knees, 'it's really good to see you.'

'Yeah,' says Robert, stiffly. He folds his arms and watches the numbers of the subway stations going past. He thinks about the platform names on the Glasgow Underground. Kinning Park. Shields Road. He thinks how small and orange and unglamorous the Glasgow Underground is.

'When is your flight tomorrow?' Paul asks.

'Eleven in the morning.'

'Shall we hook up later for something to eat?'

'I'll see how it goes,' Robert says. 'I need to pack and stuff.'

'Right,' says Paul. He clears his throat. Then he stares up at the black wall of the subway, his eyes clear and pale.

When Robert gets back to the hotel, the porter is watching an infomercial about a Steam 'n' Clean. 'Look how easy it is,' says a voice, 'to clean around the bathroom taps'.

'Hallo,' says Robert, his heart sinking, and the porter looks up.

'Hi,' he says, then he looks back at the screen.

Robert walks down a short flight of stairs, across a landing and then up another flight of stairs. He turns left at the tourist information sheets, and walks up eleven steps to his room. He unlocks the door, walks in and lies down on the bed. The room is very quiet for somewhere in the middle of Manhattan. He turns his head and looks through the window, past the iron railings, at a branch with leaves on it. He can hear someone singing in a kitchen across the yard. There is a cooling breeze, a smell of onions frying and the sound of a radio. He hadn't imagined things like that, when he imagined New York.

He picks up the remote control and switches the television on. The Steam 'n' Clean infomercial is still running; now somebody is cleaning the inside of their car. It is the kind of thing he can imagine his father using.

He can't keep his eyes open; they feel heavy, as if they've been open for days. He switches the television off and puts his head against the pillow, which smells like hotel pillows across the world: of washing powder and cigarettes and other people. He lies in the dark, closes his eyes and listens to the hotel. There is the sound of water in the pipes, and of a woman's voice shouting to someone in a different room. Now there is a man's voice shouting back. It reminds him of being at home with Paul when they were young; when they lay in their room, and listened to their parents arguing.

He sleeps, and has a curious dream, in which he is trying to measure the distance of the Atlantic with a rectractable tape measure.

When he wakes up he is uncomfortable, with his head at an odd angle on the mattress. The pillow has slipped on to the floor, and the room is strange for a moment; he has no idea where he is. He moves his head and looks sideways at the green numbers on the radio alarm. Then he sits up. He turns and lifts his address book off the bedside table. He switches the little light on, and begins to flick through the pages, looking for Paul's number, and when he gets to the right place and looks at his brother's name, the only one on the page, written in big, green capitals, he stops trying to picture him, suddenly; the imaginary Paul, living in the imaginary Manhattan. He just dials his number and waits for him to answer.

Amen

WHEN DOROTHY ARRIVES at Training Room C, everyone is standing around the coffee flasks, balancing cups and saucers and Bourbon biscuits.

On a table there is a register, a biro and some little plastic name badges. Dorothy ticks her name and finds her badge. It says DOROTHY BASSISTE: CLEANER. Her surname has been spelt wrong. Also, she is the only CLEANER, amongst all the LECTURERS and ADMINISTRATORS and RESEARCH FELLOWS.

She walks over to the table and pumps some coffee into her cup out of a flask. The flask is nearly empty, and the coffee squirts out of it in short streams, like milk from a cow.

She stands near the window, sips her coffee, and looks around. Every so often, she remembers that it is her birthday. Her daughter sent her a card that said 'TO SOMEONE SPECIAL', but she doesn't feel like someone special. She just feels like a woman standing in a room wearing a misspelt name badge that says 'DOROTHY BASSISTE: CLEANER'. When she looks around, everything in the room, the women and the chairs and the plants and the coffee flasks, looks flat. When she looks through the window, the sky looks as if it has been painted on.

She is putting her coffee cup back on the table when the door opens and a woman walks in, wearing a yellow jacket and carrying a lot of blue folders.

'Good morning,' says the woman.

She walks to a table at the end of the room and puts the folders on it.

'Now,' she says, 'I'd like you all to grab a chair and form a circle.'

There is a tiny pause. Then everyone puts their cups down on the table, trudges across the room and forms a queue beside a stack of plastic chairs. They pick up a chair each and walk back to the middle of the room. But they seem to have different ideas of how a circle should be. One group begins to create a very small circle in the middle of the room, and another tries to distort the edges.

'That's the oddest circle I've ever seen,' says the yellow-jacketed woman when they have sat down. She picks up her own chair and walks towards them. She lifts it up into the air and knocks Dorothy's head with one of the legs. The leg makes a bouncing, musical sound.

'Sorry,' she says. 'Was that your head?'

'Yes,' says Dorothy quietly. She sits still. And then, after a moment, when people have stopped looking, she raises her hand to her head and rubs it. She blinks. It is her birthday. She feels almost as if she might cry.

Because it is a compulsory course, she will have to do the cleaning this evening. When everyone else has gone home, she will have to go to the cleaning cupboard next to Lecture Room B, take off her smart clothes and put on her working clothes. She will have to yank out the cleaning trolley from behind the buckets and mops, and wheel it down the dark, emergency-lit corridors. She will dust the graffitied student desks. She will clean the laboratories and the lavatories.

The woman in the yellow jacket looks at her watch.

'OK,' she says. 'Now, this is a compulsory course as you know, but I do hope you don't feel as if you've been forced to attend.'

She pauses. Nothing fills the pause. So she begins again.

'First I'd like you all to introduce yourselves,' she says, 'and then, as a little ice-breaker, I'd like you to add some other detail. For instance "My name's Fleur and I got a parking ticket this morning".'

Everyone looks at her.

'Let's start with you,' the tutor says, frowning, and glancing at the woman beside her. The woman plays with her wedding ring and looks back at her out of the corner of her eye. 'My name's Rita Spink,' she says, abruptly, like a greyhound let out of a trap. 'I'm addicted to chocolate.'

'Very good,' says the tutor. Rita breathes out.

The woman beside Rita is a research fellow. She is researching travel sickness in pigs. Next to the pig researcher is an administrator called Evelyn, whose son fell off a wall the day before, and had to go to hospital.

Then it is Dorothy's turn. She feels her mind seize and go blank. She holds on to the papers in her lap. She can't think what to tell them. She doesn't want them to know anything about her.

'Take your time,' says the tutor, grinning horribly. Dorothy shifts in her chair.

'My name is Dorothy Baptiste,' she says after a moment, 'not Bassiste. It's been written wrong on my namebadge. I just thought I'd mention it. As something to say.'

'Fine,' says the tutor. 'That's fine, Dorothy.'

Dorothy relaxes her grip on the papers and looks down at her lap, at the day's agenda. Coffee and Registration. Introductions and Warm-up Exercises. She counts how many things they have to do before lunch.

When she looks up again, the tutor is standing in front of a whiteboard, writing with a squeaky pen. She is using long words, elongating the letters at the right end so they fit in.

CONSTRUCTIVE LISTENING, she writes: LETTING PEOPLE SPEAK.

'I think we can all be guilty of interrupting each other,' says the tutor. She puts the lid back on her pen and looks around. Her voice is slow and loud, as if she's talking to a group of simpletons. She grins and fixes her gaze, for some reason, on Dorothy.

Dorothy doesn't know what she expects her to say. She just wants not to be there at all. She is about to say 'Sorry . . .?' when the travel-sickness-in-pigs researcher speaks.

'I know I do, sometimes,' says the pig researcher.

'I think we can all be guilty of interrupting each other,' says the tutor again.

From across the room, somebody's stomach rumbles. A woman blushes and puts her blue folder across her stomach.

'Somebody's not had their breakfast,' says the tutor. She laughs briefly. Then she tells them that they are going to do some role playing. They must all get up again, she says, find a partner and talk to them. One person has to talk and the other person has to listen, without interrupting. No interruptions whatsoever. 'OK?' she says. So they all put their folders down on the ground, stand up again and look around. Friends grab on to each other quickly, as if they're being plucked to safety from a fast-flowing river. They just keep getting snapped up. After a couple of minutes, the pairs start sitting down again and talking. There is only one woman still standing: RITA SPINK, SECRETARY.

'It looks as if we'll have to talk to each other,' says Dorothy, pulling up two chairs.

'I don't know what to say,' says Rita Spink.

She sits down and looks at her notes.

'Say anything,' say Dorothy. 'We've only got a minute.'

'I don't know,' says Rita, 'if I can talk for a minute without someone interrupting me.'

'Have a go,' says Dorothy. Beside them, she can hear a woman talking about some cockroaches in a hotel room in Corsica. She wonders how people get on to subjects like that so quickly. She looks beyond Rita's head, through the window, trying to see something different about the sky; something about it that will make the day feel different. A song appears in her head that she used to sing at primary school. She hasn't thought about it for years, but suddenly, sitting here, being told what to do, surrounded by corridors and timetables and signs in the toilets saying 'Have you washed your hands?', she is reminded of school.

Now the day is over,
Night is drawing nigh
Shadows of the evening
Steal across the sky

Singing it was a little ritual that was quite nice, she thinks. In retrospect. They sang it for seven years, quickly, quickly, so they could go out and play. They stood behind their desks, mumbling about the shadows of the evening, looking down at the graffiti marks, and up at the day through the window. Then, there would always be a little pause before they sang Amen. Somehow, Dorothy always found the Amen a strange and difficult word. The drone of it, and the fact that she didn't know what it meant. Sometimes she didn't bother with the Amen.

'What shall I say?' says Rita Spink. She sits and thinks for a moment. She sighs. 'I know,' she says after a moment, 'I'll tell you about when I took my wee grandson to the zoo.'

'That sounds nice,' says Dorothy.

'My son and daughter-in-law are splitting up, so I'm looking after him a lot at the weekends.'

'I'm sorry to hear that,' says Dorothy.

'You see, you're interrupting,' says Rita.

'Anyway,' she says, 'we spent half the day there last Saturday. We saw some chimps and some emus and some reptiles, but the thing he liked most . . .'

'Time's up,' shouts the tutor.

'Oh,' says Rita, 'oh well.'

'Go on,' says Dorothy, 'what was it?'

'Nah,' says Rita.

At one o'clock, lunch is wheeled in on a trolley that Dorothy recognises. It is a college one, the same as hers without the buckets of bleach and the cleaning cloths. There are egg and cress sandwiches, or tuna and cucumber. She doesn't feel like eating either kind. The thought of them makes her feel slightly ill.

During a little sandwich-eating lull, she looks at the agenda again. There are still four things left to do:

SAYING NO AND MEANING IT
PROBLEM-SOLVING
FINAL OBSERVATIONS
CLOSE

Final Observations is not till five o'clock. Close is scheduled for five fifteen. Close is such a strange way to describe the end of a day. So formal. And she will have to start cleaning before that or she will never get out. The janitors won't realise she's there polishing the corridors at six o'clock, and she will get locked in for the night. It will be the worst birthday she has ever had. Even though she has had bad birthdays, in fifty-eight years.

She puts down her uneaten tuna sandwich, gets up from her chair and walks towards the tutor.

'I'm sorry,' she says, 'but I'm going to have to go. I have an appointment.'

'Oh,' says the tutor. She looks disappointed. She smiles.

'Well, Dorothy, don't hang around if you have to be somewhere else,' she says.

'No,' says Dorothy.

'I hope everything's OK,' says the tutor, as if she's been on a course called How to be Gracious to Difficult People. 'Don't forget to take the course notes with you.'

'Yes, I'll do that,' says Dorothy.

People are always nice at the wrong moments. She smiles at the tutor and doesn't move. She feels she should hang around now, out of courtesy.

'Go on, then,' says the tutor.

'Right,' says Dorothy.

She turns, and wonders what she will be missing. Maybe she

will miss something very important about SAYING NO AND MEANING IT. She looks around the room. 'OK,' she says, and she walks over to the coat rack, takes her coat off the peg, picks up her bag, opens the door and walks out. She walks quickly.

Heading for the cleaning cupboard, she keeps expecting the tutor to run after her. But there is no sound of footsteps. So she speeds up, calculating how fast she can do her work and be out. Maybe she can do it in an hour. Maybe she can skip washing the corridor floors and be out in three-quarters. She turns on to Level 5, her level, with the smell of formaldehyde and the darkness and the posters about Quantum Mechanics, and sees Rita Spink. Rita Spink is returning from the chocolate machine with a Bounty Bar.

'Caught me in the act,' Rita says.

'It's better than the sandwiches,' says Dorothy. She clutches the cleaning cupboard keys.

'What are you up to?' says Rita.

'Well,' says Dorothy, 'I was . . . I was . . .'

And now, she thinks, now she has been seen by someone on the course, she will have to be away. She can't start trundling down the corridors now, with her mop and her bottles of Flash.

'I was just checking the cleaning cupboard,' she says. 'I was just making sure it was locked.'

Rita looks at her. 'How odd,' she says. She unwraps her chocolate bar, and bites a large chunk off the end. 'So what were you going to say before?' she asks, her mouth full of chocolate, 'before we were so rudely interrupted?'

'Nothing, really,' says Dorothy. 'Just that it's my birthday.'

'That's not nothing,' says Rita.

'No,' says Dorothy. She feels embarrassed. Childish.

'Are you going to do something nice then?'

'I thought I might,' Dorothy says. She grips the cupboard keys tight.

'The zoo's nice,' says Rita. 'It's lovely at this time of year. Go and look at the crested newts. They were my grandson's favourites.'

'Yes,' says Dorothy, in a confessional rush. 'Or I might go to the beach.'

'Good for you. Treat yourself.'

And something about the day alters suddenly, as she's standing, talking to Rita; it changes. It feels wilder, the way she hoped it would. She takes off her name-tag. *Now the day is over*, she thinks. *Amen*, she thinks.

Whistling, Singing, Eating Fruit

In 1935 Ivy's husband gave her a book. It was called *Don't*. It had a subtitle: *Social Crimes and Domestic Mistakes.*

'Oh,' said Ivy. She wasn't sure how she was supposed to react.

'In jest, my love,' said Leonard.

'I see,' said Ivy.

She read some of it while she was sitting at the breakfast table. 'Don't read at the breakfast table,' she read. The sentence sprang out at her, like a reprimand. It was extraordinary. Out of the corner of her eye, she noticed Leonard raising his eyebrows and looking at her.

There were a lot of chapters about what to do in polite society. Advice on good manners when playing golf, when motoring and when at the bridge table. She never did any of those things; they couldn't afford them. Driving a car would have been fun, but the idea of playing golf or bridge depressed her. There was a chapter in the book called 'For Husbands' which was one and a half pages long. The one 'For Wives' was eleven pages.

Don't wear faded or spotted gowns or anything that is not neat and appropriate, said the first sentence in the 'Wives' chapter. *Dress for the pleasure and admiration of your family.*

She looked down at the tired, up-turning collars of her dress.

'Am I wearing a neat and appropriate gown?' she asked. But Leonard had started to read his newspaper, and he didn't answer.

The next day she went out and bought herself a new dress. It was very neat: blue with buttoned cuffs and a little collar. The skirt of it reached to the middle of her calves. She tried it on in the shop, and looked instantly practical, like a Wren. She wore it when Leonard came home from work in the evening.

'How do I look?' she said.

'Eh?' said Leonard.

'I'm wearing a neat and appropriate dress.'

Leonard looked at her. He didn't reply.

After supper she continued reading the book she had borrowed from the library. *Moby Dick.* She had just got to the part where Captain Peleg was saying 'Fiery pit! fiery pit! ye insult me, man; past all natural bearing, ye insult me,' when Leonard put his head around the door.

'I've invited Mr and Mrs Cramshaw round for dinner tomorrow evening, my love,' he said.

Then he withdrew his head and walked away, down the hallway. Ivy looked up from her book and stared into space. She heard Leonard stop and tap the barometer in the hall. She wondered what the hand had moved to: Set-fair, or Change, maybe.

After a while she put a bookmark in her novel and read another paragraph from the 'Wives' section of her *Don't* book.

'*Don't confine your reading to novels,*' it said. '*How can women hope to maintain their position as intellectual equals of men if their reading is confined to this one branch of literature?*'

She looked in a few recipe books the next day and decided on a stew for the Cramshaws. This was a good thing for a hostess to do, because it could be sitting in the oven while she tended to her guests. She could almost pretend that she had a servant working in the kitchen, basting things. When the Cramshaws arrived, she glittered and sparkled. She drank slightly too much wine. She moved her hands a lot while she talked, and the dining room was filled with the scent of Nights in Paris. While they ate the stew she flirted a little with Mr Cramshaw. She noticed Leonard and Mrs Cramshaw glaring at her but she took no notice of them.

'I'm reading a very good novel all about whaling, Mr Cramshaw,' she said.

'That's an unusual book for a woman to read,' said Mr Cramshaw.

Ivy looked down at the carrots in her stew.

'But commendable,' said Mr Cramshaw.

'Commendable?' she said. 'Do you think so?'

'Ivy,' said Leonard, in a snapping little voice, as if he was commanding a Jack Russell to come to heel.

'Commendable,' Ivy said, stabbing a piece of carrot with her fork. She finished her stew before everyone else: behaviour which was not recommended in the *Don't* book. A hostess was supposed to synchronise eating with her guests.

In 1939 she had a baby. He was bonny, noisy and completely bald. She and Leonard decided to call him Barry. A couple of months after he was born, Ivy discovered that Leonard was having an affair with Mrs Cramshaw. It had been going on for months; secret trysts in the clerk's office; little love-notes and guilty lunches together on a park bench near their office. So she packed a suitcase, put Barry in a pram and left to go and live with her mother.

Leonard's affair didn't last long. Mr Cramshaw turned up at his office one day and hit him, breaking a front tooth, and suddenly Mrs Cramshaw seemed to love her husband again. Leonard visited Ivy the same evening, with a swollen mouth, a black eye, and carrying a large bunch of roses.

'I'm sorry,' he said, 'it won't happen again.'

Ivy looked at him, standing on the doorstep with his bunch of flowers.

'I hope not, for your sake,' she said.

'No,' he said, 'I mean. . . .'

'Do you know,' she interrupted, 'in that book you gave me, it says "don't take your love for granted".'

Leonard's swollen mouth began to quiver, and she shut the door.

* * *

When the war started, her mother looked after Barry while she went out to work. She had found a job in Hackney. This involved growing vegetables in a park, for the war effort. When the weather was good, her mother would walk to the park with Barry in his pram, and they would sit on a bench and eat sandwiches.

'Do you think you'll ever marry again?' her mother asked her one afternoon.

'Who knows, Mum,' said Ivy, 'if I meet the right man.'

She had already started divorce proceedings. Sometimes she thought of Leonard and wondered how he was getting on. She hoped he was not unhappy. She kept the little *Don't* book on the shelf in her mother's living room, and read it sometimes, when she wanted to be amused and amazed. There was a particular sentence – '*Don't whistle, sing or eat fruit in the streets*' – that always made her smile.

In 1951 she and Barry moved out of her mother's house into a little flat in Stoke Newington. It had once been part of a terrace, but after all the bombing, it had become semi-detached, and was quite an imposing sight at the end of the street, standing tall and independent. With her salary and allowance from Leonard, she was able to afford some of the latest household appliances. She bought a twin-tub and a new gas cooker. She also bought a wooden coffee grinder and some wine glasses, and sometimes she invited her friends round for dinner. Most of the time she did things that the *Don't* book scorned:

> *Don't, when about to give a dinner party, invite more guests than can be accommodated with comfort.*

She did this all the time, seating her friends on rickety little chairs and cramming them around the small formica-topped table. She also flirted, swore, and made inappropriately risqué comments.

She met a man in 1962, whom she loved but never married. They just visited each other for twenty-five years, throughout the sixties and seventies. He was her lover; and the *Don't* book didn't even mention lovers. Lovers were unmentionable. She misses him.

She remains in the flat in Stoke Newington, although it is no longer semi-detached; there is an Indian take-away on one side and an Oxfam shop on the other, both of which she finds very useful. Barry, who is now as bald as he was when he was born and works as a washing-machine repair man, comes to visit her twice a week. Sometimes he brings her a bunch of roses, which reminds her of Leonard. But apart from that, he is not like Leonard at all.

While they're standing in the kitchen one weekend in October, Ivy asks him to look at her washing machine, which has stopped working. It just stopped, she says, in mid-spin.

'Let's have a look,' says Barry, and he frowns and kneels on the kitchen floor and tries to pull the machine forward, away from the wall. But he can't manage it. He's a little too plump and unfit. His face turns rather pink, and after a couple of minutes he stops trying.

'This is stuck fast,' he says.

'Are you sure, dear?' Ivy asks.

'It's absolutely wedged,' he says.

'Let me try,' she says, and she opens the door of the machine, puts her hand inside, flat against the steel barrel, and pulls. The machine moves forward a fraction. She pulls again and it moves a little more.

'How on earth did you manage that?' says Barry.

She stands up straight and puts her hand on his shoulder. She is thinking of a little sentence: 'Don't undermine a man's abilities. It is more becoming for women to remain the gentler sex.'

'Ha!' she says.

She is still going strong.